YOGA AND MEDITATION

Their Real Purpose and How to Get Started

YOGA AND MEDITATION

Their Real Purpose and How to Get Started

Stephen Knapp

Ocean Books Pvt. Ltd.
ISO 9001:2015 Publishers

Published by
Ocean Books (P) Ltd.
4/19 Asaf Ali Road,
New Delhi-110 002 (INDIA)
e-mail: info@oceanbooks.in

ISBN 978-81-8430-506-7
YOGA AND MEDITATION
by Stephen Knapp

Edition
2025

Price
₹ 500.00 (Rupees Five Hundred only)

Printed at
Shree Sai Printers, Sahibabad

Contents

1

The Real Purpose of Yoga

First of all, yoga is not a religion, it is a spiritual science that has been practiced and developed over thousands of years. Archeological evidence shows figures in yogic positions from the Indus Valley region that date as far back as 3000 BCE. Yoga is also mentioned in various Vedic literature, such as some of the *Upanishads*, the *Bhagavad-gita*, the *Bhagavata Purana*, and others, all of which date back thousands of years.

Religion often deals with externals, such as how we act, what we do, and customs and rituals. Spirituality, on the other hand, may also use rituals and practices, but is focused on our internal changes and development, and is, thus, more personal and individualistic. It does not depend on a church or our connection with an institution. Neither does it depend on a strict dogma, but it goes beyond all that. This is the Vedic system. The goal of religion may be to reach heaven, but the goal of Vedic spirituality, from which originates the yoga system, is *moksha*, or liberation from all forms of materialistic limitations, a reawakening of our real spiritual identity, and even entrance into the spiritual dimension.

The purpose of any true spiritual path is to raise our consciousness to the point of allowing us to directly perceive the spiritual strata. Being spiritual means to recognize one's spiritual identity and practically see the transcendental essence of all others. It also means to see that we are all parts and parcels of God and to respect each other in that light. That is one of the goals of yoga. But how can we be convinced that there really is a God?

We need to understand that all things that are spiritual function on a higher plane of existence, one that is hardly perceptible by our mind, intelligence, or senses. The spiritual dimension can only be detected when our consciousness reaches a higher level of awareness. It is similar to radio and television waves. These are not perceptible by our mind or senses. They remain invisible, yet they are all around us. In our base level of awareness, or unawareness, we may think that such things as radio waves and television frequencies are not real. Of course, we may be viewed as quite uneducated by those who are familiar with their existence. So the thing is, even if you cannot perceive them, if you have a receiver that can detect or even utilize such subtle waves or frequencies, then you will know that radio and television waves are not only a fact, but can be used for many practical purposes.

The same thing goes for a genuine spiritual path. It is meant to bring our consciousness up to a higher level of awareness, to fine tune it so that we can receive or perceive the higher vibrations of the spiritual strata. As we practice a genuine spiritual tradition, then our consciousness can become refined and focused enough so we can receive the subtle frequencies and perceive the reality of the spiritual domain. Then we can have our own spiritual experiences. The point is that the more spiritual we become, the more we can perceive that which is spiritual. As we develop and grow in this way, the questions about spiritual life are no longer a mystery to solve, but become a reality to experience. It becomes a practical part of our lives. And how to reach that level of perception is supplied in the Vedic methodologies that have been preserved and handed to us by the previous sages who have also used them for their own development and spiritual experience. And that is what the Vedic process has been giving to humanity for thousands of years.

The Vedic system is practically non-denominational. It is not for any one culture or ethnic group. It is for all of humanity and is called *Sanatana-dharma*. *Sanatana-dharma* is both a path and a state of being. It means, essentially, the eternal nature of the soul, that which always exists. We are all spiritual beings within material bodies, so the goal and our main duty of human existence is to regain that spiritual identity. This is attained by a reawakening of our higher consciousness and the perception of our spiritual identity. It is through the process of yoga and the path of *Sanatana-dharma* that we can reach this higher awareness and perceive exactly who we are. This is precisely the purpose of yoga.

The Sanskrit root of the word *yoga* is *yuj*, which means to bind, link, or unite with the object of our meditation. Thus, it is to unite the mind, intellect, the will, body, and soul to God, or the *jivatma* to the *Paramatma*, the individual soul to the Supersoul, through the discipline of yoga. Furthermore, the word *religion* comes from the Latin word *religio*, which also means to bring back or bind to God. Thus, there is no difference between the goal of yoga and the deeper goal of religion.

Nowadays people often practice yoga merely for improving their physical fitness, or for their mental and overall well-being. There is nothing wrong with that, and yoga can do that most efficiently. But there is also a higher aspect of yoga, which for some has been forgotten. The great *rishis* of old in India gave it for our preparation to reach higher states of consciousness. And such training was performed for years to attain more developed states of being. Thus, the process of hatha yoga was given to prepare one for entering the elevated stages of meditation. Hatha yoga is a beginning process for preparing the body and mind for spiritual awakening through the practice of raja or astanga yoga. Thus, it is also quite effective in reducing any diseases, physical defects, or mental disturbances. And this is why some people use it as a preventative medical therapy. It is the imbalance in the energy system that contributes much of the psychic or mental diseases that people suffer. Hatha yoga, along with breathing exercises, *pranayama*, can eliminate many such problems. However, it is not enough to use only particular *asanas* or yoga postures to remedy certain problems. It must be used holistically to treat the whole person so the student, or the *sadhaka*, can rise to a higher level of being. The person's character, thought processes, mind, senses, and physical nature, must all rise to a more refined level of existence. That is what is needed, otherwise the goal of yoga remains incomplete. This, it seems, is what has been forgotten by many modern yoga teachers.

In order for the mind to be purified, the body also has to be purified, or prepared spiritually. Hatha yoga is that preliminary process by which we prepare the body, nervous system, mind, lungs or breathing, and *nadi* channels so the energy within can flow most efficiently for states of deep meditation. This is its real objective, and this is what we will explain as we move forward.

□

2

Benefits of Yoga

The benefits of yoga are various and numerous. On the mental level it strengthens concentration, determination, and builds a stronger character that can more easily sustain various tensions in the materialistic world. The assortment of *asanas* or postures also provide stronger health and keeps ills such as diabetes, high and low blood pressure, etc., away or in check. It improves physical strength, endurance, flexibility, back pain, digestive disorders, and arthritis. It promotes detoxification of the body, toning of muscles, and relief from stress and anxiety. Certain diseases can be prevented or improved by performing yoga on a daily basis.

Students also use yoga to find relief from the stress of study, tests, homework, and pressure to keep up good grades. Yoga has been shown to provide an increase of energy, so students can use that toward school work and improve their academic performance.

Presently, yoga is rapidly growing in the United States and many Western countries. At the time of this writing, about 6.9% of U.S. adults, or 15.8 million people practice this ancient Indian discipline that has been around for over 5,000 years. People spend about $5.7 billion a year on yoga classes and products, including equipment, books, DVDs, etc., which has doubled since 2004. Thus, a growing number of the U.S. population now experience the benefits of this practice. And of those who do, nearly 25% have been practicing for over five years.

With the practice of *pranayama* and *asanas*, the glands and muscles increase in capability, which helps cure or prevent various diseases caused by bad food habits and irregular lifestyle. Problems such as constipation, cardiovascular and respiratory difficulties are examples of this. Yoga also strengthens the heart and keeps the veins healthy. It improves the entire digestion process, making every part of the body healthy, light, and active. Yogic exercises also work to dissolve fat, which makes the body light, healthy, fit, and attractive.

It is understood that physical growth or the anabolic process continues to the age of 18. From 18 to 35 there is a balance or neutral stage between the anabolic and catabolic or degenerative processes. But from 35 onward the catabolic or deteriorating process sets in. Yoga and meditation can significantly reduce that decline caused by the catabolic process. That is because our body's cells, organs, and nerves are affected by the attitude or energy we send through the body. They have their own consciousness and are influenced by the collective consciousness we create, that we live in by our thoughts, desires, words, and deeds. Thus, positive thoughts and spiritual practices bring uplifting results to the body. Since yoga and meditation can help establish a prolonged state of mind and body that is positive and progressive, it naturally helps rejuvenate the body and sustains life and good health, besides leads us to spiritual consciousness.

In the changes that the body undergoes through a serious practice of hatha yoga, the body can become more subtle, flexible, and balanced so that the affects of old age are greatly reduced. However, those who practice yoga seriously and not merely for outer beautification and health reasons can progress to the higher forms of yoga. They can develop or feel the superior indwelling pleasure and peace that is attainable through the full progression of yoga, which leads to self-realization, the real goal of yoga. Nonetheless, a person will still feel benefits from whatever practice they make. Even on an elementary level, a higher state of peace, tranquility, and even meditation can be attained.

Even if yoga is performed only for good health, the higher brain centers are still activated to varying degrees and can become further opened with steady practice in preparation for higher consciousness.

As one progresses through yoga and engages in meditation, a person can taste a mental calm that is experienced when the mind becomes stable and steady, and more closely connected with our real spiritual identity. Thus, a person becomes attracted to the meditation sessions, and other outer or sensual forms of pleasure or happiness become less significant. As one's self-fulfillment increases, it becomes easier to naturally avoid those activities that are not conducive to peaceful living and healthy well-being.

In the preliminary stages, yoga is, essentially, for controlling the flickering nature of the mind, and for developing one's finer qualities and expanding one's consciousness from material to spiritual awareness. It is explained that yoga is the process of completely calming the movements of the mind, which include perceived knowledge, misconception, imagination, sleep, and memory. When these are stabilized, then it can be called yoga, which offers the opportunity for the seer to become established in his own essential and fundamental nature. Yoga is the attempt and the process to realign our selves with the Supreme Self, God.

When you progress in yoga, you can feel the unwanted burdens of the mind fall away, such as anxiety, anger, greed, envy, hate, discontent, etc. Then other qualities like peacefulness, tranquility, contentment, and blissfulness will be felt. These are qualities everyone is trying to find and are some of the many things that can be accomplished with yoga, at least on the elementary level. As you make further progress, you may enter into the deeper levels of understanding and transcending the mind and gradually go so far as to attain realizations as to what your own spiritual identity is and what your relationship is with the Absolute. Becoming free from material life and regaining one's spiritual identity is the superior goal of all yoga.

As we progress in this way, we separate ourselves from the general vibrations of selfishness, greed, and anger that often pervade this planet. But we also contribute to the uplifting vibrations in the social or mass consciousness that this world so much needs these days. If we all can continue to work in this way, there could be a major shift in planetary consciousness for the upliftment of humanity for the greater good. Thus, our own spiritual progress becomes a positive influence on the whole planet.

□

3
Types of Yoga

The *Yoga Sutras* of Patanjali comprise the essence of yoga practice. Though instructions on yoga were around for many years, it is accepted that Patanjali was the first to codify it. However, yoga itself is a deep and serious process, and there are a variety of forms of yoga that can be performed. There are four main types of yoga. These are:

Jnana yoga (pronounced gyana), the path of intellectual development and understanding of what is real and what is not.

Karma yoga, the path of right action, detachment from the fruits of one's labor, and dedicating our activities for a higher and spiritual purpose.

Astanga or Raja yoga is the path of inward meditation and the attainment of higher states of consciousness through various practices that are part of eight essential steps.

Bhakti yoga is the path of raising our consciousness and uniting with God through developing our devotion and love for God, and by that means decreasing our attraction for the various aspects of the temporary material energy.

There are additional forms of yoga, but they are often considered branches or offshoots of these four paths. By understanding what is involved with each discipline, you will know how practical they are and what is the goal of each process.

HATHA YOGA

Hatha yoga is one of the first types of yoga with which people become acquainted. However, it is not a separate system of yoga as many people seem to think. It is one of the eight steps of raja yoga. Nonetheless, it can be used separately if only for helping keep the body and mind fit and in shape.

The word *hatha* consists of two *bija* or seed mantras, namely *ha* (prana) and *tha* (the mind or mental energy). *Ha* means the *prana* or energy flowing within the body and that associated with the sun, while *tha* means the mind or mental energy, or that associated with the moon. Thus, *hatha* means to bring in balance the energies of the sun and moon, or unify the vital energy of the body with the mental. This opens the door to higher consciousness, which culminates in *samadhi* during meditation. With the use of yoga, the body can become more subtle, or what is called a yoga body.

Hatha yoga is described in such early texts as the *Hatha Yoga Pradipika* by Yogi Swatmarama, the *Gheranda Samhita* by the sage Gherand, and the *Shiva Samhita*. Lord Shiva is said to be the originator of the system found in the *Hatha Yoga Pradipika*. This is highly regarded by the Nath tradition founded by Gorakshnath and his teacher Matyendranath, who was accepted to be a disciple of Lord Shiva. Yogi Gorakshnath wrote the *Goraksha Samhita*. A later text on yoga is known as the *Hatharatnavali* by Srinivasabhatta Mahayogindra. Of course, most people are aware of the *Yoga Sutras* by Patanjali in which he codified the steps of yoga.

The mind naturally has to become purified of all materialism or attraction to material and sensual desires. But in order for that to happen, the body must also be cleansed of all impurities. That is the purpose of hatha yoga, to help purify the body and align it and the energies within for meditation. Therefore, the preliminary step in all such yogas, like raja yoga, kundalini yoga, tantra yoga, or kriya yoga, must be hatha yoga. Thus, hatha yoga is not a system of its own, but is merely a step for reaching something higher. If the impurities of the body are not removed, then it will adversely affect the ability to meditate, or even bring abnormal experiences or difficulties in some yoga systems.

Hatha yoga is known as the time when there is a union with the Ida, Pingala, and Sushumna channels of subtle energy. It is this union that is the awakening in kundalini and raja yogas. However, it is no longer hatha yoga when the kundalini or *prana* moves to the Sahasrara chakra, when it then becomes yoga. Yoga means union, and in raja yoga it is when the *pranic* force unites with Brahman at the Sahasrara chakra, or when the kundalini shakti rises to the Sahasrasa and unites with Shiva.

As it states in the *Hatha Yoga Pradipika* (1:76) "There can be no perfection if hatha yoga is without raja yoga, or raja yoga without hatha yoga. Therefore, through practice of both, perfection is attained."

In any case, hatha yoga is one of the most popular forms of yoga, which can be done by anybody, regardless of how serious he or she may be about attaining higher levels of spiritual development. Although it is a part of a spiritual process, when taken as an isolated exercise technique it can be completely secular as well. Thus, it is practically non-denominational and non-sectarian. Anyone from any background can use it and acquire its benefits.

Hatha yoga involves maneuvering the body through particular *asanas* or exercises, along with breathing techniques for controlling the life airs within the body. This is the *prana*, the universal energy that flows through the body. *Prana* is divided into certain bodily airs that function in different ways. *Prana* is the incoming and outgoing breath; *apana*, is the air which expels bodily waste; *vyana* assists in the power of physical movement; *samana* distributes nutrition through the body; and *udana* is the air in the Sushumna channel. The main goal of hatha yoga is to help keep the body in shape and free from disease, the mind peaceful and steady for spiritual pursuits, and the inner energy balanced and flowing. This, however, is very useful in whatever spiritual process we pursue because if our body is too diseased, and if our mind is too restless and unsteady, they become a hindrance in our quest for spiritual awareness or perfection. Thus, with the practice of hatha yoga, the body and mind become healthier and our spiritual practice can continue with fewer impediments to higher levels of realizations. Thus, it is beneficial regardless of what is one's spiritual discipline, or even when there is no spiritual interest at all.

KARMA YOGA

Besides exercises to keep the flow of energy within the body balanced and smooth for the ease of reaching a higher consciousness, there must also be philosophy and awareness applied to everyday actions. Karma yoga is another system that many people often talk about. This is for attaining perfection through right action, of which this world could use much more. This sort of action is based on religious texts for one's purification and future happiness, such as a better next life, or for entering heaven after death. These activities may include ritualistic worship of God, or the demigods, as well as a variety of other things, such as avoiding the causing of any harm to all other living beings, and doing activities for the good of others who may be less fortunate, such as digging wells, giving food, building shelters, or doing other humanitarian work.

The main interest of a person practicing karma yoga is generally for accumulating pious credit and in achieving good future results rather than transcendence. In other words, this path is for one who is still attached to materialistic fruitive activities but want to apply a higher purpose to them. A karma-yogi often works for acquiring good karma for himself and, thus, a better future. But in the higher forms of karma yoga, the results of whatever a person does are meant to be offered to God as regulated by the rules in the Vedic literature. When one gives the fruits of his work to God, then the work becomes yoga or linked to the Supreme, which makes such actions free of all karma. Without dovetailing one's work for God in this way, all activities that are performed for one's own interest or development simply cause one to accumulate more karma, not to be free of it. Thus, such actions are not yoga, or the means to unite with the Supreme. And karma in any form, good or bad, means future rounds of birth and death in order to experience that karma.

So, ultimately, karma yoga is meant to be a means to work in the world not merely to acquire good karma or to reduce the accumulation of it, but to act in a way that can rid oneself of all karma and establish a strong connection with God. Then work becomes yoga. By giving the results to God, one becomes freed from the reactions of such work and also begins to make advancement on the path of yoga. Karma yoga is considered to be the transitional stage between material and spiritual life. Nonetheless, one's karma (as I have explained in my books *The Secret Teachings of the Vedas* and *Reincarnation and Karma: How They Really Affect Us*) should be a concern for everyone.

JNANA YOGA

Jnana yoga is the path to enlightenment through the process of mental speculation and the study and acquirement of empirical knowledge. On a deeper level, *jnana* (pronounced gyana) or jnana yoga is the process of discriminating between truth and non-truth, or reality and illusion (*maya*), and understanding what is the Divine. This is the knowledge of the soul and God, and the relationship between them. Therefore, the acquirement of *jnana* or spiritual knowledge is one of the first steps in spiritual development.

The aspirant of jnana yoga engages in long hours of study and discussion in the attempt to understand the highest truth. One following this path must also accept the authority of the great sages and study in their association. Without proper guidance along this path, one can easily become confused about what is actually the Absolute Truth. By merely involving the cognitive intellect, which is the main activity of the jnana-yogi, one simply remains on the mental or intellectual platform, which can, thus, easily fall into mere speculation rather than realization. Therefore, it is very difficult for the jnana-yogi to rise above material existence and fully enter the spiritual realm. The reason for this is that knowledge alone does not purify the consciousness, although it can help one understand the proper path to be taken and giver deeper insights into what needs to be accomplished. However, a person should not forever remain a seeker of truth, but should reach a stage of following the path that will give you realization of what is the Absolute Truth and enable you to reach the spiritual strata. This is the level of *vijnana* or practical and realized knowledge, which is far more developed and deeper than mere acquired or cultivated knowledge. The spiritual strata should not always be a mystery to solve or a quest to reach but a truth to perceive and experience.

However, in jnana yoga much of what we find today is *advaita-jnana*, the knowledge of the non-dual impersonal aspect of God wherein the idea is presented that the individual soul and God are the same, they are one, and that God is the impersonal Brahman. This is merely one aspect of the Absolute Truth, and complete realization means to understand all aspects and features of the Supreme. We will discuss this more fully as we move forward in this book.

The preliminary levels of *jnana* may be acquired from books, but it is generally accepted that a person must traverse the deeper avenues of this knowledge from a genuine *jnani*, a realized teacher. When a student has attained the means of accessing this spiritual knowledge, which, as I said, is generally the *advaita* or non-dualistic philosophy, he must continuously absorb his mind in the concepts that are presented until his mind and consciousness completely adopt it. This can be a long process, especially in this age of numerous distractions. Even if a student tries to do this with utmost sincerity, the *advaita-jnani's* conception of the Brahman is that it is inconceivable and unimaginable. So, it can be difficult to actually get a grasp as to what the soul's identity is in connection with the Brahman.

After following this path perfectly, the mind is expected to become purified or spiritualized to the point wherein it can perceive the reflection of the soul, which is beyond all *mayic* or illusory forms of experience, and, thus, beyond all external limitations. This level of perception, wherein one can see the obvious difference between the temporary body and the eternal soul within, is the stage of pure goodness or the pure *sattvic* level. Such a perception of the soul is when the *jnani* is said to have attained the stage of self-realization. This level of enlightenment, though still quite an accomplishment, is as far as this process can take one. Yet, it has not taken one all the way to God or to perceiving one's relationship with God. Knowledge and the perception of the soul removes the attachments of materialism and ignorance from the mind, however this is in preparation for what must come next to continue this process, if a practitioner gets this far. So, although he may be considered self-realized in his perception of the soul, he is not yet thoroughly liberated from material existence, which means this path is not complete in itself. There is another level of yoga which must be added to it. Therefore, jnana yoga is often combined with other forms of yoga, such as raja yoga or bhakti yoga.

DEEPER ASPECTS OF JNANA YOGA

From this stage of *jnana*, many practitioners add or

continue with the deeper aspects of yoga, if they have not already started it. This may be in the forms of astanga yoga, raja yoga, kriya yoga, or something of this sort. Yoga is the process to calm the mind and, ultimately, to become free of all sensual input and dictates from the mind. In that state lies the doorway to the spiritual dimension. In other words, it is the process of obtaining a perfectly thoughtless level of awareness in the state of pure *sattva-guna,* or mode of goodness, in which one can enter *nirvikalpa samadhi* – the thought-free form of meditation.

In this way, it is said that *jnana* is the theory or knowledge while yoga is the practice. By putting this into perfect balance, one can enter what is called *kaivalya,* the understanding of the Brahman, the impersonal form of God. The ancient Vedic texts, such as the *Yoga Darshana,* the *Yoga Sutras, Bhagavad-gita,* and others, mention that in order to be successful in this path it normally takes many lifetimes of continued practice. Such practice must be without falling down from the proper standard, along with following all the rules correctly, such as the *yamas* and *niyamas*. Only then can one gradually reach the *kaivalya* position, the perception of becoming one with the Brahman, which is the final or perfectional stage of *advaita* or the impersonalist form of yoga. So, naturally, this path holds its challenges for anyone who wishes to follow it all the way to its completion.

The *Yogshikho Upanishad* (1.55) also explains that to achieve *vijnana* or yoga realization, it takes hundreds of lifetimes in the continual state of *samadhi* to attain full liberation from material existence. This liberation refers to the process of being completely free from one's material identity and merging into the Brahman effulgence as a spiritual spark. So, it is an extremely rigid path in which one must be absolutely determined over many lifetimes if necessary. It is like a painstaking and manual process in which one rids himself or herself of every last drop of the many lifetimes of material conditioning that has accumulated in one's consciousness. Then a person has nothing left but an awareness of the Brahman and one's spiritual identity with it. After all material qualities, attachments, and conceptions are dissolved in the mind, to the point where you could say there is no mind, and one is in full *samadhi* meditation, absorbed in the Brahman, one can then enter that region at the time of death. Some yogis become expert enough where they can leave their body at will. However, such a yogi who can become liberated in this way has to rid himself of all desires for enjoyment or worldly pleasure, otherwise there can be no liberation on this path. Simply one material desire means another birth on some level. Even if he can leave his body at will and enter a higher realm, eventually he will be forced to return in order to seek out that one desire. It is similar to traveling in an airplane, high in the clouds, seeing so far in all directions. But one desire will dictate that you come down from your high position, to one town, to one house in that town, because you have one desire that you wish to satisfy in that particular town.

It is explained that even a sense of pleasure from the yogic path itself, such as the soothing and pleasant feeling during meditation in the mode of goodness, must be eliminated. These are all obstructions or limitations and attachments on the soul, keeping one from attaining full freedom in the Brahman. This is why this process can seem rather dry after some time for many practitioners, who then may look for something else, or quit altogether. Unfortunately, there are also those who are impatient and if they feel there is not the expected result, they become distracted or simply give up.

So, actual success in this type of yoga is the result of firm preparation that fully establishes one in the mode of goodness, the *sattva-guna,* and then raises one to *shuddha-sattva,* the level of pure goodness which is beyond the ordinary mode of goodness in material nature. *Shuddha-sattva* means the yogi has escaped all material limitations, all mental conceptions and attachments, but has still not reached the spiritual form of existence, which is *sat-chit-ananda-vigraha*, the form of eternal knowledge and bliss in which one realizes God. He may think that he has realized God, but he has still only attained the outskirts of full God-realization, or the preliminary steps in the complete perception of the personal form of God in which one can attain a loving relationship with God. This level of realization is still out of reach even for one who has attained success in the impersonal yoga system. Such a yogi has only reached the *sat* or eternal level of being, without the remaining *chit* (eternal knowledge), *ananda* (the bliss of spiritual existence which comes from variegated spiritual activities, and not merely the freedom from all material limitations or sufferings) and *vigraha* (the attainment of one's spiritual form in connection with one's relationship with God).

After many lives of practice (and for some advanced yogis, they have already been practicing for many lives) and when a yogi experiences the effects of the pure *sattvic* mind and attains *brahma-jnana* (knowledge of the Brahman) and perceives the Brahman, he may then be called a *jivanmukta*, a liberated soul, by those who honor him. If such a yogi can be absorbed in that *brahma-jnana* experience at the time of death, he can leave all material attachments and identification, allowing only the soul to enter a neutral state and merge into the eternal Brahman to drift there indefinitely in that great spiritual effulgence. Then he has achieved *moksha*, liberation from all material existence. The soul then attains all the benefits of being in the Brahman, such as eternity and freedom from all material limitations and sufferings, which itself is a lofty form of ecstatic bliss. But he is like a single particle amalgamated into a great white light and is hardly aware of his own individual existence. It is as if he drifts in a state of perpetual, actionless, spiritual dormancy. Therefore, even though this may be the goal of many types of yoga which portray the Brahman as the ultimate form of the

Absolute Truth, such a perfected yogi still has not attained the personal form of God, just as merging into the sun's rays does not mean you have reached the sun planet. Without knowing about *bhakti* and spiritual activities in the form of devotional service, one is still obstructed from entering the spiritual kingdom of devotional activities to God. Thus, if such a yogi ever has the slightest desire for engaging in activities again, there is only one place to go, and that is back into the material worlds. Since he has no knowledge or awareness of God's spiritual form and the realm of spiritual activities, he cannot move upward but must return to the material manifestation. That is why bhakti yoga is often combined with these forms of yoga. This means one thing: if you ever have the chance to learn about the process of devotional service, do not take it lightly, but add that to your *sadhana* and study.

THE EIGHTFOLD PATH OF RAJA YOGA

From either hatha yoga, karma yoga, or jnana yoga, a person may go on to practice raja yoga. Raja yoga, known as the royal (*raja*) way, also called astanga yoga, is the eightfold path leading to liberation. It is one of the most popular systems of yoga today. The process involves calming all mental agitation, which gradually helps the meditator to fuse with the objects of meditation by supraconscious concentration. The process is divided into eight basic steps.

THE FIRST STEP is understanding and following the *yamas*, the essential moral commandments or practices. Patanajali defined the following *yamas* in the *Yoga Sutras* as follows:

Ahimsa – non-violence toward all creatures. A yogi should avoid any type of violence through thoughts, speech, and actions. *Ahimsa* promotes and is developed only through love for every life. However, there is some confusion that it means to never lift a finger in any action of violence. But it does not mean that we become someone's doormat at the expense of our well-being. Sometimes we must become action oriented to defend Dharma.

Ahimsa also means to live peacefully with all other beings, not just humans. And this is shown most clearly by adopting the vegetarian lifestyle, which is the most non-violent diet with respect to all forms of life. There may still be some harm caused to other beings within vegetarianism, but it certainly reduces whatever harm we cause to others by a great extent. Regardless of what anyone may think, if a person expects to succeed in yoga and meditation, they must stop killing as much as possible, starting with being a vegetarian. Eating meat or the bodies of other creatures will certainly keep one in *samsara*, the rounds of birth and death. One will never be able to practice meditation to the point of *samadhi* if one still eats meat. Meat is produced only through violence and cruelty to others, the vibration of which is also ingested and lowers one's consciousness. This is completely contrary to our spiritual goals and simply causes more work and suffering for ourselves.

Ahimsa also means to live in harmony with nature, to work with it, not merely try to control nature and get what we want from it. Furthermore, *ahimsa* means to take care of ourselves by avoiding those habits which are harmful to ourselves, such as overeating, smoking, using harmful drugs, etc. We cannot expect to advance when our own activities are but causing a slow suicide, both individually and socially.

Asteya – non-stealing and avoiding that which is harmful to spiritual merit. A yogi should never desire to steal and never desire to have what others possess. This is a virtue of mind and action that drives away greedy, possessive desires that are detrimental to one's spiritual progress. This is simple enough to understand, but it also means to not be wasteful. This means to use our time wisely, not waste the natural resources that we have from nature, and not waste our time talking too much gossip or trivial conversations that serve no purpose. Thus, if we avoid this, we keep from reducing the duration of our lives by filling it with nonsense, along with the lives of those with whom we engage in such things, which is also a type of stealing. We also steal when we purchase merchandise that is made by people in forced slave labor, or near to it, or are forced to live in substandard conditions that have been inflicted upon them by their employers. Thus, *asteya* also means to care and give for the benefit of others.

Satyam – truthfulness in thought, word, and deed, and not hurting anyone by one's words. A yogi should always follow the principles of truth which is beneficial for all. This truth is the search for truth or the highest reality, speaking only truth, and upholding the truth.

Satyam also means we must not only speak the truth but live by it as well. And the highest truth to live by is spiritual knowledge. Thus, our lives must be balanced in thought, word, and deed with the spiritual knowledge that we acquire through our learning and by direct realization. Thus, when we know this knowledge, we should be able and willing to share and explain this truth to others, not by emotional force but by logical descriptions.

Brahmacharya – following the eternal principle of Brahma, or the control of sensual passions in thought, word, and deed. It also means celibacy and continence, which promotes one's determination and singleness of purpose. A yogi should restrain from carnal activities to advance toward Brahman, or that which is spiritual.

Brahmacharya is also focusing or concentrating on spiritual progress and purifying one's activities. This term is generally applicable to younger students, but it can also be applied to anyone, whether monks, sannyasis or renunciants, but also householders or married people as well. In this way, it is the means of moderating one's existence to keep the spiritual goal as central to one's life, and in all our relations, whether with wife, sons, daughters, friends, etc.

Aparigraha – abstinence from collecting material things. A yogi should not possess those things which are not necessary for living. Altogether this means to avoid violence, lying, stealing, greed, possessiveness, and a lack of celibacy. *Aparigraha* promotes renunciation and a thrifty lifestyle that allows one to more easily attain spiritual bliss. There is only so much we can use in life, and beyond that it becomes a distraction, not only from our spiritual goal, but becomes a diversion from what can give us peace of mind, mental balance, discrimination, austerity, and the time we need to practice our *sadhana*.

THE SECOND STEP is *niyama* or preparation and discipline for self-realization. This involves austerity or undergoing physical hardships for a higher result, along with study of scriptural texts, purity of mind and body, contentment, and devoting all one's activities to God. *Yama* means the things to avoid and *niyama* means the practice one must do. Together they help keep the yogi's passions quiet and stilled, and keep him in harmony with nature. The *niyamas* include:

Shaucha – purity and cleanliness of mind and body, keeping it as a temple. A yogi should always keep his physical body as well as mind free and pure. This means that one must bathe everyday to stay clean, but must also do his or her spiritual *sadhana* or practices to clean the mind and consciousness. This is to prepare and to keep the consciousness purified or spiritualized for our continued development, which manifests in our positive and uplifting thoughts and actions. This involves keeping all deviating and impure thoughts away, or out of what we read, hear, or watch in the form of entertainment or information. We have to be careful with the images we imbibe because sometimes they can last a long time, and it can take years to remove fiercely negative images or brutal thoughts from our minds and consciousness. So, it is better to keep out what may take a long time from which to rid ourselves.

Saucha also means to guard ourselves from putting the wrong or degrading things into our diet. The pure diet alone can do wonders to help purify and stabilize the mind, and help keep it focused on the spiritual goal of life. Impure foods, no matter how tasty one may consider them to be, only do harm to both body and mind.

Santosha – satisfaction or contentment of mind with what one has without undue endeavor. A yogi should be satisfied with whatever he gets within the dharmic (lawful) means. This refers to internal and mental contentment and not merely pleasure from external sources or objects. This means that we should only want what we need, and be happy with what we have. We should not want what is unnecessary or frivolous. The less we need to acquire, then the less we need to work for the money to spend on what will not help us anyway. Otherwise, as they say, the more money you have, the more you spend. So, *santosh* means we have more time to be happy with whatever life has given us, knowing that life is full of lessons to learn from by what it gives us.

Tapas – voluntary austerity and tolerance in body, mind, and speech for a higher cause. A yogi should be determined to endure pain, troubles, and adversities in order to achieve his objective on the spiritual path. This austerity is in regard to our spiritual practice. In other words, we undergo some hardship to attain something higher. For example, our mind may not like the idea of getting up early to do our spiritual practice and meditation. But we do it because we know the benefits we get from it. That is *tapas*. Of course, no matter what we want, we have to undergo some sacrifice to get ahead. But *tapas* means to progress spiritually, not merely undergo hardships to make more money, advance in our career, get a promotion at our job, etc. It is through the practice of *tapas*, or austerity, that we become free from the dictates of our mind and senses. These have lead us into attachment to the bodily concept of life, or *maya*, illusion, so it is now time that we break away from that enslavement and attain freedom in understanding who and what we really are. *Tapas* also means to tolerate various disturbances or urges in life while remaining devoted to our spiritual progress.

Swadhyaya – self-analysis, introspection, scriptural research, and reflection to understand and perceive who and what is our real identity and how we are progressing. This also can be interpreted in two ways. The first meaning is the study of self, contemplating on the nature of self and trying to understand the principles of yoga on one's own. According to the second meaning, a yogi should go through and study various principles of yoga again and again. He should also research the scriptures such as the *Vedas*, *Upanishads*, *Bhagavad-gita*, and other texts. This process elevates the consciousness to a higher level in which we start to realize that all creation is made for *bhakti* (devotion) to the Supreme rather than *bhoga* (enjoyment for ourselves), and that all creation is divine. Naturally, everyone should study the sacred Vedic texts, which are the foundation of the spiritual knowledge that is most deep and helpful to our development. Then by comparing our symptoms of spiritual advancement with the descriptions given in the texts or with the help of spiritual teachers, we can get insight into our own position and how we are advancing and what more we need to do and what qualities we need to attain. This should also help keep us motivated to stay the course for all the practices that are recommended.

The last of the *niyamas* is *Ishwara-pranidhana* – acceptance, devotion, and surrender to God, or the offering of the fruits of one's actions to God. A yogi should surrender his actions and thoughts to the Supreme Being, God. Such surrender is one of the highest principles of yoga. This and the realization of God is the culmination of the previous *yamas* and *niyamas*, and the epitome of following *Sanatana-dharma*.

Besides these five *yamas* and five *niyamas*, the *Hatha Yoga Pradipika* gives us ten *yamas* and ten *niyamas*, which are: nonviolence, truth, non-stealing, continence (being absorbed in a pure state of consciousness), forgiveness, endurance, compassion, humility, moderate diet, and cleanliness as the ten rules of conduct (*yamas*). (HYP 1:1ii)

Penance (austerity), contentment, belief (faith) in the Supreme Being, charity, worship of God, listening to the recitation of sacred scriptures, modesty, a discerning intellect, *japa* (mantra repetition), and sacrifice are the ten observances (*niyamas*). (HYP 1:1iii)

The *yamas* and *niyamas* together are like basic moral values that one must have if he or she expects to go further while anticipating any genuine results. You can find similar principles as the basics of most any religion. Once you can follow these, then we can move forward to the additional steps in this yoga system.

THE THIRD STEP is *asana*, which means a seat or postures for meditation that are often used in hatha yoga as previously explained. *Asanas* are the disciplines of using steady and comfortable postures, both in sitting or standing positions, which will be suitable for toning the body for the correct flow of *prana*, or psychic energy, and to heighten one's consciousness for meditation. This is used with *pranayama*, the controlled breathing and retention of breaths in a systematic way. *Asanas* help control or calm the mind, and also builds or stores the *prana* or life-force within the body for preparing the consciousness for higher awareness. This process always uses what is called *rechaka* (exhalation), *puraka* (inhalation), and then *kumbhaka* (retention).

Asanas also help promote health. *Asanas* are exercises, some simple and some quite advanced, that can be performed alone with minimal equipment, like a blanket or mat, fresh air, and room to move around, preferably outdoors. Different *asanas* develop and affect different nerves, muscles, and organs of the body and keep the system strong, limber, and free from disease. Thus, the body becomes a fit instrument for spiritual development and higher awareness. Learning *asanas* can also help in other systems of yoga, too, and helps keep the body in a good, healthy condition, which is beneficial for anyone. So, we have included the basic *asanas* and *pranayama* exercises for you to use described later in this book.

THE FOURTH STEP is *pranayama*, breath control for fixing the mind in concentration. *Prana* means life or energy, and also can mean spirit. *Ayama* indicates the length and retention of breath between inhalation and exhalation, and control of the *prana* within the body. Thus, *pranayama* is the process of controlling, stimulating, regulating, and channeling that *prana* to help us live more healthy and happy. *Pranayama* purifies and energizes the body, mind, and nervous system the same way a bath purifies and energizes the body.

Furthermore, since it is considered that a person is born with a certain number of allotted breaths in a lifetime, the yogi learns breath control to strengthen the respiratory system, soothe the nerves, and steady the mind for meditation, and to prolong one's life. Simply by controlling one's breathing a person can steady the beating of his heart. When one's breathing is not smooth, the mind is also usually unsteady and easily agitated. So, as one learns *pranayama*, the mind becomes equipoised and free from the pulling of the senses. It can also clean the *nadis* (subtle *pranic* channels) and open the *pranic* currents as well as decrease the unwanted inner mental activity.

THE FIFTH STEP is *pratyahara*, control of the senses and checking the mind's attraction to external objects. It is necessary to control the senses to advance in yoga, and in *pratyahara* the yogi analyzes the mind's attraction for external objects. By the use of his study and cultivated knowledge, he recognizes that sensual delights lead to one's destruction, and the path of sense control leads to his progress and liberation. By intelligently adjusting his consciousness, the yogi gives up sensual desires in order to achieve the proper frame of mind and freedom from the modes of nature to pursue successfully the goal of yoga.

THE SIXTH STEP is *dharana*, concentrating on the object of meditation. However, it is more than mere concentration. It is becoming so absorbed in one's focus on something that a person becomes oblivious to everything else. When the body is balanced and the mind has been completely stilled by the previous steps, the yogi can totally concentrate on a single object of meditation.

THE SEVENTH STEP is *dhyana*, when the mind is in a state of undisturbed flowing meditation. In this stage the mind takes on the characteristics of the object being meditated on, and the frequency of consciousness adjusts to that upon which the awareness is focused. So, if the yogi is merged in meditation and contemplation on the Supreme, the yogi can enter that level of reality and remain in that state of supreme bliss.

THE EIGHTH AND FINAL STEP is *samadhi*, in which, according to the eightfold path, the yogi becomes one with the Supreme, or fully engaged in thought of the Supreme. *Samadhi* means the absorption in the balanced, eternal awareness or knowledge. This is the state of self-realization for the individual. It is when a person becomes free of ego, bodily identification, sense perception, mental activity, and all time and space. This allows for one's consciousness to achieve its natural state of nonduality. This is in reference to the way the mind interferes with our perception of things around us and, thus, rather than seeing everything as parts of the Divine energy of God, we see the world of names, forms, images, desires, goals, and temporary illusions, all of which are interpreted to be separate from God. In this state of being, we become absorbed in the finite and unaware or forgetful of the Infinite. This is what we want to avoid. So, this is why calming the mind or even attaining freedom from its influence is a prime goal of yoga. Thus, in rising above the effects of the mind and then perfecting our meditation and reaching the state of *samadhi,* we can attain the Infinite. In kundalini yoga, the state of *samadhi* is considered the union of the *kundalini* or *shakti,* the female energy, with Shiva, the universal male energy. This union takes place in the top chakra, the Sahasrara Chakra.

So, in the state of *samadhi,* the knower and the known, the seer and the seen, the soul and the Supersoul, become one. Thus, the yogi loses all individuality and merges into the Supreme or in thoughts of the Supreme. This is the result of reaching perfection on this particular path of yoga and in the state of flawless meditation.

We should point out, however, that the path to *samadhi* through this eightfold system is arduous. There is no question that reaching *moksha* through the complete process of raja yoga is not easy for most people. It takes time, patience, discipline, determination, and endurance, especially in developing one's concentration. Each of the eight steps calls for its own rigorous discipline. Bhakti and karma yoga are also important in this path since it requires that karma must be reduced or even stopped, and the emotions must be purified or spiritualized as done through bhakti yoga. Furthermore, as in any science, if you do not follow the procedure properly, you do not get the results. For example, the actual form of perfection in *pranayama,* the control of the ingoing and outgoing breaths that are the last interference in one's complete absorption of meditation, means that, ultimately, the yogi should reach the stage of stopping his breathing entirely during his meditation. Just as it is said that in meditation the yogi should enter the gap between thoughts and extend it, therein finding the doorway to freedom beyond the mind, similarly the retention or space between breaths is the same space between mental and physical distractions. This is the state of being that a yogi needs to reach for entering into the deepest possible meditation, or that meditation in *samadhi* which allows one to reach *moksha,* complete liberation from material existence and any further rounds of birth and death. The breath is considered the last obstacle or distraction. So, one must overcome this. Only after this is accomplished can the yogi withdraw his senses and mind from all material and physical engagements. Then he can go on to the steps of *pratyahara, dharana, dhyana,* and possibly reach *samadhi.*

Yet, it must be mentioned that such practices of what I call mechanical attempts to completely subdue or control the mind and senses by long, difficult exercises in sitting, breathing, sense control, etc., are not likely to be completely successful for anyone in this age of Kali-yuga. This is the age of constant quarrel, confusion, and distractions of all kinds. This form of yoga was recommended for the ages many years ago when the times were more peaceful. In this age, the complete removal of our attachments and distractions through such a process is rarely attainable for the average person. Besides, in the distant past when things were easier and mankind lived longer, at least as described in the Vedic texts, this yoga system required many years of meditation for genuine spiritual development. This was not something that was done for twenty minutes a day, but was practiced all day, day after day for years on end. The people of the Vedic age were more inclined and capable of doing that. In these modern times, however, we can see that most people are so restless and have so much on their mind that they find it difficult to sit completely still even for ten minutes. So, this is not a process that was recommended or really expected to provide the means for total spiritual perfection or *moksha* in this age of Kali-yuga, which offers many forms of agitation, worries, and problems with which we must concern ourselves.

The difficulties in raja yoga are that it takes time, discipline, patience, serious practice, and control of the mind, all of which are not easy in this day and age. The real goal of raja yoga can never be reached until the mind has been balanced, the karmas deactivated, the emotions purified through bhakti yoga, and, ultimately, after the chakras and the *nadi* channels, especially the Sushumna, have been opened or awakened. All of this may not be so simple, and constant attempts without success can lead to depression or discontent or disinterest in continued spiritual pursuits. However, even minor success on this path can lead to basic progress, which can provide some insights into our own character, the nature of our own mind, and slow but sure changes. As one begins to uplift one's consciousness, the basic lures of life such as sensual desires and urges diminish, and the uncontrolled nature of the mind becomes more tame, tranquil, and less disturbing. This is positive progress that can be beneficial for anyone and will separate them from the general crowd of people who have not developed themselves in this way. We can all strive to attain this. But the real goal is still far beyond that.

In the meantime, we still need to remember that there are certain factors that will contribute to our failure in yoga, which need to be avoided. These are described in the *Hatha Yoga Pradipika* as overeating, exertion, talkativeness, adhering to many rules, being in the company of common people, and unsteadiness (wavering mind) are the six (causes) that destroy yoga. (HYP 1:15)

Furthermore, there are six qualities that will assist us in continuing our practice and bring success in yoga, such as enthusiasm, perseverance, discrimination, unshakable faith, courage, and avoiding the company of common people (who are entrenched in materialism). (HYP 1:16)

Therefore, following these principles with the serious practice of this form of yoga can still provide some preliminary benefits, depending on how deeply a person can enter into it. The point is that one must be serious if a person expects to take it to its completion. Nonetheless, any spiritual progress made is never lost. It is an asset that clings to the soul. Still, as established in the *Yoga Sutras* of Patanjali, the first goal is to become free from the dictations and disturbances of the mind. However successful we may or may not be, this can still help us distance ourselves from the external drama in which we always find ourselves and the constant conversation that goes on in our mind. This will help center ourselves in our spiritual identity. This can also bring some practical inner peacefulness into our life. And once we are free of these kinds of mental distractions, real concentration and meditation can begin. This can even lead to experiences attained only from a lofty state of consciousness.

Essentially, it is the higher taste that one attains from their spiritual connection, the perception of their true identity, that gives one the motivation to continue their practice of yoga, and, thus, reach a higher meaning of life based on direct perception rather than mere theory and practice. In that state of consciousness, whatever system we use to meditate on God can be more effective and become the key to our enthusiasm and dedication.

Once the mind has been brought to a suitable condition for meditation by performing this type of yoga, from this point, the goal of yogis may still differ. Some yogis meditate on God with the intent of merging into the body of God, or to "become" God or one with God as they say, or be equal to God, as explained in the *Yoga Sutras* of Patanjali.

This idea comes from a lack of knowledge of one's true spiritual identity as an eternal, individual part of the Supreme with an eternal, spiritual relationship with the Lord that simply needs to be reawakened. This is the real purpose of yoga. Such a relationship is not awakened by attempting to merge into the body of God. That is only another way of disregarding or even trying to nullify this relationship. Thus, to practice yoga with such a desire does not lead to the highest level of self-realization or perception of our real spiritual identity.

Limiting ourselves to an impersonal conception of the Absolute is most difficult to understand for the embodied souls because we are all persons, and we naturally relate to each other and everything in a personal way. We have a personality, and in various Vedic texts God is known as the Supreme Personality, so there are relations. However, these are spiritual relations which are quite beyond the inclinations of materialistic relations.

So, whatever we imagine as the impersonal Brahman is so tinged with our personal tendencies and conceptions that it is immediately not the Brahman that we can imagine. Thus, the question that arises is how can we ever imagine what is the Brahman, and that if we are persons in this material level of reality, which the *Bhagavad-gita* says is a perverted reflection of the spiritual world, then why should we not have the potential to be persons or individuals in spiritual reality?

In any case, if one wants to pursue this eightfold form of yoga to its ultimate goal, the *Bhagavad-gita* contains some important instructions by Lord Krishna on how this yoga process is actually meant to be performed, as related next. Many parts of the following instructions, however, can be applied towards any kind of yoga.

FURTHER INSTRUCTIONS ON RAJA YOGA FROM BHAGAVAD-GITA

It is explained in the Sixth Chapter of *Bhagavad-gita* that a transcendentalist on this path of raja yoga should be free from desires, live alone, control his mind, and always concentrate on the Supreme. He should remain in a secluded and sacred place. He should arrange a seat, neither too high nor too low, with kusa-grass on the ground, covered with a soft cloth and deerskin (which was used to help keep away snakes). While sitting on the seat, the yogi should keep his body erect and stare at the tip of his nose (closing the eyes completely may lead to sleep), control the mind and senses, purify the heart, and subdue the mind to keep it unagitated and free from fear. Thus, completely free from sex life, the yogi should meditate on the Supreme as Paramatma, the Supersoul in the heart, and make Him the ultimate goal of life. By this process of controlling the body, mind, and activities, the mystic attains the spiritual strata by ending his material existence. Entering the spiritual atmosphere and achieving liberation is the ultimate level of success in this or any other form of yoga.

Furthermore, the yogi attains the goal of yoga after he becomes situated in transcendence. This is possible only if he is temperate in his eating, sleeping, working, and recreation, and becomes devoid of all material desires. As steady as an unwavering lamp in a windless place, the yogi must meditate on the Supreme with his mind. This perfectional stage of yoga is *samadhi* or trance when the mind is free from all material engagement. The characteristic of this is that the yogi can see the self and experience boundless spiritual happiness through his transcendental senses. The yogi realizes the ultimate spiritual truth and feels nothing is greater than this. Even amidst the greatest difficulties the yogi does not give up his spiritual consciousness. Thus, he is never shaken from his position of freedom from material miseries. In this way, one should practice yoga with steady determination and abandon all varieties of material desires. Gradually, step by step, such a transcendentalist should intelligently practice yoga until he can enter the trance of thinking of nothing but the Supreme.

Since this description says that the meditation should be on the Supersoul, we should know what is that form. According to the Vedic texts, the Supersoul is the plenary expansion of God, who is situated within the heart. How we begin to understand and perceive the Supersoul is described in *Bhagavad-gita* by Sri Krishna: "I shall now explain the knowable, knowing which you will taste the eternal. This is beginningless, and it is subordinate to Me. It is called

Brahman, the spirit, and it lies beyond the cause and effect of this material world. Everywhere are His hands and legs, His eyes and faces, and He hears everything. In this way, the Supersoul exists. The Supersoul is the original source of all senses, yet He is without [material] senses. He is unattached, although He is the maintainer of all living beings. He transcends the modes of nature, and at the same time He is the master of all modes of material nature. The Supreme Truth exists both internally and externally, in the moving and nonmoving. He is beyond the power of the material senses to see or to know. Although far, far away, He is also near to all. Although the Supersoul appears to be divided, He is never divided. He is situated as one. Although He is the maintainer of every living entity, it is to be understood that He devours all and develops all. He is the source of light in all luminous objects. He is beyond the darkness of matter and is unmanifested. He is knowledge, He is the object of knowledge, and He is the goal of knowledge. He is situated in everyone's heart." (*Bg*.13.13-18)

"In this [material] body there is another, a transcendental enjoyer who is the Lord, the supreme proprietor, who exists as the overseer and permitter, and who is known as the Supersoul. That Supersoul is perceived by some through meditation [yoga], by some through the cultivation of knowledge [jnana], and by others through working without fruitive desire [no karma]. Again there are those who, although not conversant in spiritual knowledge, begin to worship the Supreme Person upon hearing about Him from others. Because of their tendency to hear from authorities, they also transcend the path of birth and death. One who sees the Supersoul accompanying the individual soul in all bodies and who understands that neither the soul nor the Supersoul is ever destroyed actually sees. One who sees the Supersoul in every living being and equal everywhere does not degrade himself by his mind. Thus, he approaches the transcendental destination." (*Bg*.13.23,25-26,28-29)

The Supersoul is here explained to be eternal, completely spiritual, the source of everything, yet subordinate to Lord Krishna, and expanded everywhere, dwelling within the hearts of everyone. He is the source of all light and knowledge, and the goal of all knowledge. Although the Supersoul appears to be divided by expanding in the Paramatma form situated within the hearts of every living being, He is still existing as the one Absolute Truth. This is confirmed in the following verses:

"Physical nature is known to be endlessly mutable. The universe is the cosmic form of the Supreme Lord, and I [Sri Krishna] am that Lord represented as the Supersoul, dwelling in the heart of every embodied being." (*Bg*.8.4)

"The one Supreme Lord is situated within all material bodies and within everyone's soul. Just as the moon is reflected in innumerable reservoirs of water, the Supreme Lord, although one, is present within everyone. Thus, every material body is ultimately composed of the energy of the one Supreme Lord." (*Bhagavata Purana* 11.18.32)

"The Supreme Personality of Godhead has created many residential places like the bodies of human beings, animals, birds, saints, and demigods. In all these innumerable bodily forms, the Lord resides with the living beings as Paramatma. Thus He is known as the *purushavatara*." (*Bhag*.7.14.37)

"As the one sun appears reflected in countless jewels, so Govinda manifests Himself [as the Paramatma] in the hearts of all living beings." (*Caitanya-caritamrita, Adi*.2.19)

The material bodies of the living entity, although seeming to appear in different sizes and shapes, are nonetheless all made of the same basic ingredients, namely earth, air, water, etc. By understanding that within the body exists the spirit soul along with the Supersoul, there is no reason to disrespect anyone. Every living entity is spiritually part and parcel of the Supreme, and the Supreme is situated within the heart next to each of His spiritual parts and parcels. The difference is that the individual soul is situated within only one body and cannot understand what is going on in the bodies and minds of others. The Supersoul, however, is present in everyone's body and knows quite well what is happening in the minds and bodies of everyone.

How to perceive the Supersoul is through one of three ways: by perfection in meditation through which one can perceive the Supersoul, by cultivation of knowledge by which one gains the knowledge of the Supersoul, or by engaging in the process of yoga. Others can understand the Supersoul by hearing from spiritual authorities. In any case, if one attains such spiritual vision he will actually see things as they are, and the transcendental destination then becomes achievable.

Further ways of recognizing how the Supersoul integrates the body and soul are described in the *Taittiriya Upanishad* (3.10.2). It is pointed out that one can perceive the Supersoul by the action of speech, as action in the hands, walking in the feet, and other bodily activities. In other words, it is by the power of the Supersoul within that we have the ability to do these things. This is further substantiated in *Srimad-Bhagavatam* (2.2.35) where it states: "The Personality of Godhead Lord Sri Krishna is in every living being along with the individual soul. And this fact is perceived and hypothesized in our acts of seeing and taking help from intelligence." Therefore, through the Vedic literature we can understand that the unifying factor between the desires of the self and the response of the brain and body to our desires can be recognized as the power of the Supersoul within.

The size, shape, and dress of the Supersoul, who is realized and seen by those sages who have reached the goal of knowledge through yoga, is also described in *Srimad-Bhagavatam* as follows, and is the way we should meditate on the Supersoul: "Others conceive of the Supreme Personality residing within the body in the region of the heart and measuring only eight inches, with four hands carrying a lotus, a chakra, a conchshell, and a club respectively. His mouth expresses His happiness. His eyes spread like the petals of a lotus, and His garments, yellowish like the saffron of the *kadamba* flower, are bedecked with valuable jewels. His ornaments are all made of gold, set with jewels, and He wears a glowing head-dress and earrings. His lotus feet are placed over the whorls of the lotus-like hearts of great mystics. On His chest is the Kaustubha jewel, engraved with a beautiful calf, and there are other jewels on His shoulders. His complete torso is garlanded with fresh flowers. He is well decorated with an ornamental wreath about His waist and rings studded with valuable jewels on His fingers. His leglets, His bangles, His oiled hair, curling with a bluish tint, and His beautiful smiling face are all very pleasing. The Lord's magnanimous pastimes and the glowing glancing of His smiling face are all indications of His extensive benedictions. One must therefore concentrate on this transcendental form of the Lord, as long as the mind can be fixed on Him by meditation." (*Bhag*.2.2.8-12)

Although the above instructions can be used in any form of yoga or religion, the yogi on the path of astanga or raja yoga is ultimately supposed to raise his life energy up through the different chakras and fix it between his eyebrows. Then in full devotion remember the Supreme Lord as described above. To be most effective, the yogi must practice constant celibacy, chant *om* properly, and remain detached from all sensual thoughts. By performing such meditation for many years, even hundreds or over the course of lifetimes if necessary, the yogi would gradually purify and control the mind until he could quit his body at will without any mental agitation or physical disturbance.

Of course, in this age no one can practice this form of yoga for hundreds of years. Neither are there many who have the mental strength to meditate properly with a singularly focused mind for hours at a time. But thousands of years ago, when this form of yoga was meant to be practiced, people could do that and actually reach perfection. Thus, the yogi would quit his body when he was ready, and at the proper time, and leave all material limitations behind. *Bhagavad-gita* (8.24) states that those who know the Supreme leave this world during the day, during the bright lunar fortnight, and during the six months when the sun travels to the north (summer).

In this way, the yogi who practices the raja yoga system should be so powerful that he can control the time when he will leave his body. Or, if a proper time is present, he should be able to raise his life air to the top of the head and, while meditating on the Supreme in devotion, immediately quit his body and enter the spiritual world. However, the *Bhagavd-gita* (8.25) states that those who leave this life during the night, the moonless fortnight, or in the six months of the southern course of the sun, or those who attain the lunar planet, again take birth in the material world. Therefore, if the yogi happened to leave his body at the improper time, or was thinking of a pleasant life in the heavenly planets, or of achieving mystical perfections, then he would not enter the spiritual world but would be transferred to the region of the universe upon which he was meditating. Or he would enter into the region where the facilities for his level of consciousness or material attachments or attractions could be best accommodated. On some of the higher material planets, in the heavenly region, the residents are born with all mystic abilities and can travel through space at will. The yogi may evolve through such higher planets lifetime after lifetime, but until the mind is pure and the consciousness spiritualized, he cannot enter into the spiritual region and will be confined to different dimensions of the material universe.

DIFFICULTIES TO REACH SPIRITUAL PERFECTION IN RAJA YOGA

However, it is significant to note that even after hearing

all about this system of yoga, Arjuna, who was being taught these things by Lord Krishna at the time, said that this system appears impractical and unendurable since the mind is so restless and unsteady. It is turbulent, obstinate, and very strong. To subdue it is more difficult than controlling the wind. (*Bg*.6.33-4) Therefore, we must ask if Arjuna, who was a far more capable person 5,000 years ago during the Vedic times than we are today, could perceive the difficulty of this system, then it behooves us to understand that we should expect the same challenges if we are to use this system today and hope to reach perfection with it. The ultimate stage with this form of yoga is that you are supposed to become so focused on the Supreme within and around you that you attain liberation from any further cycles of birth and death in this material creation. However, now that we are in Kali-yuga, an age of quarrel, difficulties, distractions, and discomfort, it is even harder for the majority of people to control the mind to such a degree.

Nonetheless, Lord Krishna continued to advise Arjuna that even though it is very difficult to curb the restless mind, it is possible by constant practice and detachment. "Self-realization is difficult work for one whose mind is unbridled. But My opinion is that he whose mind is controlled, and who strives by the proper process, is assured of success." (*Bg*.6.35-36)

However, Arjuna was not so convinced and still questioned Lord Krishna. He asked what was the destination of someone who starts the process of self-realization but does not persevere, but gives up due to worldly-mindedness and does not attain success. Does such a person perish like a riven cloud, with no position anywhere? (*Bg*.6.37-38)

Here Arjuna is not merely asking about the astanga or eightfold path of yoga. He is asking about any kind of genuine process of self-realization. What happens when a sincere person still cannot continue to reach the goal? Lord Krishna answers him that such a transcendentalist does not meet with destruction either in this world or in the next. One who does good is never overcome by evil. Even an unsuccessful yogi who cannot reach *moksha* can still reach heaven where, after many, many years of enjoyment on the heavenly planets of the pious [attained by the yogi's spiritual merit], he is born in a family of righteous people, or a wealthy family of aristocracy [due to his pious credits]. Or he takes birth in a family of transcendentalists who are already on the spiritual path and great in wisdom. Such a birth is most rare in this world. But on taking such a birth, he again revives his divine consciousness from his previous life. Then he takes up the process again and continues to make further progress in order to achieve complete success. It is by virtue of the spiritual consciousness from his previous existence that he automatically becomes attracted to the yogic principles – even without seeking them. Such an inquisitive transcendentalist, striving for yoga, stands always above the rituals prescribed in the scriptures. But when the yogi engages himself with sincere endeavor, and being washed of all contamination, then, after many, many births and deaths, he ultimately attains the supreme goal. A yogi is greater than the ascetic performing austerities, greater than the empiricist philosopher, and greater than one engaged in karmic activities for fruitive results. So, in all circumstances be a yogi. (*Bg*.6.40-46)

Herein Lord Krishna describes the positive opportunity that awaits anyone who makes any sincere endeavor on the path of spiritual advancement, even if they do not fully succeed in one lifetime. And then He concludes in the next verse the real goal of yoga, again pointing out the ease and need for the process of bhakti yoga, loving devotion to Him. "And of all yogis, he who always abides in Me with great faith, worshiping Me in transcendental loving service [*bhakti*], is most intimately united with Me in yoga and is the highest of all." (*Bg*.6.47)

Therefore, only a very few may ever be found who can be completely successful in raja or astanga yoga in one life without previous progress in past lives, although many may try and reach basic levels of progress. Such levels of expertise may even be exhibited in the form of mystic powers and might look impressive at first, but these are not the end result. Of course, many people may be fooled by those who display mystic powers and think that such yogis are great saints. Indeed, sometimes they are, but such mystic abilities are nothing more than by-products of one's austerities, and are not necessarily a sign of genuine spiritual consciousness or purification. Some yoga students, especially in the West, may be attracted by these mystic powers and engage in yoga in the hopes of attaining them. But the number of Westerners who have ever displayed such mystic abilities, which will be described next, is practically nil.

In any case, the point to remember is that these mystic powers are nothing more than added attractions that one may attain as they advance along the path of yoga. Therefore, it is advised that these mystic powers must be ignored or they will become obstacles in one's spiritual advancement, and distractions from the real goal of yoga. Therefore, if a yogi or guru makes an open display of various mystic abilities in order to attract people and make disciples, this should be taken as a warning that he may only be a fraud, like a magician performing some tricks simply to get adoration and distinction. Such things have never taken one all the way to God.

MYSTIC POWERS

Mystic powers are quite real and can be acquired or developed through the practice of yoga, austerities, or especially by mastering such things as *pranayama*. They are not the goal of yoga, but are sidelines of development that one gets along the way if one is serious and steady enough. What these yogic powers are and what they do is described in *Srimad-Bhagavatam* (11.15.3-8). There the Supreme Personality, Sri Krishna, says that master yogis have established eighteen types of mystic perfection, eight of which are primary, having their shelter in Him, and ten secondary, appearing from the material mode of goodness. The eight primary powers consist of *anima*, making one's body very small; *mahima*, becoming very big; *laghima*, becoming as light as air; *prapti*, acquiring whatever one desires; *prakamya-siddhi*, experiencing any enjoyable thing; *isita-siddhi*, controlling aspects of material energy; *vasita-siddhi*, overcoming the modes of nature; and *kamavasayita-siddhi*, obtaining anything from anywhere.

The ten secondary mystic powers that arise from the material mode of goodness through yoga are freedom from hunger and thirst, the ability to see and hear things far away, to move with the speed of mind, to assume any form, to see the pastimes of the demigods, to attain whatever one is determined to do, to hold influence over others, to have power to know past and future, to be immune from heat and cold and other dualities, to know the thoughts of others, to be invincible, and to halt the influence of fire, sun, water, and poison.

The *Yoga Sutras* of Patanjali (3:4) also described how these powers can be achieved: "When these three – concentration, meditation, and absorption – are brought to bear upon an object, they are called *samyama*." This explains the means to perceive the true nature of the object upon which one is meditating, and then absorb the real condition or knowledge of it. It is like leaving the body without traveling, or like scouting the universe while keeping the body in one place. Through *samyama* you can acquire knowledge and abilities of various kinds. For example, in the third chapter of Patanjali's *Yoga Sutras* we find the descriptions of many kind of yogic powers that one can attain by perfecting the process of *samyama*. "By making *samyama* on the three kinds of changes, one obtains knowledge of the past and the future. (3:16) By making *samyama* on previous thought waves [or levels of consciousness], one obtains knowledge of one's past lives. (3:18) By making *samyama* on the distinguishing marks of another man's body, one obtains knowledge of the nature of his mind [consciousness]. (3:19) If one makes *samyama* on the form of one's body, obstructing its perceptibility and separating its power of manifestation from the eyes of the beholder, then one's body becomes invisible. (3:21) By making *samyama* on two kinds of karma – that which will soon bear fruit and that which will manifest much later – or by recognizing the portents of death, a yogi may know the exact time of his death, or his separation from the body." (3:23)

Similarly, "By making *samyama* on the sun, moon, and polestar, one gains knowledge of cosmic spaces, the stars, and the motion of planets. (3:27-29) By making *samyama* on the radiance within the back of the head [the location of the bindu], one becomes able to see the celestial beings." (3:33) However, there is a warning about this: "When the yogi is tempted by invisible [or subtle] beings in high places, let the yogi feel neither allured nor flattered, for he is in danger of being caught once more by ignorance." (3:52) This means s couple of things. One is that such a yogi may feel pride that he can recognize or even converse with such subtle beings, the likes of which common men cannot see, but he may also be persuaded by them to act in such a way that he loses sight of the goal of yoga and human existence. He may desire to reach the subtle or heavenly realm where such beings exist. Thus, he again falls into ignorance and loses the goal of yoga and the purpose of human life for which he endeavored for so many years or even lifetimes.

Through these mystical abilities, it can seem as though the yogi can perform miracles. However, it is only the mechanics of perfecting the yoga system that make these possible. The common man may not have much knowledge of such, which make such activities seem extraordinary, yet these are the byproducts of constant practice along the way to spiritual progress. They are not in themselves the goal. Some of these miraculous activities are further described as follows: "When the bonds of the mind caused by karma have been loosened, the yogi can enter into the body of another by knowledge of the operation of its nerve currents." (3:39) In other words, by understanding his true potential, being free and unbound from the limitations of bodily identification, the yogi can actually enter into and operate the body of another being while his own body remains dormant.

Also: "By controlling the nerve-currents that govern the lungs and the upper parts of the body, the yogi can walk on water and swamps, or on thorns and similar objects, and he can also die at will. (3:40) By controlling the force which governs the *prana*, he can surround himself with a blaze of light (like a bright halo). (3:41) By making *samyama* on the relation between the body and the ether, or be acquiring through meditation the lightness of cotton fiber, the yogi can fly through the air." (3:43) For most people these would be fantastic to see, but a yogi takes them in stride and is not distracted by such things.

Although these yogic powers may seem impressive, many of them have also been accomplished by the advancement of materialistic technology. For example, the *Yoga Sutras* of Patanjali state that by controlling the nerve-currents that govern the lungs and upper body, the yogi can walk on water or thorns and similar objects. To reach this perfection, the yogi may have to struggle and meditate for twenty, thirty years, or fifty years. Or a common man may go to the boatman and pay a small fare to immediately cross the river. What is the advantage of practicing yoga for so many years simply to walk on water?

Similarly, from the *anima-siddhi* one can become so small he can enter into a stone or atom. But modern science has made tunnels through hills and mountains and have analyzed such small molecules as atoms, accomplishing similar results as the *anima-siddhi*. By scientific advancement we can also fly through the air, travel under water, or see and hear things from far away as on television or radio. Of course, there may be some things science cannot do, like the *laghima-siddhi*, which enables one to go to the sun planet by entering and then flowing into the rays of the sunshine. Or *prapti-siddhi*, which enables one to get anything by extending his hand and taking what he wants from anywhere. Although it may appear like he is magically producing the object, but actually he is just taking it from someone else.

By the yogic power of *isita-siddhi* one can create or destroy an entire planet. This power is much stronger than the atomic bombs that can only blow up a small portion of this planet and never recreate it. The *prakamya* power allows one to perform wonderful acts within nature, while the *kamavasayita* power enables one to control nature. And there are many other forms of these mystic powers.

Summarily, these mystic powers are attained by being absorbed during meditation in the qualities of the different elements that give one the ability to acquire the natural powers within them. A yogi then attains control over them, which manifests as mystic powers.

Through these mystic perfections one can derive many kinds of material happiness, but such power is still material. They are not spiritual. Therefore, yogis who are absorbed in the use of these abilities or the happiness derived from such yogic powers cannot get free from the material creation. They may be able to perform so many wonderful miracles, but this is not the business of those who are actually spiritually advanced. Saints and sages who are pure in heart have no interest in displaying their mystical abilities, though they may have many. These yogic powers signify only a preliminary stage of spiritual advancement.

Therefore, Patanjali provides a warning about getting overly familiar or dependent on these mystic powers and abilities. First, he explains that these powers may be acquired through various ways, not just by the practice of *pranayama* or yoga exercises. "All these powers of knowledge may also come to one whose mind is spontaneously enlightened through purity." (3:34) In other words, by spiritualizing our consciousness, reaching a higher level of perception, we may also attain these potencies automatically without the means of *samyama* or yogic practices. Thus, other yoga and spiritual systems may also bring one to attain such powers through the development of spiritual consciousness. Patanjali also explains: "The psychic powers may be obtained either by birth [such as from past life endeavors], or by means of drugs [that may help induce the perception of subtle realities], or by the power of words [such as mantras, prayers or gayatris], or by the practice of austerities [physical exercises done for a higher purpose], or by concentration." (4:1)

Nonetheless, he finally advises that the best thing to do is to not show such powers to anyone or dwell on them, or become fascinated by them, otherwise they could easily distract you from the real goal of yoga and spiritual practice. "These are powers in the worldly state, but they are obstacles to *samadhi*. (3:38) By giving up even these powers, the seed of evil is destroyed and liberation follows." (3:51) In other words, by renouncing such mystic abilities, the yogi makes additional progress in detaching himself from the ego and the body, which binds one to bodily existence or *samsara*. This detachment paves the way for a smooth transition to higher realms, which is the ultimate goal of all yoga and spiritual practice. There is a similar statement in *Srimad-Bhagavatam* (3.27.30) in which Sri Krishna states that a perfect yogi no longer considers using mystic powers, which then makes the yogi's progress towards Krishna unlimited and causes death to lose its influence over him.

From these descriptions we can begin to understand that yogic powers, or other supernatural abilities one may possess by other means, such as from witchcraft, Tantraism, etc., may be useful in some ways, but if we are too focused on them they become little more than another snare of the illusory energy, *maya*, to keep one bound up in the material world. And using such mystical powers is another way of lording over and trying to control material nature for one's own enjoyment. This can create more karma for ourselves and cause one to become proud and to lose sight of what we are meant to accomplish in this life.

Patanjali describes in his *Yoga Sutras* (3.56) that perfection is attained only when the mind becomes as pure as the soul itself. In *Srimad-Bhagavatam* (3.27.28-29), Lord Kapiladeva (an *avatara* of Lord Krishna) explains that His devotee actually becomes self-realized by His causeless mercy, and, when freed from all misgivings, steadily progresses towards his destined spiritual abode and never returns to material existence. That is the ultimate perfection one can achieve. In this way, we can realize that if one continues on the path of the real yoga process, regardless of whether one attains various mystical powers or not, he will still reach the perfectional platform in which everything else is automatically achieved. This is further described in *Srimad-Bhagavatam* (11.15.33-34) by Lord Krishna where He tells Uddhava that those who are expert in devotional service (bhakti yoga) claim that these mystic abilities are useless and impediments on the path of the topmost yoga, by which one attains all the perfections of life directly from Krishna, including mystic powers. Thus, as He concludes, not by any other means but devotional service can one attain the actual goal of yoga.

□

4
Other Forms of Yoga

KUNDALINI YOGA

Kundalini yoga is another system which is often talked about. It is a system in which those who practice it must understand a good deal about their body, subtle body, and the chakras and channels of energy within. One also must thoroughly understand the disciplines that help the yogi control his bodily functions and internal states. The term *kundalini* is hardly mentioned in any of the Vedic texts, and not at all in any of the *Upanishads*. However, the principles of it are related to the philosophy found therein. The system of kundalini is introduced in later texts. These include such primary yoga scriptures as the *Hatha Yoga Pradipika* of Svatmarama, the *Gheranda Samhita*, and the *Shiva Samhita*. It is primarily described in the Tantric texts. So, it is generally practiced by those who are followers of the *Tantras*. Of course, there are many simple exercises within this system that are similar to hatha yoga that anyone can do for benefitting their health or mental makeup. But herein we are talking about the means for taking this system all the way to the advanced level for complete spiritual unfoldment, which needs supervision.

The basics of most any form of yoga can be started without the help of a guru, but not with kundalini yoga. There is no doubt that to begin the serious practice of kundalini yoga, you must take instructions from an experienced guru. This is a complex system and you certainly cannot start with advanced techniques. Even basic methods can produce questionable results if not done correctly. You must prepare yourself on all levels, namely the physical, mental, and emotional, and experienced guidance in this matter is essential.

The word *kundalini* is derived from the Sanskrit word *kundal*, which means "coil," as a coiled serpent. The serpent is illustrated in three-and-a-half coils. The three coils represent three aspects of *Om*, namely the past, present, and future; the states of being or wakefulness, dreaming, and deep sleep; and the three *gunas, tattva, rajas,* and *tamas,* or goodness, passion, and ignorance. The remaining half coil represents the state of transcendence that exists above the named sets of three.

However, *kunda* also means a pit, or deep place. So, the fire pit in a fire *yajna* ritual is also called a *kunda*, as a deep water tank is called a *kunda*. *Kunda* is also the cavity in which the brain sits. Thus, the *shakti* energy while it is lying dormant is called kundalini, but when it begins to manifest it is called according to the form it takes, such as Devi, Durga, Kali, Sarasvati, Lakshmi, etc. When you are able to handle the energy and direct it toward beneficial purposes, it is called Durga. However, when it awakens and you have not learned to handle it properly, it is called Kali.

Kali is depicted as the lovely lady that she is, but with dark or smoky skin, and a large necklace of 108 human skulls. These represent the memories of previous births. Kali's protruding tongue, red and dripping with blood, represents the mode of passion (raja guna) which compels all creative activity. This gesture indicates that all *sadhakas* or spiritual practitioners must control the influence of the mode of passion. She also caries a severed head in her left hand and a sword, which represents the dissolution, especially of ego, after which is the birth of light and life.

Traditionally, as described in the *Puranas*, when Kali rises, all the demigods are fearful of her power and what she may do. So, her husband Shiva is requested to pacify her, and when he approaches her, she roars and throws him down, not recognizing him, and he lies down before her. She then accidently steps on him and sticks her tongue out after realizing what she has done. This also shows how Lord Shiva controls the material energy.

When the kundalini is aroused and becomes tamed, then it manifests as Durga, mother of the material energy, who has eight arms which represent the eight elements. She is seen sitting on a tiger, which represents her control over bodily or sensual impulses. She wears a necklace of 52 human heads, which represents her wisdom and power, and the 52 letters of the Sanskrit alphabet which are the outer manifestation of the original, spiritual vibrational energy in the *Shabda Brahman*, or spiritual sound vibration. Kundalini as Durga represents the giver of peace, power, and remover of evil. So, the technique in kundalini yoga is to arouse the energy in the refined form of Durga, otherwise if it remains in her form as Kali, it can produce some ill effects. That is why kundalini yoga must be performed properly or it can be counterproductive from the real goal we want to achieve.

Kundalini yoga is a process similar to the raja yoga or astanga yoga systems in that one must sit in the proper place and posture, control the breathing, and discipline the mind and senses. With practice, the yogi tries to awaken the kundalini, the "coiled one" or primal force, which is compared to a tiny snake or spiral of fire-energy lying asleep and coiled three-and-a-half times at the base of the spine. The yogi performs certain exercises and techniques to arouse the kundalini and raise it through the Sushumna channel to the highest chakra at the crown of the head, which is called the Sahasrara or lotus of a thousand petals. The kundalini is female, or Shakti, while the Sahasrara is male, or Shiva. When the kundalini or Shakti energy unites with the universal Shiva force, the yogi is then considered to be united with the universal soul.

What is required to be done before the kundalini can be awakened is that the Ida and Pingala *nadis* must be opened and operate harmoniously together. The chakras also have to be awakened, which requires particular practices for each chakra. The Sushumna must also be opened or awakened, otherwise if the kundalini begins to rise, where will it go, other than up through the Ida or Pingala? This may produce alternative results than what we want to achieve. The ancient texts explain that if the kundalini goes up the Ida channel, the yogi may be able to predict situations. If the kundalini rises up the Pingala channel, then a person may attain the powers to become a healer with control over certain aspects of material nature.

So, the Sushumna must be prepared properly. If the chakras and Sushumna have not been prepared, and the kundalini begins to become aroused and cannot go anywhere, there can be tremendous energy awakened in the Muladhara chakra which can create various sexual or even neurotic problems. This keeps you focused on the more base level of awareness and does not bring about experiences in higher consciousness.

Awakening the Sushumna can take more work than opening the chakras, and can lead to intense experiences that you will need to know how to handle. Even if you have taken all the necessary steps to harmonize the Ida and Pingala channels and open the chakras, if the Sushumna has not been opened properly, leaving an obstruction somewhere along the way, the kundalini will not be able to rise the way it should, and we will not reach the goal of this form of yoga, which is to become a *jivanmukta*, or a liberated soul.

The movement of the kundalini energy is spiraling when awakened from its coiled state. The means by which the kundalini becomes awakened is the process which fuses the negative ions of the *prana* (life air) with the positive ions of the *apana* (the body's functional airs). This fusion occurs in the lower Muladhara chakra after steady practice of purification consisting of yoga, such as hatha yoga, laya yoga, karma yoga, mantras, *asanas*, meditation, etc. When awakened, this energy moves through the *nadi* channels, through which flow streams of subtle energy. Veins and arteries are also *nadis* but of gross physical energies, whereas the Ida and Pingala *nadis* are not structures but are channels where the subtle energies flow.

Once it is awoken, if the kundalini keeps rising, it can go all the way to the top of the head to the top chakra. The yogi then has a chance to attain the highest goal of this form of yoga. Once the kundalini is awakened, then, for the full goal to be achieved, the practitioner must continue working at raising the kundalini until it reaches the Sahasrara chakra. Then from the Sahasrara chakra it can leave the body. Otherwise, the work remains unfinished, and the process incomplete.

The whole purpose of Kundalini yoga is to purify and then awaken the *nadis*, especially the Shushumna *nadi*. Then to awaken the chakras and remove any *kriyas* or obstructions that are found in the chakras, after which the goal is to fire up the Kundalini in stages, bringing it to the various chakras as we progress, and, of course, to be able to handle the experiences along the way. If we can do that, then we have a chance that this process will expand our awareness on many levels. As the chakras are activated, the yogi not only becomes aware of different realms of existence, but can also gain the power to enter into them, especially when the kundalini reaches the Sahasrara chakra, joining with Shiva. This union remains for some time while the *sadhaka* or yogi experiences what is called cosmic consciousness. Until the kundalini is ready to exit the body through the Sahasrara chakra, the kundalini will next descend back to the Muladhara chakra. Then the functions of the chakras return, along with the powers of their deities, and the yogi lives in an expanded state of consciousness. He is now a changed person, and if he can keep this awareness and join the kundalini with the Sahasrara chakra on a regular basis, he will reach a higher dimension when he leaves the body.

Another way this works is that as the kundalini energy ascends the spine through the Sushumna channel, it pulls the yogi's life energy and soul up to the Sahasrara at the top of the head. If the yogi is skillful enough, the skull then fractures and the yogi leaves the material body and merges into the great white light of the Brahman, or somewhere else. This is the ultimate goal of kundalini yoga. Though there may be many who try the kundalini yoga process and even make some progress on the path, few are those who can actually take it to the final goal.

The various experiences that a person sometimes has when the kundalini begins to awaken can be quite profound, and is different for everyone. When it is awakened, the body and mind can be vitalized. Mental transformations can take place, in some cases rapidly. Awareness begins to expand and intuitive powers increase. For some, it can feel like a hot burning sensation going up the back, or a severe pain. Or it can be a creeping sensation starting from the toes, or feel like the swerving of a snake's tail, or even like ants crawling up the back. If it rises smoothly and high enough, superconscious states may manifest. As the kundalini rises to the different chakras, one may have many physical sensations, such as feeling hot or cold in different parts of the body, or feeling light or heavy as the energy moves. A person may also have psychic experiences or acquire different mystic powers. A person may even have visions of other realms or view events of the future, or may mystically travel to the planets of hell or heaven or the subtle realms of existence that are described in the Vedic *Puranas*.

However, if one is not spiritually mature to understand what is happening, it can be quite confusing, dizzying, or even schizophrenic. For others, it can be quite blissful once the kundalini has finally reached the Sahasrara chakra. This is why preparation is so much emphasized, and why it is important to have the instructions of an experienced guru to assist with one's development along this path. Continued practice in spiritual activities and meditation will also help.

When the kundalini rises to the heart chakra, the heart and emotions open and one can be flooded with waves of great bliss. At the Ajna chakra, the mind becomes quiet and steady. As it rises towards the Sahasrara chakra, one can hear cosmic sounds described as the inner harmonies of the celestial spheres. These experiences can be caused by the energy within or from simply opening oneself to the subtle realm or astral plane beyond the physical dimension. One then quiets the mind thereby allowing for the destruction of ignorance and illusion, which is the cause of duality and identification with the finite. Reaching this non-dual consciousness, one is said to become enlightened, or at least enters a level of non-dual perception of that plane of subtle reality. However, this does not mean a person is making the necessary spiritual progress to enter the transcendental atmosphere, which is above and beyond the effects of the subtle realm. The subtle realm has many levels, both high and low, or awesome and horrible. Opening channels that allow us to experience these subtle energies does not mean we are in control of them. A person may have fantastic mystical experiences, or undergo nightmarish encounters, depending on the level of energy and consciousness with which one comes in contact. One may also encounter various entities from these subtle levels, both benevolent or intimidating.

Once the channels to the lower levels of the subtle realm have been opened, through whatever means, harmful entities may come through and cause trouble in a number of ways. Of course, not many are those who reach this level of practice or need worry about such things. Other stages of kundalini yoga are described in the next section on the chakras.

The ways through which the kundalini can be awakened include intense devotion to God, repetition of particular mantras, continued practice of prayer, meditation, or by yogic exercises under the guidance of an empowered guru. Intense practice in *pranayama* can be very powerful, and is also a method that can awaken the kundalini. *Pranayama* not only increases *prana* in the body, but it can also create yogic fire to heat and awaken the kundalini. But this heat needs to be directed to the proper centers to propel the kundalini upward. It is also helpful when a person's health is in good condition, when one lives in a spiritually conducive environment, and when one is receptive to spiritual awakening. Rarely is it spontaneously aroused because of one's progress in past lives, but it can happen, which may create confusing experiences if the person does not understand what is taking place. The kundalini can also be aroused when the guru transmits his energy to the disciple through touch, called *shaktipat*. This causes the disciple to have an awakening of superconsciousness, but only to the degree to which the guru is empowered.

This also happened with Sri Chaitanya Mahaprabhu in Bengal 500 years ago. Whoever came in contact with Him or heard His ecstatic chanting of the Hare Krishna *maha-mantra* would be imbibed with His potency and become immersed in ecstatic love of God. Some people relate this form of God-realization to the arousal of the kundalini, while others refer to it simply as being a reawakening of one's spiritual position. Even though Sri Chaitanya gave this powerful ecstasy to many people, He never put any emphasis on rousing the kundalini. He only taught that the goal is to reawaken one's spiritual love of God through the process of bhakti yoga by absorbing oneself in the chanting of the *maha-mantra*, which can bring complete spiritual enlightenment and transform one's vision on every level.

To master the kundalini energy may take many years. One must also take instruction from a guru who is well experienced in this practice because the aspirant must know how to handle the kundalini force when it is awakened, otherwise negative reactions can take place. The flow of the kundalini has to be controlled or guided properly. If it flows downward, or up through the Ida or Pingala channels, serious health, mental, or psychological problems will ensue. It can only flow up the Shushumna channel with smooth, steady progress to attain positive results. If the kundalini is not controlled properly once one is able to begin raising it, or if it is awakened forcibly by one who is improperly trained, it can be more than the person can handle. The kundalini may become active, but in an irritated manner. In such a case, it can cause serious damage, both physically and psychologically, up to the point of mental agitation, confusion, illusion, or even insanity. Thus, the practice of kundalini yoga can be dangerous if one has not been thoroughly trained by an expert guru.

This does not happen often, but I have personally seen the damage this form of yoga can do if one does not know what he is doing. One boy who used to visit a yoga center I was staying at years ago also practiced kundalini yoga. He started becoming good at awakening this force. He could raise it a little, but never learned what to do with it. At one point the force went up his spine and all the way to his brain. What exactly happened I cannot say, but it obviously affected him psychologically and damaged some of the nerves in his brain. From then on he acted very peculiar, as if he was mentally challenged. Before that he was quite normal and enthusiastic and talkative. But afterwards, you could not even have a coherent conversation with him. He simply lost his ability to communicate well, even though he would try. So, a neophyte must not rush in and begin trying something for which he is not prepared.

You first have to ask yourself why you are engaging in yoga. Are you sincerely trying to attain spiritual enlightenment, or are you just trying to see some white light or hear some cosmic sounds? Are you actually longing for a purified consciousness, or do you simply want a little excitement, another cheap thrill? If all you want is some new sensation, then what is the difference in your pursuit of yoga and your sensual desires? Sex can produce a thrill, too, although very temporarily. But if such is the case, then the real goal of yoga is missed. Engaging in yoga for such purposes is like undergoing the struggle of digging a deep well in order to find water to satisfy your thirst while residing on the banks of a clear, fresh water lake. In other words, it will reward you with only shallow results after much work, while, on the other hand, attaining the real goal of yoga through the purification of your consciousness allows you to experience the bliss within, which is like an ocean of joy.

THE CHAKRAS AND KOSHAS

If you are interested in raja yoga or kundalini yoga, you must know the science of the chakras and *koshas*. Within the gross physical body there is the subtle or *sukshma* body, which is divided into layers. As *Bhagavad-gita* (3.42) explains, the working senses are superior to dull matter; mind is higher than the senses; intelligence is higher than the mind; and the soul is higher than the intelligence. This describes the way the body has layers or sheaths called *koshas* that cover the living entity, the soul, and become decreasingly dense as one goes inward.

The physical body is called the *annamaya kosha* that is made from food. Then there is the *pranamaya kosha* made of the vital air circulating within the gross body. Deeper is the *manomaya kosha*, or mind body, and then the *vijnanamaya kosha*, or intelligence body. Finer than all these is the *anandamaya kosha* wherein one attains spiritual bliss.

Within the subtle body are the chakras that are the psychic centers of energy situated along the spinal column. Each of the *koshas* are connected with the different chakras. The *annamaya kosha* is made up and connected with the elements of earth, water, and fire, which are centered respectively in the Muladhara chakra at the base of the spine, the Svadhisthana chakra along the spine near the genitals, and the Manipura chakra at the level of the solar plexus. Composed of air and ether is the *pranamaya kosha* that is centered in the Anahata chakra near the heart, and the Vishuddha chakra along the spine behind the throat. The *manomaya kosha* and *vijnanamaya kosha* are centered in the Ajna chakra situated between the eyebrows. And connected with the *anandamaya kosha*, the Sahasrara chakra or lotus of a thousand petals is located just above the crown of the head.

The chakras are related to different levels of consciousness in this way: the Muladhara and lowest chakra is principally related to establishing security and maintenance for oneself; Swadhisthana is related with the search for pleasure; Manipura is connected with the consciousness of attaining assertiveness and power; Anahata at the heart chakra is associated with the search for and expression of love; Vishuddhi with outward communication; and the Ajna chakra relates with intellect, intuition, and psychic powers.

Below the Muladhara chakra are seven other chakras that are associated with those of animal bodies and the lower or tamasic phase of consciousness. These focus on the senses and instincts of eating, sleeping, mating, and defending, not higher awareness. But these do not affect us because humans have ordinarily transcended them. There are seven of these chakras, which, starting at the lowest level of animal consciousness, are named as patala, mahatala, rasatala, talatala, sutala, vitala, and atala. It is in the patala chakra wherein total darkness is the main dimension where nature no longer functions and only static matter is dominant, where instincts are the only motivating factor. Human consciousness begins with the Muladhara chakra, which is the rajasic or passionate phase of consciousness, and goes up to the Sahasrara chakra, where begins the *sattvic* phase, or consciousness in the mode of goodness.

The subtle sheaths that are mentioned have particular connections with the physical body at numerous points that are linked with many subtle energy channels known as *nadis* that flow through the whole body. These points also correspond to acupuncture points. The *Shiva Samhita* describes 14 major *nadis*. But the most important *nadi* is the Sushumna, the central channel that runs from just below the Muladhara chakra and extends up the spine to the forehead. On the left side of the Sushumna is the white lunar *nadi*, called Ida, and on the right side is the red solar *nadi* called Pingala.

The Ida *nadi* is connected with the mental processes, and Pingala is connected with the vital processes. The Pingala carries the active, yang, dynamic, solar, creative, and masculine energy within our bodies. Ida is the more femine, lunar, intuitive, yin, receptive energy. The Ida and Pingala channels are considered to be the powers of the mind and body, or the sun and moon. They are more like currents that flow through the body and can be utilized as such in the process of yoga. The Sushumna is the central channel through which the rising spiritual consciousness is carried.

Therefore, the Ida and Pingala *nadis* must be opened and balanced, and working harmoniously, and, more importantly, the Sushumna must be awakened and open through the chakras before the kundalini or the *prana* can properly begin to rise. If these have not been done first, if the kundalini begins to awaken, adverse affects cannot help but happen because there will not be a proper channel for it to reach the Ajna or Sahasrara chakras. It will only produce unwanted complications by rising through the Ida or Pingala channels. Or worse, it will stay in the Muladhara chakra, obstructed, and will create various neurotic problems. Thus, it must be obvious that a lot of work must be done in order to open the Ida and Pingala channels and clear the chakras. Simply awakening the Sushumna channel can cause experiences that are more intense than awakening the chakras.

Once this process begins, various psychic powers may develop, but, as we have already explained, these must all be given up or they will distract one from the goal, which prevents progress. It is only after the kundalini rises through the Shushumna to the Sahasrara chakra that one has the opportunity to become a *jivanmukta*, or liberated soul. But even that depends on how one handles and utilizes the experience when the kundalini shakti unites with Shiva in the Sahasrara chakra. After all, we have to remember that once the kundalini rises, it will again descend through the chakras and return to the Muladhara chakra.

The conjunction of the Sushumna, Ida, and Pingala is called the Yukta Triveni. This is where the fusion of the *prana* and *apana* takes place to charge the kundalini upwards. When that happens, two currents of psychic energy flow through the Ida and Pingala *nadis* in opposite directions, spiraling around the Sushumna from the base of the spine and up to meet at the forehead at the Ajna chakra. Within the Sushumna are three more channels called Vajra, Chitrini, and Brahmani. It is the Brahmani in which the kundalini travels upwards toward the Brahma-randhra, or Sahasrara chakra.

In this process of raja yoga or kundalini yoga, both the *pranic*, or the internal flow of subtle energies, and mental forces interact in a way that transforms our bodies, minds, and awareness. When the *prana* energy unites with the Ida and Pingala channels at the Ajna chakra and then lifts up through the Sushumna channel, passing through the chakras to the Sahasrara chakra, then it is called yoga or union, and is no longer considered hatha. But this is why the obstacles in the chakras must be broken, or I would say smoothed out, so the energy can easily pass through them. Chakras are the energy junctions wherein the *pranic* forces get distributed through the other 72,000 channels that circulate throughout the body.

As one raises the life energy or kundalini, there will be a transformation of awareness from the physical to the subtle. This can be understood in the way each chakra corresponds with one of the elements. The Muladhara relates to earth or solidity, Svadhisthana with water or liquid, Manipura to gases or fire, Anahata with air, and Vishuddha with ether or space.

At the Ajna center, known as the third eye, the energy reaches the hollow space between the hemispheres of the brain known as the Bhramara Gupha (cave of the bumble bee) and the Andha Kup, known as the tenth gate of the body. The nine other gates are the two eyes, two nostrils, two ears, the mouth, and genitals and anus. The tenth gate opens only when one has reached perfection in this kind of yoga. The tenth gate is the soft spot on top of the skull, especially noticed in babies before it is developed and becomes hard. By the practice of this form of yoga, a person prepares himself to leave the body through this gate, especially during the last breath. In this way, he becomes liberated from further cycles of rebirth.

When the energy reaches the Ajna chakra, the third eye is said to open, in which a person can see beyond the affects of time. He becomes *trikalagya* or *trilkaladarshi*. This means the yogi has risen above the influence of the three modes of material nature to be the knower of the past, present, and future. At this time one also becomes merged in divine consciousness; yet, the identification with a separate ego still remains and keeps the practitioner from attaining perfect unity with Brahman. Only after reaching the Sahasrara chakra is there the possibility of perfect *samadhi* and unity with the void or Brahman.

In this way, the practitioner or yogi passes progressively through elevated planes of consciousness. This means that one not only acquires new realizations as each chakra becomes opened and reached, but the person must also give up attachments or hangups on the plane of consciousness related to that chakra, which are the basis of the blockages along the path. These must be cleared for complete unfoldment to take place. In other words, one has to leave his or her habitual and preconceived conceptions of things behind before full perception of the realizations at the next chakra can begin. But when one is very inclined toward activities related to the *annamaya kosha*, or the physical body, it is very difficult to go upward to the more subtle bodies or raise the kundalini or *prana* to higher chakras. Basically, consciousness goes no higher than the first three chakras if one is absorbed in worldly thoughts. Thus, the aspirant must penetrate these lower levels of consciousness if he or she expects to make any progress at all in this form of yoga. And getting past the Muladhara, the Anahata, and then the Ajna chakras are the most difficult.

For the average person in the West, this is quite a formidable path to attempt and it takes serious determination to be successful. Of course, there have been reports of those who have been able to raise the kundalini *shakti* to some degree, but there is more to reaching perfection in this system than raising the *shakti* and experiencing whatever mystic powers, bliss, or other feelings that come along. You must also finally completely release the *jiva*, your soul, from the body if you are going to take it to the final step. This is its real purpose.

This is done by sitting in the proper *asana* and restraining your breathing, and leading the *jivatma*, your individual soul, into the heart of the Muladhara chakra. Then by contracting the anus and following the rules for this yoga process, you awaken the kundalini. As the kundalini awakes, you merge the Paramatma in the impersonal form as the *prana* or life-force into the Sushumna *nadi*. Then you raise it up along with the soul through the different chakras to the Ajna chakra. There you merge all the diverse elements, from the gross to the subtle, into the kundalini, along with the *jivatma*. Then you merge the kundalini with the universal Shiva at the Sahasrara chakra and pierce the Brahma-randhra at the top of the skull and leave the body altogether and finally become merged with the Brahman. If, however, you cannot accomplish this last step, then all of your efforts on this path remain incomplete.

This science of chakras is, essentially, a part of the mechanical yoga process. In other words, if you follow it properly, certain mystic powers or other results will be achieved as the chakras become open, but they are not necessarily in relation to the Supreme Being. In fact, some aspirants do not care about occult powers or opening the chakras. They are only interested in realizing God. Thus, they learn to meditate and when they make progress through meditation, the chakras open automatically. The opening of the chakras may be compared to steps along the path toward God-realization. But many times the achievement and distraction of mystical powers that take place along the way has taken sincere seekers away from the path that leads toward the Absolute Truth. Such powers are often a curse rather than a blessing, as previously explained.

At the ultimate stage, the science of chakras is used mostly for merging into the void or Brahman effulgence, called Shiva in kundalini yoga. As we have established by *shastric* evidence in my book, *The Secret Teachings of the Vedas*, the Brahman effulgence is simply the spiritual rays that emanate from the body of the Supreme Being, which consists of innumerable spiritual sparks or souls. These sparks, the liberated living entities, indefinitely drift in the eternal spiritual sky without any spiritual engagement. But when there is some tendency for activity, they must return to the material world for engagement since they have no knowledge of, nor did they develop the inclination for, the devotional activities to the Supreme Being that fully manifest on the eternal spiritual planets that exist within that everlasting and self-effulgent spiritual sky or Brahman.

In this way, after returning to the material worlds by their own free will due to their desire for activity, they again start over and proceed through the rounds of birth and death, going up and down throughout the various levels of planetary systems within the material cosmos, until they start a spiritual process again. Of course, by their previous experience they may automatically be inclined to search for it. Thus, it is considered by the topmost sages that even if one does fulfill all the requirements to reach complete perfection on the path of raja yoga or kundalini yoga, he or she still has not reached the ultimate stage of spiritual realization and occupation. This reiterates once again the importance to learn the process of bhakti yoga, as it is needed along with whatever other yoga or spiritual process you may practice.

LAYA YOGA

Laya yoga is very similar to kundalini yoga, but as one raises the feminine energy at the base of the spine through the chakras towards the crown of the head, the emphasis is on meditating on the inner sounds that one experiences at each chakra. The final goal is to raise the feminine energy up to the crown chakra and merge with the Brahman.

KRIYA YOGA

It is explained in the *Yoga Sutras* (2.1,2) of Patanjali that kriya yoga consists of austerity, the study of sacred texts, surrender to God, and the practice of what is learned and realized. In this way, all external and mental obstacles are removed to bring about the realization of the Absolute.

This is the method of cleansing and activating the physical, astral, mental, emotional, and subtle bodies. Thus, it is a means that leads to a state of purity and good physical, mental, and spiritual health and progress. Kriya yoga incorporates various exercises, called kriyas, that can purify the *nadis*, awaken the chakras, and prepare for awakening the kundalini. It also works with hatha yoga to help control the *prana*. The kriyas help arouse the kundalini in controlled and smooth stages rather than allowing it to become awakened suddenly or without sufficient control over it, the danger of which can lead to experiences that may be difficult to understand or comprehend.

Kriya yoga is a system for those who are inclined towards the mystic process. *Kriya* means "action," which can include physical austerities for a wholesome life, study of spiritual knowledge of the soul and consciousness, and the yoga exercises for meditation and the transformative and regenerative processes that assist the body and mind for the upliftment to spiritual awakening. It is a type of *sadhana* or regulatory set of routines for cleansing and activating the body, clearing the mind, and adjusting the consciousness to perceive higher levels of reality. So, kriya yoga is meant to combine the most useful parts of all yoga systems.

Among its purposes is to provide a method for recharging the blood with oxygen through its recommended exercises. From this extra oxygen, the atoms are turned into life energy to rejuvenate the chakras and brain. By reducing the toxins in the blood, the yogi is able to reduce the decay of tissues and improve his health and prolong his life. One who is advanced is able to get energy from his cells or turn the cells into energy. By mastering it completely, a yogi's body can even dematerialize or materialize at will.

Kriya yoga is also meant to help clear and purify one's consciousness from unwanted or regressive thought patterns. As the yogi continues to advance, he can turn the energy used for bodily maintenance, such as for breathing and heart action, and use it for higher purposes such as raising inner subtle energies to higher levels. Thus, by breath and mind control the ultimate goal is to unite the mind with divine realms, allowing the yogi to concentrate on the cosmic consciousness or Supersoul within.

Kriya yoga is also outlined in the *Garuda Purana*. It is stated there that any person who in gladness sees the worship of the Deity in the temple will obtain the results of kriya yoga, which are described in the *Pancharatra* scripture. In other words, one can learn to concentrate on the Supreme in the heart by years of practice of kriya yoga, or one can simply walk into the temple and immediately absorb oneself in seeing and meditating on the Deity form of the Lord and obtain a similar result. Kriya yoga is a system much like devotional service, or bhakti yoga, but it is especially meant for those who are attached to the performance of mystic yoga and merging into the impersonal Brahman.

MANTRA YOGA

Mantra yoga is one of the oldest forms of yoga and an easy system for enlightenment. It is especially used quite well within the process of bhakti yoga, in which case many people chant the Hare Krishna mantra. It is also recommended as the best means for focusing the mind on the Supreme in this age of Kali-yuga, so it is often and easily used with other forms of yoga and spiritual processes.

The word *mantra* literally means to deliver (*tra*) the mind (*man*). The instrument used to accomplish this is the secret power of vibrations arranged in a particular formula, called a *mantra*. Different mantras have different purposes. Some are meant for bringing happiness, some fulfill material desires, some are used in the worship of various demigods and deities, some simply focus and steady the mind, some help raise the life energy up through the chakras, while others are incantations for casting spells and so on. But mantras used for spiritual enlightenment release vital energy, strengthen the mind, and prepare the consciousness for perceiving higher realms of existence. By concentrating on the mantra, the mind associates with the energy within it and takes on the characteristics found within the sound vibration. The more powerful a mantra is, the more it can invoke the higher energies in the mind and consciousness. In this way, the mind can be purified by the spiritual vibrations within the mantra. One who chants a mantra generally repeats it a particular number of times each day while using a string of beads like a rosary, called *japa mala*. A powerful way to chant is to sit down, do some *pranayama*, and then focus the mind and simply listen to your chanting. We will describe this form of yoga more elaborately later in this book.

MUDRA YOGA

You could say that mudra yoga is the language with which we communicate with the body. It is used to adjust or direct the inner energies within the body to help clean and heal one's body, mind, or astral body. These are of four types:

1. Yoga Tatva Mudra Vigyan.
2. Yoga Pranayama Mudra.
3. Yoga Dhyan Mudra.
4. Yoga Asana Mudra.

The Yoga Tatva Mudra Vigyan is used with breathing. This is the knowledge of how the finger postures are related to the elements. In this practice, the fingers are folded in particular postures that put tension on certain nerves of the fingers to produce curative effects by the currents of subtle energy caused by the tension.

Every human body consists of the basic elements of nature, which include water (*jal*), earth (*prithvi*), space or ether (*akash*), air (*vayu*), and fire (*agni*). The hands are made up of five fingers, and each finger represents an element and its energy, related as follows:

1. The little finger is related to water.
2. The ring finger is related to earth.
3. The middle finger is related to space.
4. The index finger is related to air.
5. The thumb is related to fire.

Yogis have discovered that the energy within the body is enhanced when the finger that is related to that element is activated. This is done by bringing the tip of that finger to touch the tip of the thumb. However, when the tip of that finger is pressed against the base of the thumb, that same energy decreases. Thus, mudra is the process of holding the fingers in particular ways and knowing how it impacts the entire being.

How effective these mudras are depends on how they are used in practice. The ideal length of time to hold any mudra position is 45 minutes a day without break. However, you can also break it up into sections of 10 to 15 minutes at a time. The issue here is that some mudras will produce an effect immediately, while others may take a month or more. But which mudra do we use for which purpose? Let us explain.

The Jnana or Dhyan Mudra

This is the most common mudra and often used while doing hatha yoga or meditation (*dhyan*), especially when you sit in the lotus position before starting your yoga routine. It is also said to help produce knowledge and peace, which is why it is called *jnana* mudra. This mudra is performed by touching the tip of the thumb with the tip of the index finger, while keeping the other fingers straight. It becomes more activated when using it during *asanas* or *pranayama*.

The thumb represents fire and the index finger is air, so when they are combined it motivates energy to move. Furthermore, when sitting in Padmasan or the lotus position, the body is positioned in a triangle, or like a pyramid, which brings the energy toward the center of the body, thus also making the mind peaceful.

Yogis have said that if you want to remember something, than hold this position while reading or listening, and you will remember it. So, try it and see if it helps. Plus, holding this mudra will also increase your focus, concentration, and power in your meditation. Also, if you feel too tired, doing this *jnana* mudra will give you more energy.

When you touch the index finger to the base of the thumb, it is called the vuya mudra. This helps relieve one of gas and problems caused by lumbago, sciatica, knee pain, and other effects that are caused by inappropriate airs in the body.

The Akash Mudra

This is when you touch the tip of the middle finger to the tip of the thumb while keeping the remaining fingers straight. This strengthens the bones and should be practiced 15 to 45 minutes a day to feel its effect. Cardiac and ear problems may be eased by this mudra.

The Shunya Mudra

This is performed by touching the middle finger to the base of the thumb, resting the thumb over that finger and keeping the other fingers straight. Performed 15 to 60 minutes a day, this can help reduce ear problems such as pain in the ear or reduced hearing.

The Prithvi Mudra

This is when you touch the tip of the ring finger to the tip of the thumb, while keeping the other fingers straight.

Practiced 15 to 45 minutes a day, it can increase the earth element or the weight of the body and give it strength.

The Surya Mudra

This is done by touching the tip of the ring finger to the base of the thumb, allowing the thumb to rest over the ring finger while keeping the other fingers straight. This is especially good for burning off excess fat and slimming the body. It is especially effective when performed while sitting in the lotus or easy posture, and done for 60 minutes once or twice a day.

The Varun Mudra

You do this by touching the tip of the little finger to the tip of the thumb, while keeping the other fingers straight. This is effective for counteracting dry skin or the lack of water in the body. It increases the water element and assists in problems with excess acidity. It can be done for any length of time.

The Ruksha Mudra

For this you touch the tip of the little finger to the base of the thumb while resting the thumb of the little finger, and keeping the other fingers straight. This mudra reduces the water in the body, which can assist problems with over-urination, and too much sweat. Do this mudra only as much as needed and not too much.

The Apana Mudra

This is done by bringing the middle and ring fingers together and then touch the tips of them both to the tip of the thumb, while keeping the other fingers straight. This mudra purifies the body from waste, and helps expel toxins with ease. It eases problems with urination, constipation, gas, phlegm, and diabetes. This also enhances the purity of the mind naturally with the release of toxins.

The Apana Vayu Mudra

This one is done by bringing the tip of the index finger to the base of the thumb, and then bring the tips of the middle and ring fingers to the tip of the thumb, while keeping the little finger straight. Do this about 15 minutes, especially in the morning or after meals. It helps the release of gas from the stomach, and helps relieve a bloated stomach or chest pains.

The Pran Mudra

Bring the tips of the ring and little fingers together and touch them to the tip of the thumb, while keeping the other finger straight. This can be done anywhere and anytime to increase the energy, or the *prana shakti*. It also increases the strength of the immunity system. This mudra done for ten minutes after a meal can help digestion. It also can improve vision.

The Shankha Mudra

This mudra combines both hands like a *shankha* or conch shell. You do this by clasping the thumb of the left hand with the palm and fingers of the right. You grip the left thumb in such a way that the tip of the index finger of the left hand comes up and touches the tip of the right thumb. The remaining fingers of the left hand are folded over the fingers of the right hand. This can also be done in the opposite way as well, with the left hand grasping the thumb of the right. This mudra assists in any disorders of digestion, appetite, or speech.

The Linga Mudra

First, interlock the fingers of both hands and bring out

one thumb of either hand so it extends straight out, while the other or vertical thumb must be enclosed by the other thumb and index finger. This mudra increases the heat in the body and helps reduce chills, phlegm, colds, and even helps increase the fire of digestion to reduce fat.

□

5
Starting the Practice of Yoga

After we have understood the eightfold steps of yoga as explained earlier, starting with the *yamas* and *niyamas*, and have put them into practice, we can proceed to the next step, namely the *asanas*.

ASANAS

For those just beginning and who want to learn an easy but thorough routine of *asanas*, the following is recommended for starters. Many additional *asanas* or extended variations of the following can be found in other yoga books. However, before we get started, there are a few rules to observe for precautions to get the most out of the practice.

Rules For Performing Asanas

1. *Asanas* preferably should be performed in the morning before eating and with empty stomach. If doing it in the morning is not feasible, then they should be performed 5 to 6 hours after lunch in the evening or at least 2 hours after eating.
2. *Asanas* should be practiced according to one's age, as well as physical and mental ability. Thus, one should do them as effectively as possible, but not overly push oneself into doing *asanas* that feel uncomfortable or stretch the body more than one

can handle. A pulled muscle can be extremely painful, which we want to avoid. So, you may have to work or practice various *asanas* until your body easily adjusts to doing them. *Asanas* should be given one's full attention and not done while watching TV or listening to the radio.

3. If you are feeling lethargic after doing yoga *asanas*, consult an expert. Yoga should increase your energy levels and not decrease it unlike other physical exercises.
4. Women should not practice yoga during their menstrual periods. Pregnant women should take care to practice moderately.
5. Initially you should take training from a teacher for the more complex *asanas* and *pranayama*.
6. If you suffer with any chronic disease ask your doctor before practicing *asanas*, or any other exercises for that matter.
7. Never extend yourself beyond your capabilities.
8. Do not perform fast actions. Yoga *asanas* need to be performed slowly and smoothly.
9. Perform *asanas* that stretch the same body parts in opposite directions preferably one after another. Thus, if you perform one *asana* in which you bend backwards then also perform an *asana* in which you bend forward.
10. *Asanas* should be performed on a soft mat or blanket and on a firm surface. Do not perform *asanas* on bare ground as being grounded in such a way can deplete or sap you of your energy. Especially avoid performing *asanas* on tiles and unclean surface mattresses.
11. Relax in between two *asanas* for 6 to 8 seconds. Take 2 or 3 normal breaths between them.
12. Food should not be consumed immediately after doing *asanas*. Have some light food after half an hour. Fried and spicy food should be avoided.

13. Avoid tea, coffee, and carbonated drinks after *asanas*.
14. If you do not have much time, at least do the Surya Namaskar three times, followed by *pranayamas*.
15. You should be relaxed before doing *asanas*.
16. Sit in Sukhasana or the easy posture while using the *jnana* mudra. Chant Om three times followed by Shanti three times.
17. Do some *pranayama* for a few minutes before starting.
18. When doing the *asanas*, do each one at least three times, hold each *asana* as long as comfortable, and for at least three deep breaths, chanting Om with each breath. In this way, the *asanas* are like prayers to God with your body.

Chanting Om

Often we start a yoga session with the chanting of *Om*. So, while sitting in the Lotus position, first take a deep breath and then slowly begin chanting *Om* with a slow exhalation, starting with the mouth open and then closing the mouth and finishing the chant while humming through the nose. Do this thee times. (There is a specific technique to chanting *Om*, which is more fully described later in this book.)

Pranayama

Now we can do a preliminary and short *pranayama* technique. While sitting in the easy posture or lotus position, inhale slowly, either through the mouth or the nose, and then exhale quickly and deeply through the nose, letting the stomach area deflate as much as possible. Do this at least three times.

Next, do fast inhaling and exhaling. Inhale quickly and deeply and then just as quickly exhale. Do this at least three times. This practice stimulates the respiratory system and creates warmth and prepares us for doing our *asanas*.

A GOOD ASANA ROUTINE

The *Yoga Sutras* of Patanjali defines yoga *asanas* as *sthiram sukham aasanam,* which means a position which is comfortable and steady. The yoga *asanas* are postures that are meant to train the body and mind to be disciplined and balanced. Used with the *pranayama* techniques, the *asanas* are meant to help charge the body with *prana* and life force to enhance one's meditative abilities and reach deeper levels of concentration and awareness. There are numerous books that describe many hundreds of *asanas,* or the many variations of the primary *asanas,* but we will include the main ones which will be all you need in order to proceed with this course on yoga and meditation.

However, we must remember that we are trying to have a posture that is comfortable for sitting in meditation. So, in spite of the descriptions that follow, we may also use cushions, folded blankets, or mats that can help in this way. They can be placed under us in a way that helps keep the spine straight while sitting, and elevates the body by about two inches, and help keep the legs resting lower on the floor. The legs and hips will be more relaxed this way, and without as much pressure on the pelvis. To help keep your back straight, you may even sit against a wall. If your legs are too uncomfortable even in this position, you can also use a straight back chair, or sit on the edge of the chair seat.

By working through these *asanas,* they will also help relieve any tension in the body, thus making the body more nimble and loosening the channels through which the energy or *prana* flows. In this way, the body becomes a more useful vehicle for highly focused meditation.

Sukhasana

This is one of the most common of the yoga *asanas,* as seen on the right. It means to sit down cross-legged in a comfortable position. *Sukh* means easy position. This is especially recommended for beginners doing *pranayama* exercises and meditation. It is one of the best to relax the body's muscles for prolonged positioning. In the yoga tradition, a comfortable position is properly executed when one can maintain it for three hours and 48 minutes, with a sufficient inward focus. Of course, while this simple posture is easily done by Indians and yogis, it is not quite so easy for those who do not often sit on the floor. So, if even this easy posture is too difficult for long periods, you can also sit on the edge of a chair with a straight spine, and feet on the floor. However, by practicing these primary *asanas*, you will soon be able to do this Sukhasana quite easily.

The Lotus Position (Padmasana)

This is probably the most popular of all *asanas*. Many yogis use it and are pictured in this position, just as the Buddha is often viewed sitting in this posture. This *asana* can be regularly practiced, and many people can take to it easily. However, for beginners it is suggested to start slow as it may take time for the leg ligaments to grow into shape. It is another cross-legged position, but with the soles of the feet resting on top of the thighs, not below them as most people sit. The position has a calming effect on the mind and nerves, which is needed for long-termed meditation. The pose helps keep the spine erect and provides good posture. Keeping the body's joints flexible is another of its benefits. First, sit down in Dandasan or Sukhasana (the easy sitting posture) and place the right foot on the left thigh and the left foot on the right thigh. (If you cannot do this properly, then just assume the normal sitting posture.) The spine should be straight. Keep the left hand below the right hand and place them on the lap (*anjali*). Or place your hands on the knees in the Dhyan Mudra. Focus the mind on the front portion of the nose, or focus on an image or deity of God or Goddess, or any symbol that you prefer.

Starting with the Corpse (Shavasana) Pose

Shava means corpse, and this is the corpse pose. It is one of the simplest to perform, and some of the *pranayama* exercises ask for this *asana* to be performed afterwards.

Basically, this is the relaxation technique that is performed at the start and at the end of each session. To do this you lay on your back, feet spread about 18 inches apart, arms at your sides palms up. Close your eyes and breathe deeply and slowly from the abdomen, and feel your abdomen rise and fall. You relax completely, both in body and mind, laying motionless and with a perfectly quiet mind. Allow yourself to go deeper into relaxation and vacate the mind of all concerns. This reduces your body's energy loss, lowers your respiration and pulse rate, and rests the whole system. However, it is also difficult because if you relax too much you are likely to go to sleep, which is not wanted. To avoid sleep, it is suggested that if you notice yourself getting drowsy, you increase your rate of breathing. Many yoga sessions begin and end with the *shavasana*, which is generally done for about 10 to 15 minutes at the end of the session. But for now, once you have relaxed for about five minutes or more, then rise and sit up for the next step.

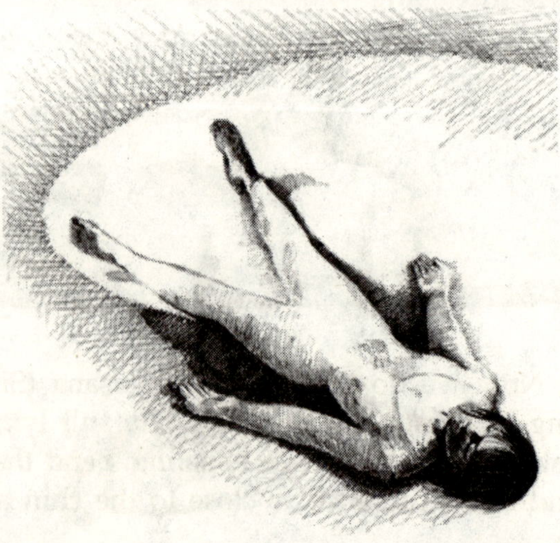

Vajarasana

This is another often used *asana* in a sitting posture. Do not cross your legs, but bend both the legs at the knees and put them on the floor and place your feet under the hips, sitting on the feet. The ankles are under the buttocks while protruding outward with the toes pointing inward, each foot pointing toward the other with the big toes touching each other. The hands should be resting on the knees. The back, head, and neck should be straight. This *asana* is good for concentration or meditation. It is one of the few that can be done after meals and is good for digestion, acidity, or constipation problems. In normal practice, this *asana* can be held for about 3 minutes.

Leg Raises and Bends

(A) Now while lying on your back, raise one leg upward to 30 degrees and hold it there for 20 to 30 seconds while inhaling, then lower it while exhaling and keeping the leg a few inches from the floor, and then raise it again. Do this several times. Then do the same with the other leg. Then do it with both legs together, raise them about 30 degrees while inhaling and hold them there for 20 seconds, and let them down while exhaling. This is called Uttanapadasana.

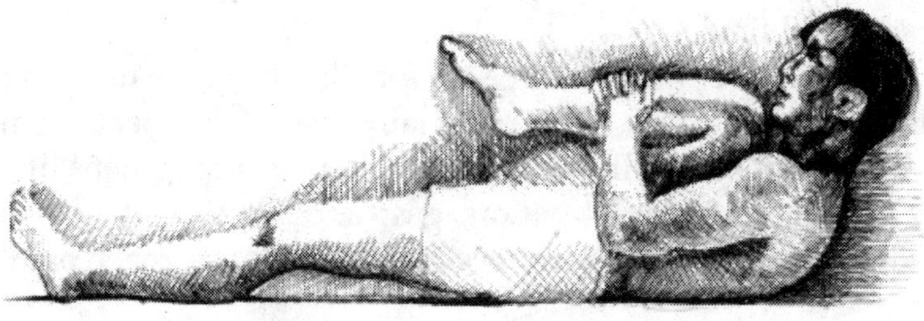

(B) Now we do the Pavan Muktasana (Single Wind Relieving as illustrated above). While still lying on your back, take one leg and while exhaling, bend the leg at the knee and bring the knee as close to the chin as possible.

Lock both the hands and keep them around the knee. Exhale and press the knee closer, resting it on the chest. The nose or chin should touch the knee. Remain in this position for about 10 to 30 seconds. Repeat this 2-4 times. Repeat with the other leg. One can do this with both the knees also (called Double Wind Relieving). Now hold both legs and massage the back, which means to rock yourself a little by bending forward, backward, right-left. This *asana* gives benefits as per its name. It is extremely beneficial for gas related stomach problems. It is also beneficial for acidity, heart disease, gout, and backache. It is beneficial for gynecological problems, mild menstruation, painful menstruation, and uterus related diseases as well. It also reduces the fat on the stomach and increases the flexibility of the hips.

(C) Now while lying down on the floor straight, raise and bend the right leg at the knee and bring the knee over the left thigh to touch the floor near the left hip while keeping both hips as close to the floor as possible (or without twisting any more than necessary), and keeping the shoulders flat on the floor. Naturally there will be some twisting. Then bring the right leg back and do the same with the left leg, bending the leg at the knee and bringing the knee over the right leg and to the floor, and then back again. Do this at least three times.

These are great exercises for the back, waist, and abdominal muscles. It is especially useful for back pain when done while lifting a single leg. It strengthens the intestines, cures constipation, gas, and obesity. It is also useful for heart and respiratory problems and stomach pain.

Two Wheels (Dwichakrikasana)

Lie down straight on your back with arms at your sides and hands palms down next to your hips. Raise one leg and bend it at the knee and rotate it like you are riding a bicycle. Repeat this from 10 to 30 seconds. Then do the same with the other leg. This then can be done simultaneously with both legs and in the opposite direction as well. Once finished, lower the legs and rest in the Shavasana or Corpse pose. Repeat this 5 to 10 times. This is a good *asana* for losing weight and to tone the middle area of the body. It also helps cure constipation and other stomach problems. However, those with heart disease and backache should not do this with both legs at the same time.

Shoulder Stand (Sarvangasan)

Lie down straight on your back. The legs should be together. Place the hands at the sides and rest the palms on the ground. Inhale and raise the legs slowly to 90 degrees upward. If you need to, support the back with your hands while lifting the legs. Keep the legs as straight as you can. Now bring the legs back further at 120 degrees and lift your hips off the floor and begin shifting your weight to the shoulders. Then bring your hands up to rest them on the back above your hips, giving support to your back. The elbows should be on the ground with the paws straightened and the eyes closed glancing at the toes above the head.

Then keep the legs straight and bend backwards slightly so they are now pointing straight up. Remain there for a few seconds, and if you can, remove both the hands from the back and rest them on the ground keeping the arms straight. Now press the floor with the palms and lower your back and then your legs so that you return to the same position so that they are again laying straight on the floor. In the beginning do this *asana* only for less than a minute and then slowly increase the time while breathing slowly and deeply. To finish, the duration for Sarvangasan and Shavasan (Corpse pose) should be the same.

This *asana* activates the thyroid and pituitary glands. It reduces obesity, weakness, tiredness, and increases height. It strengthens the adrenal glands, semen glands, and ovaries. It is also beneficial for initial stages of asthma. The diaphragm gets toned due to participation in the inhale and exhale process. However, those with cervical-spondylosis, hypertension, or spinal problems should be cautious with this *asana*.

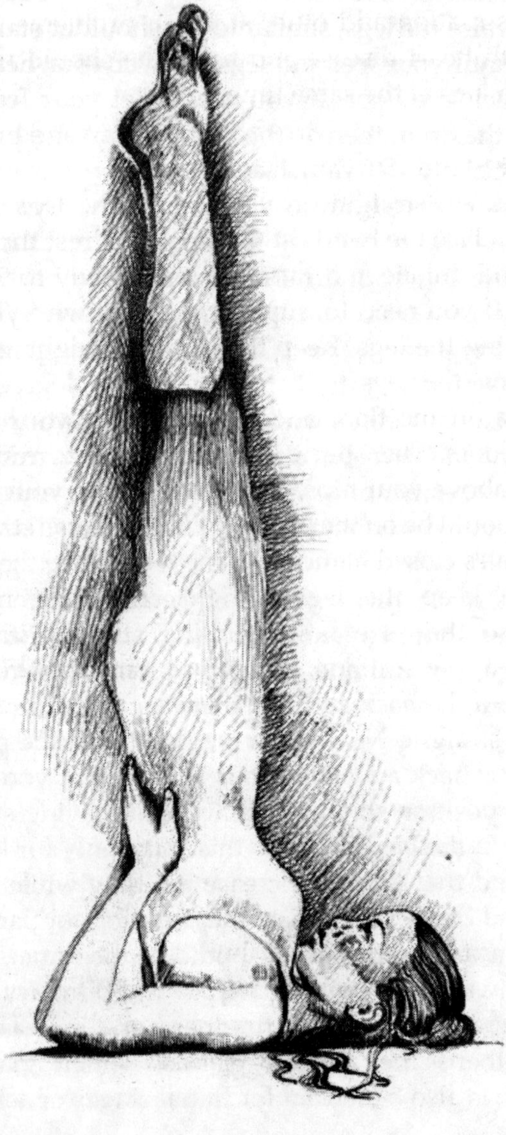

The Plough (Halasana)

Lie down straight on your back with your palms down on either side of your hips. Inhale and slowly lift the legs up together, keeping them straight, and then the hips. Lift your hands to your back and support your back at the hips as you raise the legs, similar to the shoulder stand, but keep going until your feet and legs go over your head and your feet touch the floor. If you cannot let your feet go all the way to the floor, then do the best you can and breath deeply in this position. If your feet can go all the way over to the floor, try to keep your legs straight, and let your hands and arms descend back to the floor, clasp your hands together and stretching your arms out behind your back. Stay in this position for 30 seconds breathing deeply. When ending, follow the same steps as used while going up but in the reverse order.

This *asana* helps make the spine and the back muscles healthy and flexible. It also activates the thyroid glands and reduces obesity and stunted growth. It benefits indigestion, dysentery, gas, constipation, and heart diseases. It can also help with painful menstruation and gynecological problems. However, people suffering from enlarged liver or spleen should avoid this *asana*. Patients with high blood pressure, cervical and spinal problems should also not do this *asana*.

The Headstand (Sirshasana)

If you can do the shoulder stand easily, you may want to go on to do the headstand. First kneel down and bend over, and put your forearms in front of you on the floor, with your hands grasping your elbows for proper distance (right hand grasping left elbow, left hand grasping right elbow). Then, keeping your elbows in the present position, cup your hands together in front of you, interlocking your fingers. Then place the back of the head in your hands with the top of the head on the floor. Now with feet on the floor, straighten your legs. Then raise your hips up into the air, and by using your toes, walk your feet close to your head. Then bend your knees while raising your feet up into the air, bringing your knees close to your chest, and raising your hips straight up into the air. Try to maintain your balance, and then when you are ready, keeping your knees bent, raise your knees toward the ceiling, letting your feet hang behind you using the muscles of your abdomen. Then raise your feet up into the air, straightening yourself completely, and allowing your weight to be supported by your forearms. Breathe deeply and stay in that position for as long as you can, meaning a few to several minutes.

When you are ready to come down, simply bend your knees and bring your feet down behind you. Then bend your legs at the hips and bring your knees to your chest, bring your feet to the floor, bend your knees and then bring your knees to the floor. Once fully back on the floor, knees under your stomach, straighten your arms by bringing your hands back toward the knees and rest in this position while breathing normally. The headstand is a most healing position and helps relieve problems with the heart, circulation, and the lower back, and helps bring a supply of fresh blood and oxygen to the brain. This helps in all matters of brain function, such as memory, concentration, etc., which is what we want for meditation.

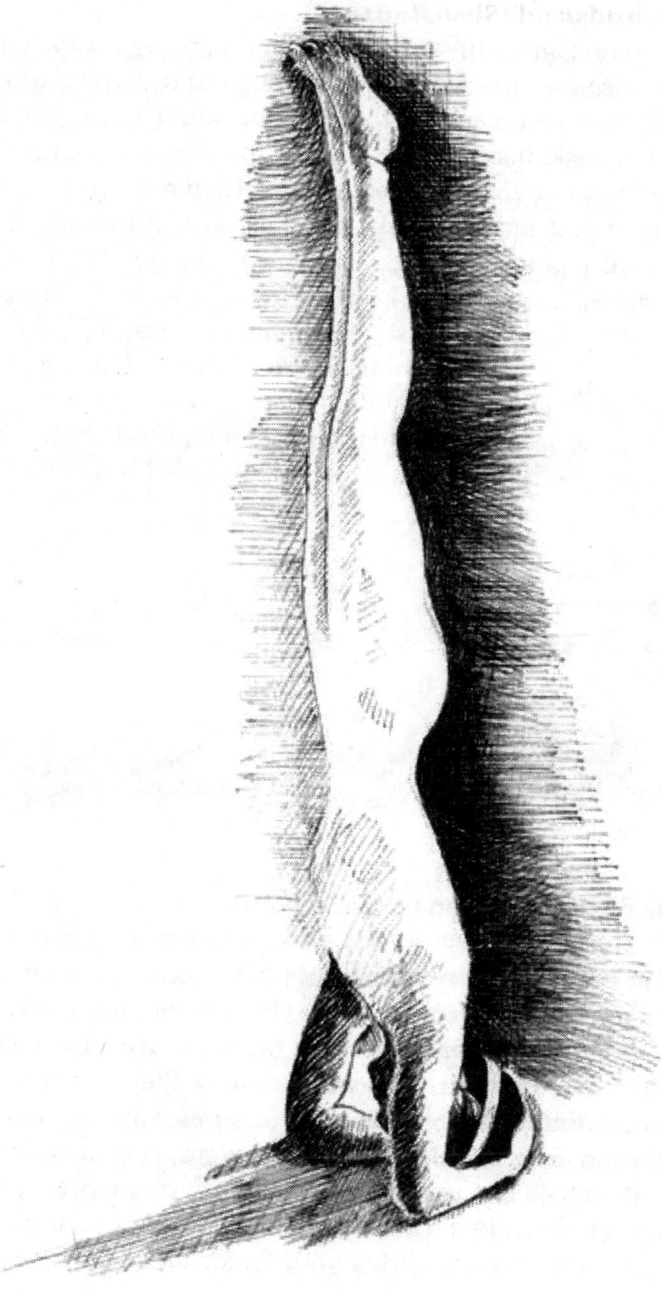

The Bridge (Setubandh Asana)

While lying down straight, bend both legs at the knees and raise the hip area while keeping your heels on the floor. Then raise both hands to the lower back area to support and lift the back, bending the arms at the elbows, but keeping the elbows on the floor for support. Then raise your hips as high as you can while still keeping your feet on the floor. Then straighten the legs with hips still off the floor, as illustrated below, while keeping the shoulders and head on the ground in a relaxed state. Remain in this position for 5 to 10 seconds while breathing deeply. Then slowly lower the waist back to the floor while offering descending support from your hands. Rest and then repeat for 5 to 10 times. This will benefit the back, which is the pathway for much of our nervous system.

The Fish (Matsyasana)

There a few ways you can start this *asana*, either from lying down or from the sitting (Padmasana) posture. If in the Padmasana, keep your knees bent in the sitting position and simply bend backwards at the waist with the help of both hands on your back while resting the elbows on the ground. Bend the neck backwards as much as you can. The back and chest should be arched upward, keeping them off the floor. Make sure that the knees are on or close to the floor. Then while the head is arched backward, the back of it resting on the floor, bring your hands to the feet and hold the toes while the elbows rest on the floor. Inhale and stop the breath for a few seconds. To end it, merely straighten the legs and let the torso relax and rest on the floor in the corpse position.

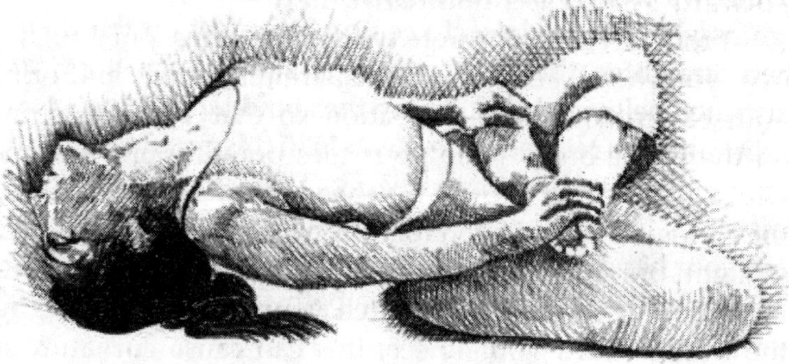

If starting this position while lying down with your legs straight and feet together, put your hands under the back of your thighs or buttocks with palms down. Then press down on your elbows, inhale and arch your back and neck while resting the back of your head on the floor. Breathe deeply and keep your legs and torso relaxed. To end it, lift your head and relax your torso and release your arms, letting them rest on the floor again, and let yourself relax in the corpse position.

This Fish or Matsyasana position helps activate the intestines and cures constipation. It also makes the thyroid and adrenal glands act properly. It's also good for respiratory or lung problems.

Forward Bend (Paschimothanasana)

From a lying position with your arms outstretched over your head, keep your arms straight, inhale and bring yourself up to a sitting position so that you are sitting on the pelvic bone. Keep your toes pointing upward and stretch your arms above your head. Now exhale and pull the abdomen in, and bend forward while keeping your back straight. Bring your chin toward your shins and your chest toward your thighs. (If you arch your back as in bringing the head toward your knees, this can cause curvature of the spine.) Continue until you are bent all the way forward without your legs bending. You can then hold onto your toes with your fingers. Or your arms and hands can go past your feet while your elbows rest on the floor. Hold the pose for several seconds and then inhale while you come out of the pose back to the lying position. This *asana* invigorates the internal organs and the nervous system, while reducing fat.

The Hands to Feet (Pada Hastasana)

This is a simple pose to do. First stand erect, inhale and raise your arms and hands so they are going straight above your head. Then, in one smooth motion, exhale as you bring your body, bending from the waist, straight forward, arms outstretched, and down to grasp your ankles or feet. Hold the big toes with your thumbs and index fingers. Pull your head as close to your shins as possible. If you cannot go all the way without bending your knees, which is often the hard part, then do as best you can. Do not strain yourself, but get used to it. Hold this pose for several seconds, then raise yourself up while inhaling, reaching out in front of you until you are straight, arms extending toward the ceiling. Then bring your arms down to your sides while exhaling. This again helps digestive problems, works the stomach and hip areas, and also helps bring nutrients and oxygen to the brain.

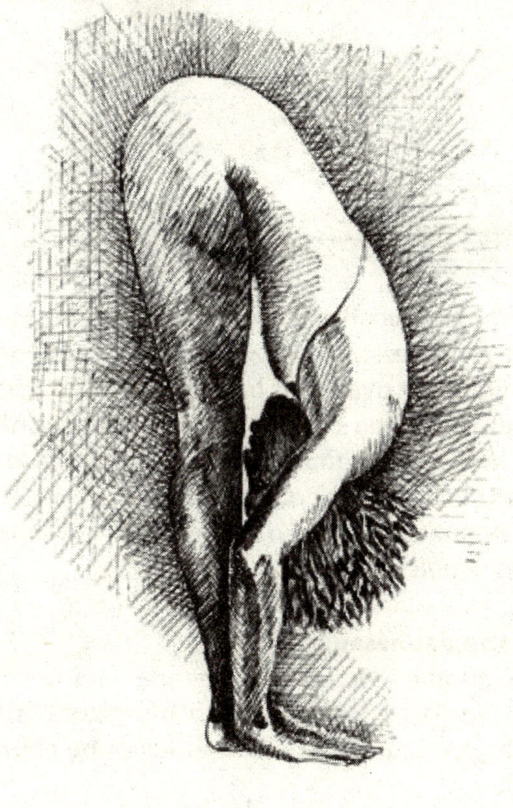

The Cobra (Bhujangasana)

For this *asana,* first lie down on your stomach, keeping the legs straight and together. Bend your arms at the elbows and place the palms on the ground near or under the shoulders. Then inhale and begin lifting the shoulders and chest upward, bending from the stomach, arching your head backwards, keeping the navel on the ground. Try to do this as much as possible without using your hands for support. If necessary use your hands only to help the body go up higher. Arch the head back as far as possible.

The complete position, however, involves bending your legs at the knees, keeping the knees on the ground, and raising your feet over your back and arching your torso until the feet touch the back of the head. Remain in this position for about 30 seconds breathing normally, and then exhale as you bring your body back down. Repeat 3 to 6 times. This benefits any slip disc, cervical, and almost all spine related problems.

The Locust (Shalabhasana)

This is another leg lift, but while laying on your stomach. So, lie down on the stomach and place both hands under the thighs. Raise the head and keep the chin on the ground. While inhaling, lift the right leg without bending the knee. Maintain this position for 10 to 30 seconds and while taking two full breaths. Repeat this 5 times and then do the same with the other leg. Then do this with both legs simultaneously, raising them up so the feet are as high as possible without bending the knee.

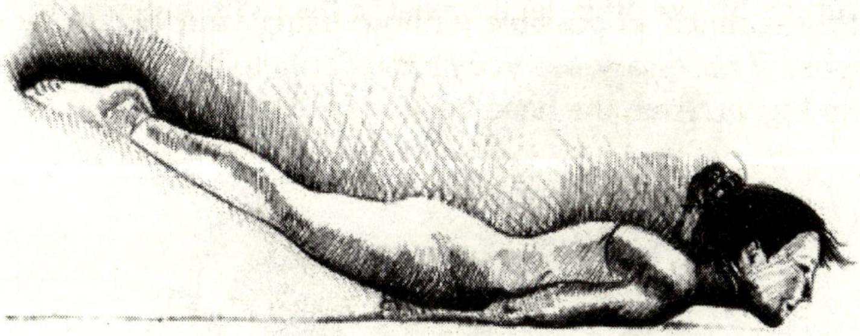

Then to complete this *asana*, take three full breaths and while holding the third breath bring both legs up and arch the body at the waist while bending the knees and bringing the feet up over the back as far as you can go, or until the feet touch the top of the head if possible. Breathe normally and then exhale while bringing the legs back down to the floor. This is good for helping strengthen the back to relieve lower back pain.

Half Spinal Twist (Ardha Matsyendrasana)

This pose does not merely bend the spine but twists it. Kneel down with your legs together, and rest your buttocks on your heels. Then move your buttocks to the right so you are sitting to the right of your feet. Then lift your left leg over your right, placing the foot against the outside of your right knee, resting it on the floor. Then bring your right heel close to your buttocks while keeping the spine erect. Now stretch your arms out straight from your shoulders (left arm going straight out to the left, and right arm going straight out to the right) and keep them level with your shoulders, and then twist your torso to the left, keeping the arms in line with your shoulders as they turn. Now bring your right arm down toward the floor on the outside of the left knee and hold the left foot in the right hand, placing your left hand on the floor behind you. Exhaling, twist as far as possible to the left while turning your head to look over the left shoulder. Then return to the sitting posture. Now do the maneuver starting with the other leg to twist in the right direction.

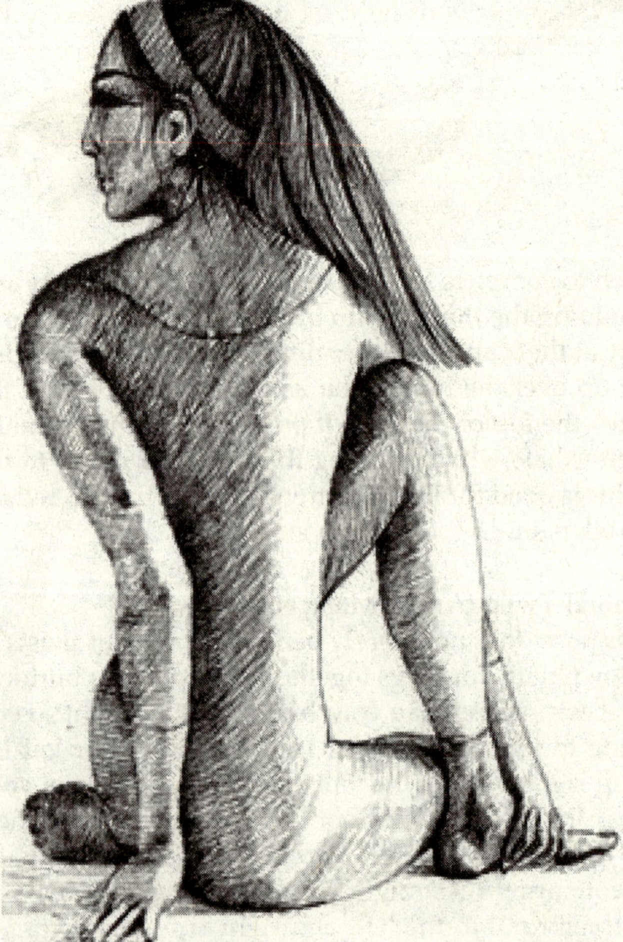

The Bow (Ardhachandrasana)

There are a few ways to start this *asana*. One way is to begin from the sitting posture in Vajarasana. So bend your knees and sit on your ankles. Keep both hands on the chest. Inhale and then bend the head and neck backwards from the stomach. Support yourself with your legs while you lift your waist and stretch up. You can reach back and touch your feet. If possible, keep bending or arching backwards until you can rest your head on the floor near your ankles. This is then called Puma Chankrasana. To come out of it, just relax, straighten your legs, and lie on the floor.

You can also start the Bow from laying on the stomach, while moving from the Cobra or the Locust positions. First, while laying down, forehead on the floor, inhale and then bend your legs at your knees, and raise your feet up, and then grasp your ankles with your hands behind your back. Then exhale. Then while inhaling, lift your ankles, raising your knees and thighs off the floor, which will also pull your head off the floor. While looking upward, arch yourself from the stomach and raise your chest, which will look like the illustration below. Take three deep breaths in this pose before lowering your legs back to the floor to relax.

This *asana* is very good for the respiratory system because of the intense stretching to the lungs. It also cures cervical, spondylitis, sciatica, and other spinal problems. Plus, it is good for thyroid when you can reach the Puma Chandrasana. However, people with hernia and severe hypertension should not strain themselves in this *asana*.

The Triangle (Trikonasana)

This is not a difficult position to fulfill, as long as you

keep your arms and legs straight. First, take a standing position with your feet about 3 or 4 feet apart. When turning to the left, the left foot should point to the left (the right foot points to the right when we turn to the right). Then from the shoulder bring your right arm straight out, and bring your left arm straight up against your left ear. Then inhale, hold it and then exhale as you bend to your right side from the waist, keeping your arms in position as you do so, until your right hand touches your right foot. Slide the hand down as far as you can go. Then look out toward the top of your head to view your left hand, the left arm still straight and touching your left ear, or pointing straight up, as illustrated below. Stay there and take several deep breaths. Then straighten yourself again and repeat the *asana,* this time while turning to the right. This move helps the spine and spinal nerves, along with assisting the digestive system, and improves our ability to perform the other *asanas*.

Returning to the Lotus Position (Padmasana)

Sit down in Dandasan or Sukhasana (the normal sitting posture) and place the right foot on the left thigh and the left foot on the right thigh. (If you cannot do this properly, then just assume the normal sitting posture.) The spine should be straight. Keep the left hand below the right hand and place them on the lap (*anjali*). Focus the mind on the front portion of the nose or any one place such as an image or deity of God or Goddess or any symbol that you prefer. You can relax a bit before ending the session with the Corpse pose.

Ending with the Corpse (Shavasana) Pose

Again you lay on your back, feet spread about 18 inches from your sides, palms up. Close your eyes and breathe deeply and slowly from the abdomen, and feel your abdomen rise and fall. Allow yourself to go deeper into relaxation. This reduces your body's energy loss, lowers your respiration and pulse rate, and rests the whole system. Once you have relaxed for about five minutes or more, then rise and sit up for the next step. After a yoga session, it is easy to fall asleep in this position, but do not let yourself do that. Now you are ready for meditation.

MEDITATION

For some people, ending the hatha yoga routine is only a preparation for the final step of the session, which is meditation. Now that the body is relaxed and in good shape, and all of the energy channels have been opened, now it is time to sit in the lotus position again and with deep breathing quietly engage in deep meditation. One can end the session by chanting *Om* three times again, but with more concentration and a deeper affect. Or one can enter into more inward forms of reflection and introspection for realization. Only after 20 to 30 minutes of meditation do some people consider their yoga session complete.

However, meditation can go on for some time, hours even, if one enters into the more profound aspects of it.

There are many more *asanas* that a person can learn. However, the more complex or difficult they are, the more you may need to be guided by a qualified yoga teacher so you can learn how to do them properly. Nonetheless, all the *asanas* that you do are only meant to prepare the body and mind to help you reach a higher consciousness in which you can attain a perception of the spiritual dimension, up to and including the Divine Reality or Supreme Being. Many are the sages who have glimpsed this reality, and some are those who have actually entered into it and live in it every moment of their lives. They are the examples we need to follow, and *asanas* alone are not enough to take us to that level of understanding. There is more to yoga than merely keeping the body and mind in good shape, but it certainly helps. And for those who want a deeper glimpse into the final frontier, or the spiritual reality, we go on to the practice of *pranayama* before ending our yoga session.

□

6

The Surya Namaskar Salutation to the Sun

Before we end our *asana* session with the corpse pose, we can include the Surya Namaskar. Some people feel a yoga session should be started with the Surya Namaskar as a warm up. However, the Surya Namaskar can also be done as a separate routine. It is one of the best exercise techniques available. So, even if we cannot do a full yoga routine, some suggest that we do at least three Surya Namaskars every day to keep ourselves in the best condition.

Many people in the West look for the best exercise routine to help them stay in shape. Here is something that has been around for thousands of years and has withstood the test of time. It strengthens the body, circulation, the breathing, and keeps the body limber and in shape. And you can have this completely free of charge, without a fitness coach, by simply using the following instructions.

Surya Namaskar is Sanskrit which means obeisance or prostrations (Namaskar) to the sun (Surya). It implies that one awakens before sun rise in order to do this exercise or pay obeisance to the rising sun. This is around 5 to 5:30 AM. Of course, this exercise is good no matter what time you may use it, but it is best done while the stomach is empty, before eating. It is a yogic exercise which consists of twelve particular postures done in a routine, one following another in a fixed, cyclic order to ensure improvement and good health in one's digestion, agility, rejuvenation, beauty, and longevity. It will also help one lose weight and trim the waist. There is no equipment to buy, or membership to a gym or fitness club that must be purchased. You just need a little space in your apartment or home. If, however, you begin to feel short-breathed or dizzy, then take a break. Women can do this during their period because it can help digestion and the flow of energy and outflow of waste needed at that time. But pregnant women should not practice it.

It is also recommended that a person chant the names of the Sun god in each of the twelve positions to increase the connection with the cosmic rays of the sun and the exercises that are done. These are the offering of obeisances (*namah*) to the sun in each of its twelve aspects:

Om Mitraya Namah (Obeisances to the sun as friend of all)
Om Ravaya Namah (Praised by all)
Om Surya Namah (Guide of all)
Om Bhavane Namah (Bestower of Beauty)
Om Khagaya Namah (Stimulator of the Senses)
Om Pushne Namah (Nourisher of Life)
Om Hiranya Garbha Namah (Promoter of Virility)
Om Marichay Namah (Destroyer of Disease)
Om Adityaya Namah (Inspirer of Love)
Om Savitre Namah (Begetter of Life)
Om Arkaya Namah (Inspirer of Awe)
Om Bhaskaraya Namah (Radiant One)

The idea is that you do about 100 Surya Namaskars every morning, and the time to do them should not be a consideration. With practice, these poses will flow more smoothly and quickly. If each pose lasts about a second, then the full Surya Namaskar can be done in about 10 seconds or so. Of course, if you cannot do so many, then start with 3, 5, or 10 Surya Namaskars every day and you will still notice the improvements.

POSTURE 1: As illustrated on the next page, first you stand erect, ready to face the early morning sun. Stand straight with chest out and spine erect, looking forward with hands folded in respect in front of the chest where the heart is located. It is like a stance of prayer. Once you start doing the routine, you spend about one second in this pose and the others that follow. Of course, if you are weak or aged, or if you are new to the routine, you may take this a little slower.

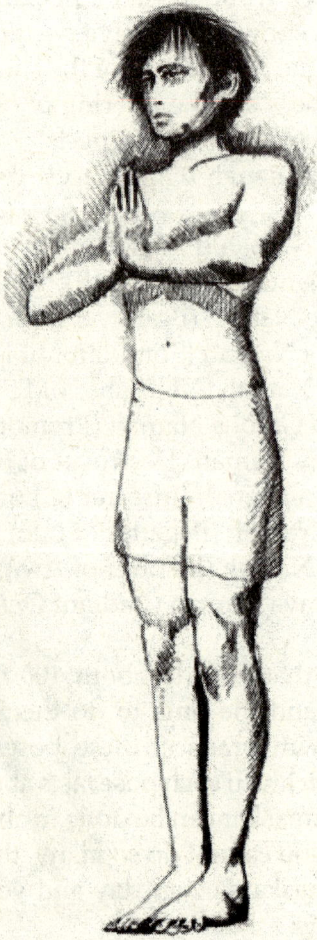

POSTURE 2: Now, while inhaling, raise your arms up in the air while keeping the hands together, and arch your self backwards as far as you can go, forming a crescent-like curve from your feet to the hands. This posture helps retain the flexibility of the spine.

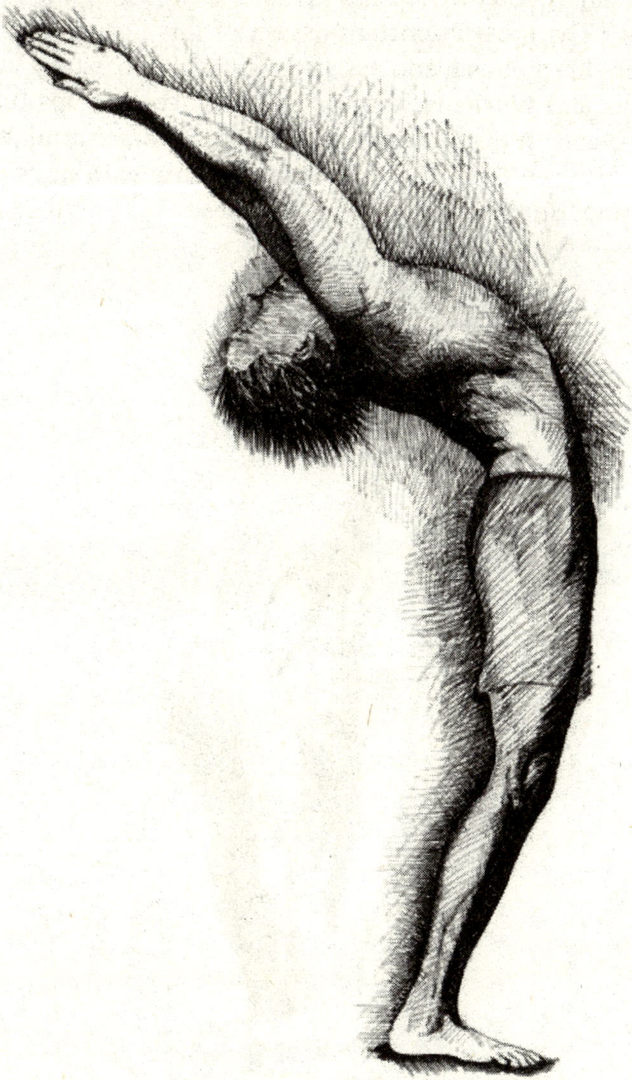

POSTURE 3: Now, while exhaling, bring your hands down to your feet so that you quickly bend forward at the waist, while keeping the legs as straight as possible. The best position is to bring the hands flat to the floor on either side of your feet, while keeping the head as close to the knees as you can. If you are not that flexible, then just do the best you can. The most important aspect of this pose is that it squeezes the stomach and assists in digestion to extract any vitamins and nutrients from one's food, which helps turn it into blood. It also loosens any fat that has accumulated there. Postures 2 and 3 are actually the easiest to do, so if you cannot do the others, at least do these.

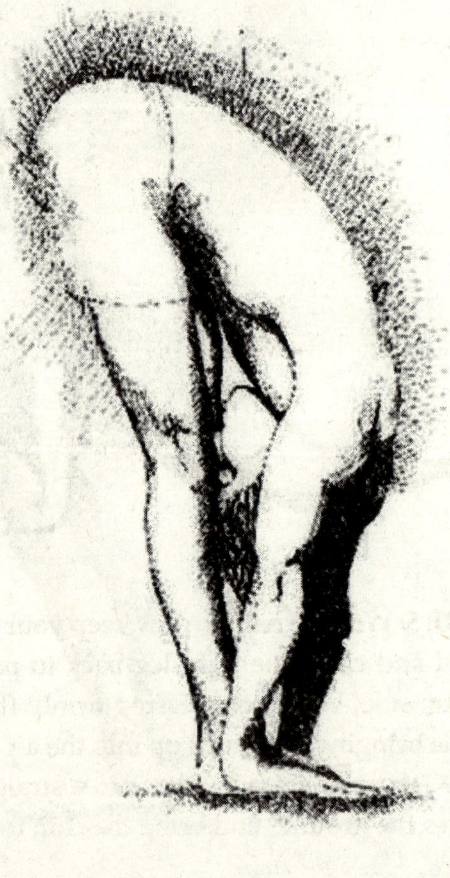

POSTURE 4: From position three, while inhaling, put your hands on the floor and lower your hips and stretch your left leg back as far as you can, letting the foot rest on the toes and the knee touch the ground, while you bend your right leg in a crouching stance, letting the right knee come up to your chest. Keeping your hands flat on the ground, your arms straight, arch your head upward and back so you are looking at the ceiling or sky. This forms a crescent shape from the left heel up to the top of your head. This position helps ensure flexibility of the spine and immunity from diseases in the left leg muscles and ligaments.

POSTURE 5: While exhaling, now keep your hands flat on the ground and carry the right leg back to parallel the left leg, side by side, both feet pressing firmly flat against the floor, while bringing your hips up into the air as high as they will go. Keep your arms and back in a straight line as your head faces the ground, and bring the chin to the chest,

making you look at your knees. This makes your body form an upside down "V" or a triangle between you and the floor.

POSTURE 6: Now, while keeping the hands and feet in the same places, having fully exhaled, hold the breath and bring your hips down while moving the head and shoulders forward, straightening the whole body near the floor with your hands now under your chest. Keep the face downward with the forehead, the chest and knees lightly touching the ground, and the hips slightly raised. With the forehead,

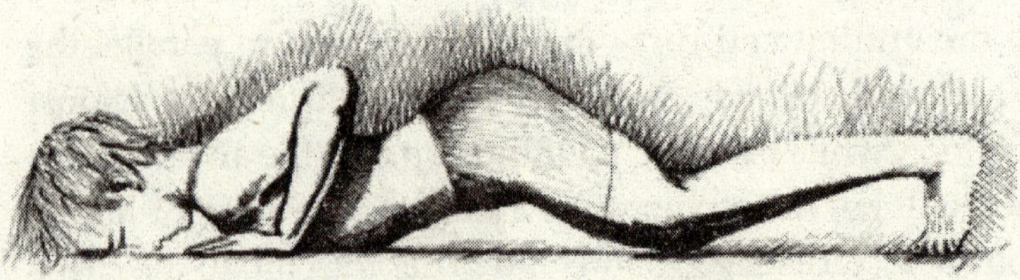

chest, and two palms, knees, and feet touching the floor, it is called Sashtang Namaskar, or prostrations with eight points touching the floor.

POSTURE 7: The next posture, while inhaling, flows from position 6, which is done merely by straightening your arms and arching your chest forward and arching your head back so that you are looking at the ceiling. Your feet and knees rest on the floor while your arms hold the rest of your body a little above it. Again you form a body-length crescent, from your feet up to your head. This yogic position is similar to "the cobra."

POSTURE 8: Now exhale and let your body flow into position 5 again by lowering your head and chest, keep your arms and legs straight, and raise your hips as high as they will go. As your head faces the ground, keep your arms and back in a straight line and bring the chin to the chest, making you look at your knees, which forms an upside down "V" again.

POSTURE 9: Now, while inhaling, we flow into the same position as posture four, but stretch the other leg. So we first bend the left leg and bring the left foot forward on the floor. Then, keeping your hands flat on the ground,

bring your hips down while moving the chest and head forward, allowing the left knee to reach up to the chest, and then arch your head up and back. The right foot stays in its place, letting the foot rest on the toes, which makes the right leg get stretched backward when your chest moves forward. This gives the body a crescent shape from the right heel up to the top of your head. This position helps ensure flexibility of the spine and immunity from diseases in the right leg muscles and ligaments.

POSTURE 10: Now we go back into posture three as in a forward bend. Keep your hands in place as you bring your right leg forward to be parallel with the left leg. With both feet flat on the floor, and the legs kept straight, the body is bent at the waist, while exhaling, with the forehead touching the knees (if you can bend this much). If you are not this flexible and cannot bend like this, then simply do it as best you can and keep the head as close to the knees as possible.

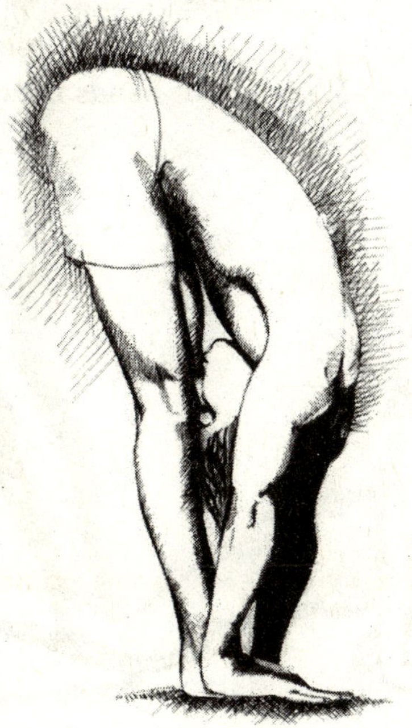

POSTURE 11: From the above position, while inhaling, raise your arms up in the air while keeping the hands together, and arch your self backwards as far as you can go, forming a crescent-like curve from your feet to the hands. This posture helps retain the flexibility of the spine.

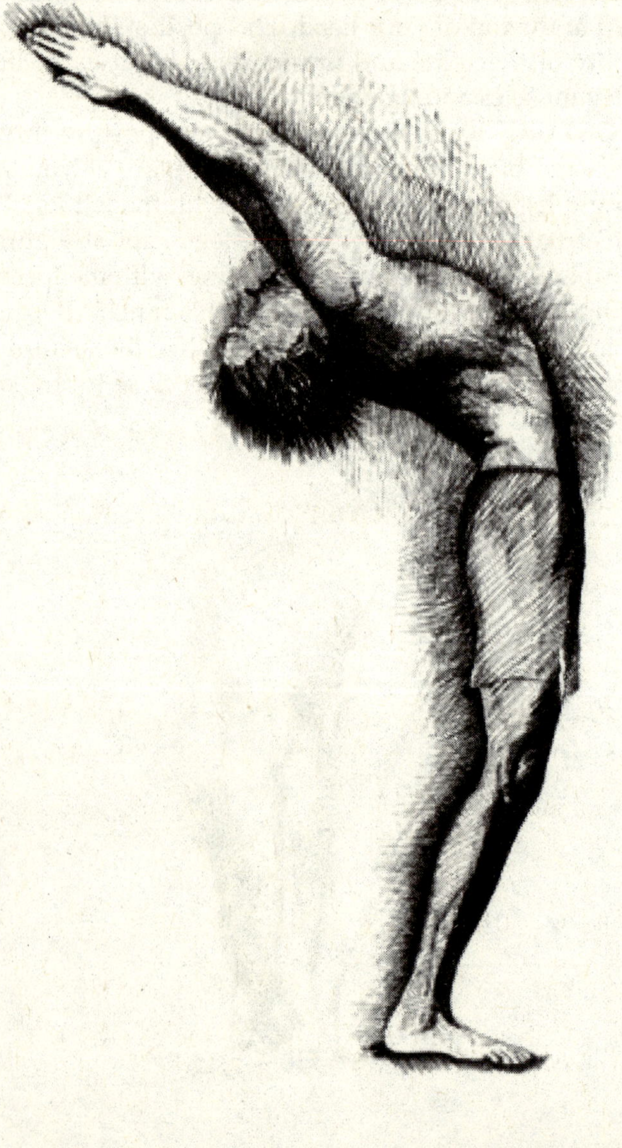

POSTURE 12: Now lower your arms and straighten your body to stand erect as in posture number one and exhale. Then join the palms in front of your chest as in prayer. Hold this for a second and then begin to go back into posture number 2 to start the whole cycle of postures again for the next Surya Namaskar.

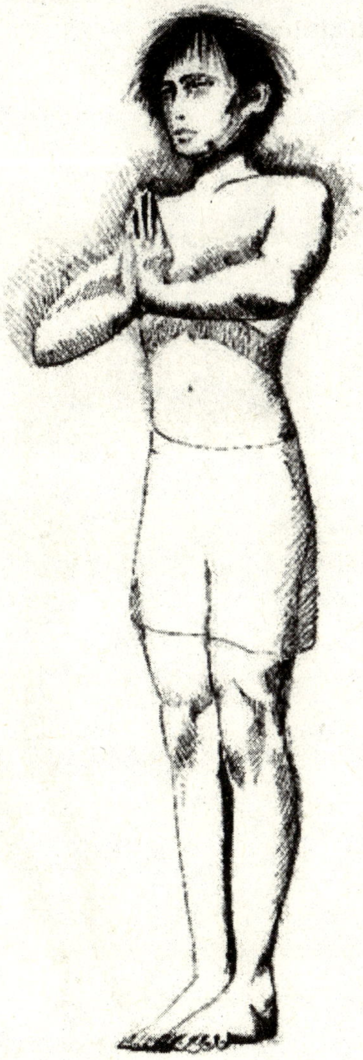

You may want to do each posture separately the first time you do this to familiarize yourself with each one. Then begin to do it as a flowing movement from one to the other, through all twelve postures. Do it as a cycle of 100 Surya Namaskars, or even more if you want. Or set a number that you can do regularly. You will certainly notice the difference in your health, weight, flexibility, energy level, and even overall attitude.

□

7
Pranayama

PREPARATION IN BREATHING

Pranayama is the science of breath. It is part of the hatha and raja yoga systems. It consists of particular exercises to control breathing in ways that it will bring more oxygen into the blood and to the brain. It also helps control the flickering nature of the mind. *Prana* in Sanskrit means breath, wind, respiration, but mostly the life energy. *Ayama* means stretch, extend, expand, or lengthen. And that is the purpose of *pranayama*: to manipulate, lengthen, or extend the breathing to increase and manage the circulation of vital energy, *prana*, through the *nadis* or subtle nerve channels through the body. This assists in the health, vitality, and longevity of the body. It is also said to awaken the cerebrospinal nerve centers or chakras to their full potential.

The practice of *pranayama* will help control the *prana*, the vital force within the body, and also capture the *prana shakti* or force from nature, and result in more mental, physical, and spiritual energy for assisting the *sadhaka* in his or her *asanas* and meditation.

The *prana* or living force within us is not static but dynamic. It is always moving. When it stops moving, as when we are in stress, or from shallow breathing and similar factors, physical disorders can result. Therefore, practicing *pranayama* helps remove toxins and mental as well as physical ailments. It helps stabilize the mind and reduces bodily stress. It slows the heart rate and makes the lungs more efficient and allows us to take in more oxygen in a shorter time. Thereafter, it helps energize the body and mind. This in itself will assist us in raising our consciousness for spiritual purposes.

Pranayama also directs energy through the *nadis* in the subtle body and open those inner channels. This also deepens our meditation, helps us focus our concentration, and opens our consciousness to higher realms of existence. This helps us reach higher levels of enlightenment and to more easily reach *samadhi* and even *moksha*.

Pranayama is also the process which brings in the energy to ignite the generator of the Muladhara chakra and begin pressing the *prana* up through the Shushumna channel. This is what must happen first if we are going to pursue raja yoga. The Shushumna must be awakened or opened to establish a connection between the higher or lower dimensions of consciousness. This is also what allows the awakening of the kundalini to commence.

Most people take little notice of the way they breathe. Many breathe quick and shallow breaths, which is not healthy. Such breathing allows for only a small amount of oxygen to be accepted by the body in the upper portions of the lungs. This causes low energy levels and susceptibility to disease. *Pranayama* can help change that.

When one practices correct breathing, one must breathe through the nose and then do a full inhalation followed by a complete exhalation. A deep breath means that the abdomen expands along with the lungs, and the shoulders move back. A full exhalation means your abdomen contracts and your chest moves in.

The whole point of *pranayama* is that the rhythmic breathing patterns improve the respiratory system and steadies the mind and nerves so they can be prepared for focused concentration or meditation. The process also reduces mental cravings and unnecessary desires that often distract one from the spiritual goal of life. However, it also improves the general health of the practitioner as well, making the body a balanced vehicle for further spiritual development.

However, *prana* is the energy that is imbibed by the blood, not only through breath but also through food, water, and even sunlight. *Pranayama,* as well as yogic *asanas,* help amplify the *prana* and increase the amount we take in. This, of course, increases our own energy, and also helps pave the way for increased awareness and brain activity, as well as the means for perceiving deeper levels of reality and consciousness. *Prana* exists and moves primarily through the subtle or astral body in the *nadis,* or nerve channels. The *asanas* are especially for opening the *nadis* and chakras to allow for an increased flow of *prana* through the system.

The main *nadi* is the Sushumna that flows along the spine. On either side are smaller *nadis* called the Ida (connected with the left nostril) and Pingala (connected to the right nostril). These are near the spinal ganglia which spiral around the Sushumna. The Ida *nadi* is the moon current, the influence of which is cooling and calming, while the Pingala *nadi* is the sun current, which is warming and stimulating. The dominant air currents usually change from one nostril to the other about every one hour and 50 minutes. When the right nostril and *prana* current dominates, a person tends to be more lively, outgoing, and intellectually active, and more left-brain oriented. When the left nostril or *prana* current dominates, a person tends to be more inward, quieter, imaginative, and meditative, and more right-brain active. When both nostrils and *prana* channels flow equally, it indicates that both sides of the brain are interacting equally. This is a good time for meditation.

While doing *pranayama,* the correct breath should be that you first exhale, then inhale and retain the breath, then exhale completely. Exhalation is the most important part. It is said that the inward breath is the Sanskrit prayer "Soham," which means *Sah Aham*, "the immortal spirit I am." While the outgoing breath is the Sanskrit prayer "Hamsah," which means "I am He" or I am part of the Divine. Thus, with each breath we unconsciously perform a *japa* or personal prayer that indicates our spiritual nature. In this way, the yogi who is conscious of this prayer and realizes its meaning can see his or her true spiritual nature with every breath, every waking moment. Thus, he frees himself from the illusions of life.

Entering meditation can help harmonize the flow of the *prana* through the Ida and Pingala channels. However, practicing *pranayama* can also do that, which then helps balance the mind and body. This is how you can regulate the flow and accumulation of *prana* in the body.

THE UJJAYI PRANAYAMA TECHNIQUE

In preparing for a meditation session, doing some *pranayama* beforehand can be most helpful to quiet the mind. If you have ever been to a yoga class, then you have probably done this common technique. If not, then here is a description of one that has been used for many hundreds of years.

This is one of the most basic techniques for doing *pranayama*. You sit comfortably in the lotus or cross-legged position. Keep your back straight, but lower the head to the chest with the chin touching the place between the collar bones. Then stretch the arms out to the knees and rest the back of the wrists on the knees. Keep your fingers straight except for joining the tips of the index fingers to the tips of the thumbs. This is known as the Jnana (pronounced gyana) Mudra, meaning the sign of knowledge. The index finger represents the individual soul while the thumb represents the Universal Soul. The tips of the finger and thumbs being joined represents the exchange of knowledge.

1. Now close your eyes and focus inward.
2. Exhale completely, bringing your stomach in.

3. Now take a slow deep breath through the nose, allowing it to make a sound, until the lungs are full, but not allowing the abdomen to expand.
4. Then retain the breath for a few seconds.
5. Now exhale slowly and evenly until the lungs are emptied completely.
6. After a few seconds, gradually relax the diaphragm.
7. Wait another few seconds (*bahya kumbhaka*) and now take another slow and deep breath through both nostrils.
8. Repeat this cycle five to ten times.
9. When finished lie on the floor with legs slightly separated from each other, and arms slightly away from the body (in the Shavasana or corpse posture). Relax for a few minutes.

THE KAPALABHATI BREATHING TECHNIQUE

This is basically a way of doing a forced exhalation. The way this works is that you sit comfortably, cross-legged on the floor or mat or somewhere. Breathe normally for a few breaths, and then,

1. Exhale quickly and deeply by pulling the abdomen in with your stomach muscles, and letting the air out through the nostrils with an audible sound.
2. Relax your abdomen and let the air enter the lungs again. The inhalation should be twice as long as the exhalation.
3. Again pull in the abdomen and exhale with a quick gasp through the nose.
4. Do this 20 times or so. You should do two or three of these per second.
5. Then end this session by inhaling slowly and completely.
6. Retain the breath as long as comfortable.
7. Then exhale slowly and deeply.
8. You can repeat this process another 2 times or so.

This exercise helps clean the lungs of all stale air, allowing for a full inhalation of clean oxygen. The name Kapalabhati means "skull shining" in reference to the additional oxygen that helps clear the mind and consciousness. The movement of the diaphragm also tones the internal organs like the stomach, liver, and heart.

THE ANULOMA VILOMA BREATHING TECHNIQUE

This is also a common technique but quite beneficial. This is for breathing through alternate nostrils. The left nostril is connected with the Ida *nadi,* the path of the Pingala *nadi* is the right nostril. Throughout the day, if you will notice, your breathing changes from one nostril to the other. Breathing through the right or solar nostril indicates the time for action, doing things. While breathing primarily through the left or lunar nostril indicates a time for thought or meditation. As previously mentioned, this change usually happens about every hour and fifty minutes when we are healthy. However, most people experience disturbances in this pattern. So this technique helps restore a balanced flow.

When ready, bring your right hand up to your nose and use the thumb and ring fingers. Fold your index and middle fingers toward the palm. This is called the Vishnu Mudra. Then,

1. Take a deep breath and exhale completely two times.
2. Then inhale and block your right nostril using your thumb.
3. Exhale a slow complete breath through the left nostril.
4. Inhale through the left nostril.
5. Hold your breath while closing both nostrils.
6. Open your right nostril and close the left nostril with your ring and little fingers and breathe out a slow and complete breath through the right nostril.

7. Keep the left nostril closed and breathe in through the right nostril.
8. Hold both nostrils closed and retain the breath.
9. Now close the right nostril with the thumb and breathe out through the left nostril.
10. Now start again from # 2, and do this routine several times for one session.
11. Gradually, slow the breath to a 5 second inhalation and a 10 second exhalation.
12. End the session by bringing down your hand and inhaling through both nostrils.
13. Exhale completely.
14. Sit quietly, aware of the energy going through your system.

A variation on this technique is that all inhalations are through both nostrils, and exhalations are through alternating nostrils.

THE BRAHMARI, SITKARI AND SITHALI BREATHING TECHNIQUES

Three other simple techniques are the Brahmari, Sitkari and Sithali. In the Brahmari, you partially close the glottis in your throat while you inhale through the nostrils, producing a snoring sound. Then as you exhale slowly, produce a humming sound which helps slow the exhalation. Repeat several times.

The Sitkari is when you press the tip of the tongue to the roof of the mouth and slowly inhale through the open mouth, producing a hissing sound. Retain the breath as long as possible and exhale through the nose. Repeat several times.

Both of these techniques cool the body and stifle hunger and thirst, while the Sitkari is said to also increase one's beauty.

The Sithali breath is when you stick your tongue out a bit and curl the sides of it. Then you suck the breath in as if sucking it through a straw. Then close your mouth and hold your breath and exhale slowly through the nose. Repeat several times.

□

8

The Purpose of Meditation

Everyone is looking for happiness in some way. It is our natural state of being. However, we need to understand that the real source of fulfillment lies within us. We may try so many ways to attain external happiness for the mind and senses, but that means of success is always elusive.

The self or soul exists within all of us in purity, peace, bliss, and knowledge, and is free from mundane and temporary forms of happiness, sadness, or any earthly conditions. To attain that inner state we must turn inward, and one of the prominent ways of doing that is through meditation.

There are numerous ways to meditate, and each school of thought seems to have a different system. These can include the Buddhist process, such as the Noble Eight-fold Path for reaching nirvana. Or there is the raja yoga process, the ashtanga yoga process, the kundalini yoga system, and so on. It also seems that new systems are being developed on a regular basis these days, not only for achieving peace of mind, but to develop such things as one's creativity, prosperity, or mental clarity.

However, we are going to focus on the ultimate goal of meditation, which is to reach a higher consciousness for realizing our true spiritual identity and awareness of God. Meditation can help accomplish many things. But without understanding the true and full purpose of meditation, it is like digging a well for water without being aware of the fact that you are sitting next to a river. In such as state, you do not know the full potential you really have through the meditative process. Deep meditation that is free from the affects of the mind culminates in self-awareness and spiritual realization. That is the ultimate and age old purpose of meditation.

The four main goals of meditation include making the body healthy and stress-free; to steady the mind and make it peaceful; to feel full of love and joy; and to reach enlightenment and to realize your spiritual identity, by which you can attain *moksha,* liberation from material life.

This liberation or *moksha* means the release and freedom from any further births and deaths in the cycle of *samsara.* It is when one enters the spiritual dimension. But it also means the liberation from the bodily concept of life, wherein one attains freedom from anger, greed, envy, hatred toward others, and from selfish and sensual desires. This is also a liberation on a practical level that can be felt right here and now. It is the way toward peace of mind and a balanced view of life. It is difficult to make any spiritual progress without having attained this kind of freedom.

The meditation process begins with the means for calming the mind. That is the first principle of consideration. It is the state beyond the influence of the mind in which a person can first begin to perceive or get a glimpse of the spiritual dimension. Meditation is meant to bring our outward awareness, which always focuses on the external activities of our senses, inward toward the self. This is our true identity and source of consciousness, and a part of the unlimited Absolute Truth.

Too much focus on the external world keeps you from your inner self, your spirit, and from inner peace. The doorway to discovering a new you, a new dimension of your self, is within. You have to learn how to go within and then keep practicing to go deeper. Often times we look outside ourselves for completion – a new object, a new career, a new relationship, a new outlet of creativity. But that will never make you a complete and whole person if you are not already complete and whole within. Furthermore, you will never be fully satisfied with your life if you are not full within yourself.

When we talk about being happy, sad, or peaceful, that feeling exists primarily in the mind. As it is said, it is the mind that is the cause of either our freedom or our bondage to material existence. The attitude and demands of the mind are what has brought society into great levels of progress, as well as into horrible eras of wars and terror. Meditation is a way to gain some control over the restless mind and direct its energy into constructive channels of purpose, or toward a spiritual object or higher understanding and awareness.

Many people look to meditation to achieve peace of mind. This benefit takes place when the constant internal dialogue that goes on within us begins to die down. That happens when our attention becomes increasingly focused within, toward a single object or level of awareness. The contentment and happiness we feel comes from the inner awareness of our real identity that increases the deeper we go within. Therein we can also become free from the problems that go on around us. We can free ourselves from the drama that we may too often accept as our real identity.

So, meditation starts with calming and centering the mind, turning it within or to bring it home. Thereafter, it is the process of connecting to your inner self and getting to know the real you, and to make inner realities a part of everyday life. It leads to infinite possibilities waiting to be discovered, waiting to emerge from within us. It can help clear away the emotional blues, limitations and hang ups. As you tune in, you will be able to see a fuller spectrum of life and its possibilities. A new energy can come into your life for inspiration and transformation.

Meditation can undo the complexities that bind and twist our lives, and make us feel less than full and fulfilled. It can give us the insight to perceive more clearly our place in the universe and our connectedness to all things. It can bring spiritual harmony and contentment within us that helps us find a self-sufficient happiness wherever we go. Yoga and meditation is the way we can gain insights and answers through experience rather than mere mental speculation or philosophical research. Tapping into new possibilities and perspectives in this way also gives us the chance to open the door to more ideas about our situation or problems at hand.

As the center of the senses, the mind's business is to always look for happiness by deciphering what is pleasant or unpleasant, happy or sad, comfortable or uncomfortable, wanted or unwanted, and to dream of what is desirable and think of how to avoid what is undesirable. When the mind acquires what it wants, it and the senses are often satisfied for a while. It is like being totally diverted by the taste of a good meal. Or when you are fully focused on the story in a movie, all other thoughts are gone, or simply not allowed entrance into the intensity of your concentration. But when the meal or movie is finished, the mood of the mind changes and then it wants something else. For example, you first may feel that the stomach needs filling. It wants tc eat. Then it thinks of what it wants to eat. Maybe a pizza. Then the intelligence kicks in to plan how to get it. Then once it gets the pizza, the stomach, tongue and mind are content. But then it wants something to drink, not just anything, but a drink that tastes good and supplies tingle to the tongue. Once you get that, then there is some satisfaction for the tongue and mind, which are dictating to you what you should get. Plus, they also translate the sensation on the tongue as to whether it is pleasant or exciting enough. If it is, then maybe you feel happy. Or is it merely the mind being temporarily calm that makes you feel a little content?

But then after the pizza and drink are finished, the mind begins to suggest something else, just one more thing, like a desert, like maybe some ice cream. Wouldn't that be nice? Then everything will be complete. And away you go again. Another thought develops into another desire, and then another desire needs to be fulfilled, which then requires action. It never ends.

So, meditation is the process of reaching that source of joy, happiness, and contentment that is within you that does not require the constant pleasing of the mind and senses. This process can help us learn how to live in peace.

The first step is concentration which is a focused or even forced awareness of something. Then comes meditation, which is a natural flow of thought and absorption toward an object or state of being.

When one becomes successful at meditation, you can reach that state of consciousness that is completely beyond the effects of the mind. This is a state of superconsciousness, beyond mind and the influence of time, space, body, and ego. Or beyond the sense of separation from ourselves and the object of meditation.

Meditation also helps heal the mind of imbalances and habitual thought patterns that need to be corrected. Regular practice of meditation helps streamline one's energies towards the true understanding of life and our spiritual purpose. It helps us separate ourselves from the illusory drama that goes on all around us, and to realize that we all have a spiritual identity. It is through this means that we unveil the layers of ignorance that cover our own divinity.

I have always said that the doorway to higher levels of exploration are within us. They are only waiting for us to open them. Meditation is that gateway which helps open us to the Infinite.

Ultimately, the purpose of yoga and meditation is to discover and realize our true spiritual nature. It is not merely to keep the body fit or enhance our material life.

This, however, takes place automatically with the sincere practice of yoga, but it is only a sideline to the spiritual realizations that are the real goal. Cutting through the layers of ignorance and lack of understanding of who we really are, and realizing our eternal and blissful spiritual identity is the real purpose of any spiritual path, especially of yoga and meditation. It rids us of the inherent feelings of fear, inadequacy, and insecurity that we often encounter while living in this unstable world.

TWO TYPES OF MEDITATION

When it comes to meditation, there are two basic types, the Saguna (meditating on something with qualities like a mantra, a deity, a yantra, a picture, symbol, or object) and Nirguna (something without qualities like the void, the Brahman, or a concept of the Absolute). Nirguna meditation is more difficult. Even Sri Krishna in the *Bhagavad-gita* explains that advancement for one who meditates on the impersonal aspect of the Absolute is very difficult and not advisable. That is because, in essence, our spiritual and material nature is individual. We are parts and parcels of the Supreme, the same in spiritual nature. In that respect, we are all one in spiritual quality, but we do not have the same quantity or potency as the Supreme. The Supreme is infinite while we as spirit souls are infinitesimal. Thus, we share many of the same qualities as the Supreme, but not the same powers, similar to the way an electrical spark is the same as that produced in the powerhouse, but the powerhouse or generator is the source of such power while the spark is not.

PROBLEMS IN THE MEDITATION PROCESS

Problems that most people have in being unable to make satisfactory progress in meditation usually comes from a lack of seriousness, sufficient purity, and especially a lack of sense control. The downward tendencies from uncontrolled senses and wrong habits in life make the mind too disturbed and restless. A person may sit down to meditate, physically unmoving, but the mind may be in a whirl, thinking of so many issues, and protesting and straining against doing meditation. This is what often makes it a frustrating and tiring experience.

For such people it may be better to go on to mantra meditation and focus the mind on something in particular, like the mantra, rather than trying to completely still the mind in order to achieve stable and fixed concentration for self-reflection and inward meditation. Mantra meditation is also extremely beneficial and is actually recommended in this age of Kali-yuga more so than the form of meditation we are presently discussing. So, we will elaborate on mantra meditation more thoroughly later in this book.

MANTRA MEDITATION

Most people that are new to meditation may sit, go through the steps for preparation, try the techniques, and still remain focused on feelings of the body, thoughts, ideas, or the external sounds that are heard around us. In fact, it is understood that most people in this age of Kali-yuga can hardly sit quietly for even ten minutes or calm their mind. That is why it is recommended that they use the process of mantra meditation to more easily focus their mind and attention on something, like the vibration of the mantra, and then, by placing their focus on the mantra, remove their attention from distractions and sensual inclinations or stimuli. This technique of filling the mind with transcendental sound is easier than trying to empty or void the mind of anything and everything.

The word "mantra" means to deliver (*tra*) the mind (*mana*), and it is one of the easiest methods to use. The mantra itself, depending on which one is used, often incorporates a vibrational formula to call various energies or powers to oneself, or to awaken one to higher states of awareness and perception and realizations. In this way, layers of illusion and confusion are peeled away giving one clarity and focus. So, a few techniques of mantra meditation are included later.

STARTING THE PROCESS

When you feel you are ready to begin a spiritual discipline, you have to ask yourself if you are serious. Have you decided that you really want to be spiritually awakened during this lifetime? Are you ready to be committed? Is spiritual progress the primary importance in your life? Are you ready to change your lifestyle in the necessary ways to assist in whatever mental, psychological, intellectual, and physical transformations are necessary? If so, then begin with steady determination.

When beginning to engage in meditation, one of the first experiences you may have will be an attractive state of mental calm. As one engages in regular sessions of meditation, it may provide a private but privileged form of refined pleasure that will bring the distaste toward the more mundane forms of happiness in material existence. With a higher sense of self awareness, one may attain a more refined set of values. Thus, it becomes easier for a person to follow a more balanced and wholesome way of life, and avoid those actions that may cause distractions and lack conduciveness to spiritual advancement.

The spiritual path is often one of inner singleness of purpose and may thus require one to appear as if alone and independent from the influences that affect so much of the rest of society. This does not mean that one will be lonely, but one must be determined to fulfill the real purpose of life. We have to understand that people who are completely absorbed in material affairs are in need of awakening with spiritual knowledge from holy beings. Most people will not be interested, but we need to help bring such light and wisdom to humanity. And we have to make the decision to be one those people.

Therefore, we have to first help ourselves, and one of the things we must do is pick our association carefully. We must pick those people who are positive, uplifting, and supportive of us and our intentions. We must stay away from those who are negative, overly critical, always complaining or fighting, or who suck us dry of our energy. However, we must be just as discriminative about the music we listen to, the magazines and books we read, or the kind of entertainment we watch and news we observe. It all affects us in various uplifting or depressing ways. So, we must be careful about this if we want to progress or have the right attitude. But especially pick those people who are spiritually inclined to assist our own spiritual progress whenever we can.

Furthermore, we should not feel that we need to be recognized for whatever spiritual progress we make in our practice. We should know that our spiritual awareness will contribute to the collective human consciousness throughout the world and our sphere of influence just by being spiritual. It is said that to move one grain of sand on a beach is to change the face of the world. Similarly, we may also do outward activities to help humanity, but the consistent upliftment of our own consciousness can certainly and subtly affect the world in a positive way, especially those within our sphere of activities or influence.

Of course, it can be difficult at times to deal with normal frustrations or problems of existence, as well as with people who are spiritually stagnant and unawake, or who have dismal attitudes toward life. However, with applied spiritual knowledge and growth, living a constructive life with a positive attitude, in spite of whatever challenges come our way, will be a natural by-product of our inner development.

If we are successful on the spiritual path, we will become aware of what we really are and have been all along. As we attain higher states of consciousness, there will be revealed new ways of knowing ourselves, and loftier ways of perceiving and relating to the world around us. We may ultimately uncover our own divine self. It is merely a question of becoming free of the wrong and distracting and misleading thoughts, feelings, and actions. Those are things which keep us tied to the wrong image of who we are, and to the temporary and fleeting level of reality. We simply need to apply ourselves with faith to the *sadhana*, the spiritual practice at hand.

Also, do not judge yourself by your progress or how much or how little you have attained in realizations or awareness. Do not expect to be seeing bright lights and hearing cosmic sounds as a means to judge your progress. Such things may mean you are on your way, but that is still not the goal. You have to reach much farther than that. We often progress in simple ways more than we have realized. Most people will merely slide quietly into perfection with little notice of any miracles or spectacular results. It is like eating a meal and afterwards you simply know, without much thinking about it, that you are no longer hungry. Spiritual progress is similar. You simply keep working at it and one day, through self-analysis, you realize how far you have come along.

Meditation also becomes easier and more joyous with time and practice, and when there is sure and simple faith and love for God. After all, any success in spiritual life depends not only on our own determination and sincerity, but also on the grace of the Supreme. In all our spiritual progress, including meditation, devotion to God is one of the most profound aids to our success and direction. It helps keep our spiritual purpose in focus, and helps prevent us from becoming self-serving and egotistical in the view of ourselves. The more humble our devotion is to God in our practice, the more likely it will result in a complete level of realization.

It has been said that the mind is like a pond. When the concentration is on one object, it is as if one throws a single stone into the water and you observe beautiful rings expanding out from one point on a smooth surface. When there are a multitude of thoughts, it is like many stones hitting the surface of the lake, and ripples are going all over in different directions, running into each other, making any sort of clear reflection off the surface of the water impossible. Similarly, when the mind is full of mundane thoughts it is impossible for any deep awareness to manifest, or any deeper reflection about oneself to take place. And this is the way the mind exists most of the time. In that condition, all we can do is attend to one thought before another breaks through, whether we like it or not. Thus, we are continuously forced to deal with the constant agitation of the mind, as if it is pulled by our senses, desires, goals, dreams, attachments, aversions, or attempts to serve the demands of others. In such a situation, where is there any peace?

So, the basis or foundation of meditation is to first reach a state of being free from this agitation, to calm the mind, like allowing the surface of the pond to become smooth after stopping the throwing of any stones into it. Then once the surface becomes smooth, we can begin to see the reflection on the surface of our self, our true nature of *sat-chit-ananda*, eternity, full knowledge and bliss. However, the real goal of meditation is to not only see the reflection, but to go deep enough wherein we make direct contact with our real, spiritual identity. That is like being able to see through the water of the pond and perceiving what is actually at the bottom. Steady contact with the spiritual self is not only meditation but becomes *samadhi*, an uninterrupted absorption in our real constitutional position of being a spiritual being, *jivatma*. Then we actually begin to enter into that higher and eternal awareness of recognizing ourselves for who and what we really are, and where we are going in this life.

□

9
Preparation for Meditation

The beauty of meditation is that you need no special equipment. You do not need to go anywhere special, or be a member of a fitness club or have certain machines to work with. You only need your own mind.

First we hear about who we are from higher authorities, such as a spiritual teacher or from sacred texts. Then we reflect on what we have heard and understood. Then we engage in meditation to allow the knowledge to unfold or manifest in our awareness. In this way, meditation, if developed appropriately, can allow us to perceive who we are as spiritual beings and then act as a channel to prepare and allow contact between the individual soul and the Supersoul, Paramatma, within us.

In the first few weeks or months of meditation, the mind may not be willing to cooperate. You may have to spend time disciplining it. As you observe your concerns and the turbulence that goes on within the mind, you may be surprised that you even have such thoughts. Later, however, with steady practice the mind will become more easily subdued, with fewer thoughts. And finally, after some experience, it may not take any time at all for you to calm and quiet the mind, which will become more accommodating for you to go beyond its influence.

If you have your own house or apartment, it will be nice to have a separate or special room in which you do your meditation, yoga, or prayers and worship. Keep it sanctified with holy pictures, incense, maybe some candles or flowers. Use it only for this purpose. Then go in when you have the proper time to engage in serious yoga, prayers, or meditation. Only allow into it those who share the same interest and vibrations as you. Keep the vibration of holiness in it. Get so that whenever you enter the room, that vibration will uplift you. Furthermore, when you have practiced your sacred activities in the room and imbibed the holy atmosphere, learn to carry that holy vibration with you throughout the day, wherever you go.

Beginners can practice meditation 2, 3, or 4 times a week until they get accustomed to the routine and the habit of taking time out just for themselves. Then you can practice everyday, even twice a day. It is the time to be with yourself everyday.

WHEN TO MEDITATE

Traditionally it is accepted that the best time to engage in any spiritual practice is before sunrise, during the *brahma-muhurta* hour as it is called. This is the time when you are often the most clear, and before you begin the course of the day and the mind becomes cluttered with concerns and activities. It is often quiet at this time, and your mind is also the most peaceful. Furthermore, early meditation prepares you for whatever else may happen through the day. And if you cannot get up early, then go to bed earlier.

However, for beginners it can be best to do your *sadhana* or spiritual practice whenever you can. Evening meditation can also be very good, especially to calm yourself after a busy day and bring yourself back to the real you. Then you can realize that you are only within the body and separate from the seemingly crazy drama that goes on around you.

The main point is to try and pick a time once or twice a day and be consistent about it. It should be a discipline that becomes a normal part of your day. Do not easily let other things get in the way. This makes for steady spiritual progress, in spite of whatever else may happen. It is also the way to train the mind to conquer itself and enter increasingly deeper states of awareness and concentration.

DIRECTIONS FOR MEDITATION

Vedic wisdom gives advice for all aspects of life, including the best directions to face while engaging in meditation. For meditation, one should face north, east, or west, but never south. For chanting *japa,* you should face east or west for the best results. And the best direction for sleeping is to have your head toward the south or east.

The reason is that thermal electricity generated by the sun travels from east to west across the earth. The North Pole is the negative magnet, while the South Pole is the positive. Our head is negative while our feet are positive thermoelectric magnets. It is the same way in which like poles repel and opposite poles attract. When we align ourselves in this manner, it helps create harmony and balance. Thus, the use of directions will also help our meditation, raising our consciousness, and maintaining our health.

As it is explained in the *Vishnu Purana*, a man who sleeps in the directions above becomes wise, while sleeping in contrary positions a person will become diseased. Sleeping southward prolongs life, while sleeping westward and northward brings ruin.

OVERCOMING THE IMPEDIMENTS

The *Bhagavad-gita* explains that there are six major impediments to meditation, or spiritual progress in general, that reside within each of us. It requires self-inquiry to see where these obstacles affect us the most. These are *kama* (sensual desire), *krodha* (anger), *lobha* (greed), *moha* (delusion), *mada* (pride), and *matsarya* (jealousy). Again, these are functions or feelings that exist within the mind. When we are functioning only on the *mayic* or illusory platform of existence, under the influence of the mind and senses, these feelings are at constant play to varying degrees. Spiritual progress means that these must be controlled and not controllers of us. However, we cannot falsely suppress these, or they will crop up in some other more damaging manner. But we must explore how they affect us and why. We must sublimate them by rising above their influence. This can be done by using meditation to perceive the difference between our mental existence and our internal and spiritual existence. The more spiritual we become, the less we are affected by these six enemies of spiritual progress, and the less we need to exist on the mental and sensual plane, which is also like the instinctual or habitual level.

The habitual thought patterns that are so often given free reign are the impulses which make us act with little thought behind it. This is what needs to be corrected. Observance of such thoughts and meditation to rise above them is the process to overcome such a base level of existence.

BASIC ELEMENTS OF THE PRACTICE

The basic practice of yoga, which culminates in a perfected state of meditation, also incorporates the eight steps previously described known as *yama* (restraints), *niyama* (positive developments), *asanas* (postures), *pranayama* (breath and psychic energy control), *pratyahara* (withdrawal of the senses), *dharana* (focused attention), and then *dhyana* (meditation) followed by *samadhi* (a perfect flow of attention on something that provides a superconscious experience).

At this point, we should already be practicing the beginning four steps, which we have provided instructions for doing, and now be ready to start the next.

Pratyahara is next, which is the withdrawing of the senses from the external stimuli that often creates distractions in the mind and in one's concentration. This is like seeing but with no vision, or hearing sounds but not listening. It is when we break the link between the mind and senses. This disconnect helps us overcome the mind's constant activity of judging what is favorable and likable, and what is unfavorable or not to one's liking. It is like starting to turn off the continual internal dialogue the mind has with itself, thus bringing about emotional balance. Once the senses are under control, or no longer providing input to the mind, or maybe we should say when the mind is no longer accepting such input, then there can be *dharana*, or fixed concentration.

It is said that when there is the cessation of the ingoing and outgoing breaths in our practice of *pranayama*, there is an unbroken continuity of *kumbhaka* or retention. This is the gap in between breaths and body functions, and in between thoughts in which there is the potential for full awareness outside the influence or affects of the mind. It is this gap which needs to be extended and where there is freedom from any distractions, and in which there is the suitable situation for *dharana*.

It is the activity of the mind which forces our interplay with the *mayic* plane of existence. Through the use of intelligence and wisdom, the individual must make the mind stable and tranquil. When the mind is no longer concerned with the past or future, but focused only on the present moment in an effortless way, then suffering and sorrow will diminish. It is this restraint of the mind's activities that will help bring about the freedom from further bondage to the wheel of time and material concerns.

Dharana, the following step, is reached after the body has been prepared through *asanas*, and the mind has been treated with *pranayama*. *Dharana* has its root in the Sanskrit word *dhri*, which means "to hold." *Dharana* is the fixed attention toward a single point or object, or state of awareness. This is the area that is probably the hardest for anyone to achieve in this day and age. The mind is accustomed to wandering about and to think or dwell on anything. So, it is not easy to fix the mind on any one object or thought. Most people tend to give up on meditation at this level if it is too difficult. This is another reason why meditation may be easy to dabble in, but most difficult to use for substantial spiritual progress. In *dharana*, the differentiation between oneself and the object of meditation becomes removed. You become absorbed in the object of meditation, or the plane of existence of the object. This is the first step in entering the higher states in which one can unite with Ishwara or God through meditation. There may still be the sense of the person, the object of meditation, and the process of meditation. However, in *dharana* there is the potential for *dhyana*, real and absorbed meditation. In *dharana*, objects can help promote fixed attention on a single object, such as religious symbols, sacred items, or pictures of one's guru or of Bhagavan and the Vedic divinities, or a mantra.

Dhyana takes place when *dharana* becomes sharpened. In *dhyana*, when the consciousness is free from the affects of the mind and senses, it can begin to recognize the pure self, *shuddhatma*. If *dharana* is the drop of water, then *dhyana* is the steadily flowing river in which the drop is carried. When the flow of attention and thought is uninterrupted toward the object, this meditation is called *dhyana*. Therein a person enters a state that has no qualification. In his contemplation and focus on the Supreme Spirit, he may enter a state of eminent bliss. Then he sees the light of his own self. He becomes filled with clarity regarding his own identity and position, and is secure in knowing who and what he really is. He feels and is filled with bliss from which he can never be shaken. He carries this consciousness and awareness wherever he goes.

This is beyond mere concentration, but when the meditator and the object of meditation become one. In other words, the flow between them is balanced, even, and without endeavor. All boundaries between them are lifted and disappear. Then we perceive the oneness between all.

An example is in the case of bhakti yoga, wherein *dhyana* is when the object of love, namely the Supreme Being, and the individual spirit soul, *jivatama*, become one through the unceasing flow of loving exchange between them. It gradually becomes spontaneous and automatic. Thus, even when the *bhakta* or devotee pulls out of *dhyana* meditation, the loving exchange or feeling does not stop, even in ordinary daily activities. Thus, everything the devotee does becomes an act of devotion, which brings one ever closer to the Supreme. Through this love, every minute of life can become an act of meditation based on the perpetual devotion that exists within the heart of the devotee. It is this kind of meditation that allows you to plug into the spiritual dimension.

Regardless of which path a person takes, this love for God, and all of the parts and parcels or energies of God, is one of the main goals of all spiritual life. There may be different paths that can take you to this level of perception, but somehow we need to get there. Reaching this perception, seeing God everywhere and in everything through love, should be accepted as one of the most important stages of spiritual realization. That is when you can begin to see the real oneness between you and all other beings. This is also one of the easiest ways to enter into what could be called a functional trance or *samadhi* wherein the devotee remains fixed in thought of the Supreme while still engaging in various activities throughout the day. The Vedic texts, such as the *Bhagavata Purana*, explain that this is how a devotee may be able to breathe, act, go through bodily functions, while the mind and attention is always fixed on the object of love, the Supreme Being. This is what truly can lead to Divine Union. The next step is *samadhi*.

The word *samadhi* is made up of *sama* which means "equal," and *dhi* which is "reflection" or "to perceive." The *Hatharatnavali* (4:3) states, "When the mind becomes motionless as a result of (deep) concentration, that is called *samadhi.*" And the *Gheranda Samhita* (7:3) also explains, "Detaching the mind from the body, one should make it one with the Paramatma. That is known as *samadhi,* which is not a state of any kind of consciousness as we understand this word." Thus, *samadhi* is a state of awareness or supraconsciousness but does not mean *moksha* or liberation. It is focusing on that which is beyond normal, temporary existence, which can open the doors toward the higher perception needed that leads toward *moksha* if we continue our development.

However, we cannot attain the level of *samadhi* by our own efforts. For this we also need the assistance of a knowledgeable guru. In such texts on yoga as the *Hatha Yoga Pradipika* (4:9) we find where it says, "Without the compassion of the true guru, renunciation is impossible, perception of the truth inaccessible, and *samadhi* unobtainable." Therefore, by the grace of the guru one is able to enter into the secrets of yoga. Without a qualified guru and following the instructions faithfully, enlightenment is still beyond reach.

It is explained that an enlightened guru is the manifestation of the inquiries of the soul. In other words, when we are ready and deserving, a guru will appear in our life who is a reflection of the needs of the soul to give us the lessons that we are meant to attain according to the progress made in previous lives. However, there are rare occasions when a genuine guru or purified soul will appear in society to give spiritual instruction due to his own causeless compassion whether we are qualified for it or not. This is our opportunity to become a suitable candidate for spiritual progress when we may actually be in a most fallen condition, and, thus, hardly able to understand higher spiritual knowledge, or even appreciate our good fortune that may be given to us by such a genuine guru. It is this kind of guru who can change our whole existence. It is this kind of guru who can pave the way for one's spiritual progress. Therefore, it is imperative to recognize and receive a qualified guru, for one who is not genuine can also pave the way downward as well.

The *Gheranda Samhita* (7:1,2) also explains: "*Samadhi*, the supreme (stage of) yoga, is attained by great merit earned previously. It is achieved by the grace of the guru and by devotion to him. That yogi soon acquires this exquisite experience, who is convinced by what he has learnt and heard from his guru, who has developed self-confidence, and whose mind is becoming more and more enlightened." Then, if we become qualified and ready, we may be able to enter into *samadhi*.

Samadhi is when the awareness is so deep that the identity of oneself becomes lost in the object upon which one is meditating. The root words of *samadhi* are *sam*, which means together or integrated, and *dha*, which means to hold. Thus, the literal meaning of *samadhi* is "wholeness." This is in reference to the way in *dharana* and *dhyana* there may still be a sense of separation between the meditator and the object of meditation, while in *samadhi* there is no longer a sense of separation.

In *samadhi* a person becomes oblivious to the outer world. The sense of ego, or of oneself, is now completely lost. The meditator or yogi is aware of only the object of meditation. There is no sense of his or her own identity, for the working of the mind has ceased, or ceased from being noticed. Then God, as the object of meditation, will become the sole point of awareness. In this sort of *samadhi*, one begins to know God, and also begins to see nothing outside the energy or existence of God. There is only unlimited bliss and freedom to expand such bliss. The peace surpasses all that could describe it. Then also *bhakti* or devotion increases immensely so that one no longer sees anything as being separate from the existence of God. In that state of consciousness, a person's love for God is ever-growing and ever-existent. There is no longer any *maya* in his awareness.

Whatever he sees is all a display of the energy of God, who is the source of all that is. In such a state of awareness, one is never outside the perception of the Supreme Being. Whatever beauty the person sees is but a reflection of the cause of its beauty, which is the Supreme Creator. In this awareness, a person is practically already in the spiritual domain. The goal is that if one can maintain this level of *samadhi* at the time of death, then the person can achieve *kaivalya*, or liberation from material existence.

When we meditate, we want a continuous flow of concentration toward the point or purpose of our attention. This process essentially involves reaching a state of pure meditation in which a person enters an uninterrupted flow of contemplation on God. Then, as one proceeds, the meditator loses all awareness of the body and external or sensual stimuli. Then you can enter the freedom to experience superconsciousness.

Samadhi does not mean to be in a trance all the time. But it also means how one's attention is completely fixed and absorbed in the object of meditation without boundaries or limitations, even when moving about, or not sitting in meditation with eyes closed. In this state, all problems or obstacles are but temporary illusions that soon disappear. The reason is that this state of consciousness can bring us such peace, bliss, and ecstasy that all such difficulties can no longer reach us. We are somewhere else, though apparently functioning normally in this world.

Meditation and the performance of chanting mantras at particular times of the day is the way to open and prepare oneself for higher awareness and to perceive lofty levels of reality and consciousness. Repeated practice of this process will cleanse the mental fields of habitual thought patterns of material desires and bring in increasingly deeper levels of illumination.

As a person practices and becomes more experienced, the preparation for meditation decreases. One can soon find that all that has to be done is sit in silence, breathe evenly, calmly, focus within, tune into a higher consciousness, and then away you go, immediately losing contact with the dictates of the mind and senses, and sailing into higher awareness or even new levels of awakening. However, this will take time to achieve, and it takes practice and experience to reach this level of familiarity with the process. So, let us explain a few of these steps a little further.

□

10
The Meditation Process

Yoga is not just physical fitness, but the preparation for the further stage in our spiritual development, which is meditation and what lies beyond. There are many techniques for meditation these days, and many levels of awareness we can reach. Many primary meditation techniques incorporate the basic step of focusing on our breathing. Our breathing also reflects our mental state. For example, when we are excited or angry, our breathing is often rapid, uneasy or shallow. When we are calm, our breathing is more slow and deep. Control of the breath automatically affects the mind and begins to calm it. This can prepare it for deeper thoughts and awareness. Also, first concentrating on our breath helps exclude other stimuli and bring our awareness closer to the self within, or closer to simply being the observer of our thoughts and actions. From there we move further along.

The mind will naturally focus on objects of its liking. The senses will drag the mind toward the objects with which they want to engage. The mind works in the *mayic* realm and is not equipped to rise above the area or awareness of the senses. It is the mind which interprets the stimuli and makes demands of the senses. It is then the intelligence that makes the plans to fulfill the wants of the mind. And the mind interprets what is favorable or unfavorable. So, for one to reach the area of perceiving a higher reality, one must rise above the influence and limitations of the mind.

Meditation on the path of knowledge and enlightenment is to focus the mind on the Ultimate Reality, the Supreme.

If you have had problems or troubles during the day, try not to take them with you to your place of meditation, or into your mind while trying to meditate. It will only further distract you when trying to reach higher states of awareness, free from mental impulses or habitual thought patterns.

If, however, you plan to meditate for guidance or solutions, feel that God is aware of your concern or situation. Make your prayers to God before you meditate so that as you go into meditation you can listen for answers or awakenings. Know that God manages the whole universe, and though we have free will to do as we like, if we are sincerely seeking help, then God can let us know in due time in the way we need to learn our lessons, and what we should do for our progress. No problem is unsolvable, but it only needs a plan or some insight in order for us to know how to deal with it or understand it. You are a spiritual being whose real identity is beyond mundane or material situations, or the problems that appear to go on around you.

For sessions of deep meditation, I personally like to meditate in the dark, before sunrise or after sunset, all lights out, with no noise. Then, even when eyes are open, there is no sensual distraction from hearing, seeing, smelling, tasting, or feeling. Then I can go as deep as I like.

You may also want to turn off the phone. Also, wear loose clothes to allow for ease of sitting and not to impede your smooth and natural breathing. The first step is to sit cross-legged but comfortably on the floor, and sit on a mat, a cushion, or even on the edge of a chair. It is important that you can sit without any difficulties or feelings of constraint. Simply keep your spine tall and straight. Let your hands relax, resting on your thighs or knees, palms up with thumbs and index fingers joined at the tips, in the dhyan or jnana mudra. Or they can be folded in your lap. Broaden your shoulders so you can breathe deeply.

The best positions for meditation consist of siddhasan, when you sit cross-legged with one leg under the other thigh, and that leg over the opposite thigh. Or the padmasan, the lotus position wherein you put one foot on top of each thigh, with the hands outstretched to the knees and in the dhyan mudra, wherein the tips of the index fingers are touching the tips of the thumbs with the other fingers pointing straight out. Or simply use the sukhasan or easy posture when you simply put the feet under the thighs.

When you have found your best position, then breathe in deeply while the mudras bring in the energy toward the center. Next, when you are ready, place your hands in your lap palms up and begin meditating. Then do some *pranayama* and breathing exercises, if you choose to, beforehand to help prepare for the meditation session.

Now close your eyes. Remember, this is time for your higher self. So, let go of all outer concerns and let yourself relax while keeping the back straight.

MEDITATION TECHNIQUE BASED ON OUR BREATH

So now begin to observe your breathing as it adjusts itself automatically to your position and relaxed state of mind. As you relax, release yourself of all stress. Turn your attention more inward, and deepen your inhalation, taking your time before you give a longer exhalation. Inhale easily and if you count to 4 on the inhale, give a count to 6 while you exhale. Let the breath bring in energy to heal, sooth, and give light to all parts of the body. Enter an increasingly calm state of mind.

As you continue to breathe, extend your breaths as it is comfortable to you. So, if you breathe in at a count of 5, hold your breath within for a count of 5, and then exhale slowly for a count of 10. This is when your breathing becomes *pranayama* and allows the mind to increase in calmness and inward perception and heightened awareness. Keep breathing like this for several minutes. This prepares you for continued inward focus.

Now begin to breath as is most natural for you, without counting, and in whatever way is most easy for you. And sit straight but easily. This meditation begins to filter out all external stimulus and prepares you for deeper focus. You can feel how your inner energy and well-being fills your consciousness, and how it extends to spread throughout the universe and all around you. You are connected with everything, and everything is in balance. No matter where you are, you are already home.

You can sit in this meditation for as long as you like, realizing the spiritual essence within you. This level of meditation may be enough for you, or you may also want to go farther.

Now simply sit in awareness of your being for a few minutes. Keep your eyes closed. Focus on being the observer, watching and listening to your inner attention on whatever you are aware of. Start with listening to the sounds outside of you. This may be birds, the wind, or something else. Keep your mind at peace if this causes an inner dialogue to begin, or if the sounds start your thought processes. Stifle your thinking and simply remain the observer, not the commentator. Remember, if thoughts enter your mind as reactions to what you hear, simply observe them coming and going, knowing they are not you but merely reactions to sense perceptions. Just watch your thoughts as if they are but the flow of water in a river, or clouds in the sky that form, change shape, and later disperse. You are the observer. As you watch this, focus on who is doing the observing. Is it the mind, or have you gone deeper to the self within the body, deeper than the mind, deeper than the intelligence? With practice this will become more clear.

Now bring your awareness even deeper, more inward, and listen to what is inside you. Maybe you can hear your heartbeat, or just listen to your breathing. If your mind wanders as you listen to your breath, quiet it and bring it back to center. Do not let it go one way or the other.

At this point you can use your meditation to focus on your breathing as a means to get closer to the Divine. View your breathing as a means of offering all that we are to the Supreme as we exhale. Then as we inhale, we bring into our body the higher life energy of the Divine. We perceive our very breath as the energy of God that supports us, enlivens us. We see that God is life all around us as well as our life force within us. This life force is the cause of all creation, the cause of all life, and the center of all bliss and eternity, of which we are a part. In this way, we become more in tune with the Supreme that manifests throughout the creation. We are dovetailed in our purpose to become and remain more united with the energy of the Divine. As we become absorbed in this awareness, it dissolves the thought forms from our consciousness along with the seeds of desire that keep us here on the material platform. This is one way we can use our breathing in meditation and to bring ourselves closer to God in the process.

Now, when you are ready, go deeper, and as you breathe, you will notice the space between your breaths. Similarly, as you watch your thoughts, notice the space between thoughts, between the end of one and the start of another. Meditation is the focus on that space or gap between thoughts. It is the process of lengthening that space. It is within that space wherein we can become free of the influence or input of the senses and mind, and more aware of our deeper selves. Therein we can become aware of a deeper dimension, and the realm of spirit, if we can go deep enough. Our higher self is beyond the mind, which is where we want to go.

As you continue to focus on the space between the breaths and thoughts, let it deepen even more. Let it widen. Let it open up to the point where you are no longer even aware of your breathing, or of any thoughts. Let this space open until you are absorbed in it. That is when you can go beyond the mind. That is the doorway into another realm wherein you can get in touch with your higher self.

This new experience beyond the mind may itself give you an initial feeling of bliss or wonder, a feeling of new possibilities that could unfold before you. But remember, this is merely the beginning, and there is much farther to go. There is also the need to become steady at this technique through practice if you are to truly attain the results that are possible.

As you free yourself from outside influences, be open to Infinity, to the omnipresent God both within you and all around you. Be alert to exploring the higher consciousness you experience or find yourself in, or the awakenings and realizations you have. When you enter higher states of awareness you are bound to have moments of clarity that allow you to reassess your identity, your position in the universe, and the possibilities that are available to you.

Now, in this deeper level, just meditate on being, on awareness. As you focus inward like this, as you go deeper, observe how the things that have happened outside in the world of the senses, the exterior drama, are no longer a distraction or disturbance. You do not listen for them, but you are only aware that they are no longer an influence. You are at peace. You see yourself as a being of light, in harmony with the flow of the universe. The seeds of suffering dissolve. You are your own person, you are whole, full of light, love, energy, and unlimited possibilities. In this state of consciousness, you have access to unlimited intelligence, clarity, and the energy or vibration for healing, and for inspiration and guidance.

It is said that prayer is like petitioning God for guidance or blessing, while meditation is listening for the answer. It is in this higher state of inner awareness in which we may hear or sense the answer, or attain the guidance. Sit quietly for some time, your awareness focused inward, and realize your wholeness, the joy available to you, and the completeness that is always there within.

After being absorbed in this way for a while, at this point, if there was something in particular you had a question about, or some quality you need to have in the outer world, now is the time when you may address that issue. If you need something like a better outlook, improved dealings with others, or a higher sense of self-assurance in yourself, now is the time to use an affirmation if you want, and to bring that back to the outer world as you begin to come out of your state of meditation.

Feel that quality throughout your whole being, as if it is blessing every part of you. When it has penetrated every cell and every corner of your mind, when you are full with this new or helpful quality or perception, and you feel empowered, then you can begin to bring your attention back first to your breath, then to listening to what is around you, and then feel your body and your surroundings.

Or if you have a particular question about which you seek guidance, you may also start the meditation session with that in the back of your mind. Then, after going through the steps of entering meditation, dwell on that a bit during your state of deep awareness, and take a sense of clarity about it with you as you come out of your meditation. Spend some time in this level of awareness in your meditation. When it is enough, then prepare to slowly return to the outer world. [If you are ready to go deeper or are not concerned with questions or guidance, then proceed to the Deep Meditation section.]

ENDING YOUR MEDITATION

As you prepare to leave your higher state of consciousness or end your meditation session, feel yourself to be more closely in tune with the Divine will, the Universal Consciousness, and that the higher energies of God are flowing through you. Feel that you are connected to everything in the universe and especially connected with God, always. The closer you get to God, the more closely God will guide you and inspire you with proper ideas, direction, motivation, inspiration, and action. Feel that you have been rejuvenated on every level, physically, mentally, and spiritually. Visualize yourself as being completely whole, a vehicle of positivity, wishing the highest good for yourself and everyone else, like a reflection of God's unconditional love on anyone, and that every living entity is a part of God. Open this view to encompass the whole universe, and pray that peace prevails through an enlightened society.

When you are coming out of your meditation, remain conscious of the presence of God, and the sense of your spiritual identity. Be aware that through the grace of God you will be assisted in whatever transformations you need to develop. The deeper you go in this awareness, the more you will become sensitive to the idea that everything is in balance. That everything that is happening to you, and throughout the world, is taking place through cause and effect. And to change the effect starts with altering the cause, or the initial action that starts the reaction. The point is to balance your external actions with internal knowings. Thus, meditation becomes a process of working within your own consciousness to reach a higher state of spiritual perception that manifests in your everyday life, and in your own sphere of influence. Thus, you will be doing your part to uplift the world. When a perfect balance is reached within you, you will feel a sense of completeness, a higher sense of purpose, a clearer sense of where you are going and where you want to go. And, certainly, a deeper perception of who and what you really are.

Once you have regularly practiced this, you can go deeper each time. You can also move to that deep space within you more quickly. Such a session may last only 15-20 minutes, or if you really get into it and get more out of it, it can be much longer. I've had sessions for 2 hours and came out of it thinking I'd spent only 30 minutes in meditation. The time is up to you, as well as how much time you can give to it. You may also do this technique once a day, preferably in the morning before the day begins, or anytime, even twice a day, morning and evening. It will change your outlook and attitude for the rest of the day.

The more you practice it, the more you take that feeling of wholeness, self-sufficient happiness, completeness, and confidence with you wherever you go. You will see that it adds quality to your life and enhances your attitude toward the world and realigns your position in the universe and your perception of who and what you are. It also helps increase the possibilities that are available to you and what you are capable of at both the outer and inner levels of your being.

DEEP MEDITATION

In doing deep meditation, instead of ending our session as we did in the previous description above, we continue to go even deeper. We continue to extend the gap between thoughts, between external influence, and go deeper within ourselves. There is no limitation. In fact, we go so deep that we lose all contact with our bodily identification. We no longer notice whether we are breathing or not breathing, or if our heart is beating or not. We become only awareness, drifting in pure consciousness, and nothing else. In fact, if we can go deep enough in this level of awareness when we observe our new identity that is separate from the physical body, then we will not even discern whether we are male or female. That becomes a foreign idea that belongs only to the *mayic* world. Otherwise, we are not connected with such an identity at all. In fact, it no longer has any meaning to us. We are only a spiritual being that is aware of our eternal and transcendental nature. We have no past, we have no future. There is only the moment, the NOW, completely independent of time and all temporary or *mayic* forms of existence. We begin to recognize the true potency and eternality of the soul, of who we are, and our connection with the Supreme Divinity.

In any case, in this level of meditation we are not concerned with attaining guidance or clarity, or even taking back certain perspectives or affirmations with us when we leave our meditation. It is the experience itself which gives us all the guidance and clarity we need. It is this level of awareness and perception alone that is enough to provide us with all the understanding we need to see things in a totally different and new or fresh way when we end our meditation. Our perception of our eternal nature, the blissfulness that is always within us waiting to be tapped by mere awareness, separate from any bodily condition, is all we need. This profound reality will cling to your consciousness, and open your awareness in all aspects of your life once you have experienced it. This itself will change the way you view your existence forever. And you will more easily want to engage in meditation as a definite part of your life on a regular basis.

I have to confess that the first time I entered into this level of meditation, when I ended the session and came back to my senses, I was not sure if what I had experienced was real. The bliss I felt was indescribable. But was it merely my mind, or was it a definite level of reality that I had entered which is beyond the body and mind? But just afterward, a friend of mine had returned from Puerto Rico and had met someone who had a near-death-experience. He had fallen off the back of a truck and hit his head, and went into that altered state of consciousness. The description of what he had experienced in his near-death-experience was the same as what I had experienced, but I did it through deep meditation rather than falling off a truck. And his feelings and awareness afterwards when he came out of it was the same as mine. You simply do not look at life the same way. The things that you took so seriously are no longer that serious. The things that kept you from living more clearly and more aware are simply not worth allowing them to have so much control over you and your life. And the problems that took up so much of your mental energy are no longer so important. It is truly like getting a fresh start in life, a new perspective of who you really are and what your place is in this universe. It is seeing what lies beyond the veil of death, how you will continue regardless of whether you have a body or not. It instills in you that there is nothing to fear about the future. The worst that can ever happen to you is that you die, and that can be the greatest day of your life.

Once you have attainted this level of meditation, the weight is off your shoulders. You know that the universe, God, will take care of you, and that you will meet whatever it is that will help take you along to a new level of growth. No matter whether it appears to be negative or positive, it is all positive because it is all meant to give the lessons or support for you to develop yourself further.

I have not really described this experience before, and I usually keep such things to myself. So, there is much more I could say about it, but in many ways it is indescribable, words do not do it justice as I am sure you can understand. When it is an experience beyond the mind and senses, how can the mind and senses fully grasp what is being described? Practically speaking, such an experience is beyond words, or the means to describe verbally. This is why some teachers or sages say that those who know, those who are experienced do not talk of it, while those who do talk of it do not know. Nonetheless, we can describe something about it to provide a little insight into it. The rest you will have to acquire from your own experience.

In any case, this level of deep meditation that I have now elaborated on to a small degree is merely on the higher level of *sattva-guna*, the mode of goodness which is still within material existence. It is not the end for perfect spiritual development, or for attaining full entrance into the spiritual domain. There is more ground to cover and more work to do in this process of meditation and spiritual realizations.

Nonetheless, as we get closer to realizing our actual identity as the soul, we can perceive that it abides in complete bliss, knowledge, and eternity. It is free and undisturbed by all the drama and commotion that goes on all around us. This state of being, which is our natural constitutional position, can be realized through the yoga process when followed sincerely and steadily. This is the process of spiritual, self-realization. The doorway to the final frontier is within.

INSTRUCTIONS ON MEDITATION IN THE BHAGAVATA PURANA

So, where do we go from here? Where do we go after having attained the deep form of meditation we have just described? Here is a description of a high form of meditation on the Supreme as found in the Vedic text known as the *Srimad-Bhagavatam* (*Bhagavata Purana* 11.14.31-46). In fact, this summarizes much of what we have been presenting but takes it further. Herein we find that while Uddhava was talking with Sri Krishna, Uddhava asked Him by what process should one meditate upon Him when they desire liberation from material existence through the yoga process. Also, he wanted to know what specific nature should the meditation be, and upon which form should a person meditate? So, Lord Krishna explained what a person should do. The instructions that follow are similar to Lord Krishna's instructions to Arjuna as we have previously presented from *Bhagavad-gita*, and also similar to the instructions given by the *avatara* of Lord Krishna known as Lord Kapiladeva, who taught His mother Devahati, as found in the Third Canto, Chapter Twenty-eight, of the *Bhagavata Purana*. But Lord Kapila's instructions contained some additional points. So, I have combined the instructions together to get as comprehensive a view as possible regarding the way to meditate. Furthermore, it may surprise some people how detailed the personal form of the Supreme Being is described within this process of meditation. Simply hearing and listening to these descriptions of the Lord's form is itself a type of uplifting and highly spiritual meditation. So, here are the full instructions:

As Lord Kapiladeva said to His mother, by practicing this system one can become joyful and progressively advance towards the path of the Absolute Truth. The *sadhaka* should perform one's own duties responsibly. He should be satisfied with whatever he achieves by the Lord's grace and worship the spiritual master. Such a person should cease performing conventional religious practices and should only be attracted to the traditions that lead to ultimate liberation. The yogi should also eat frugally and remain in a secluded place to raise the consciousness to the highest perfection of life. A person should also practice truthfulness and nonviolence, and avoid stealing. He should be satisfied with owning only as much as one needs for maintaining oneself. The *sadhaka*, practitioner, should also abstain from sex life, perform voluntary austerity, be clean, and study the Vedic literature, and worship the Supreme Lord [all of which are outlined in the *yamas* and *niyamas*]. One must also observe silence, acquire steadiness in the practice of *asanas*, sitting postures, and learn to control the breath. One must also withdraw the senses from sense objects and concentrate the mind on the heart.

As Lord Krishna further explained to Uddhava, one who wants to meditate properly should sit on a seat that is not too high or too low. Keep the body straight and erect yet comfortable. Place the hands on one's lap and focus the eyes on the tip of the nose. Then purify the pathways of breathing. Once the senses are controlled, one may practice *pranayama* step by step.

Lord Kapila takes this part a little farther and explains that the yogi should clear the air passages by inhaling deeply, hold the breath in and then exhale. Or, one can reverse the process by first exhaling, hold the breath outside, and then inhale. This is done so the mind can become steady and free from external disturbances. By practicing such *pranayama*, one can concentrate the mind and become free from the desire for sinful activities and material association. By meditating on the Supreme Lord, one can become free from the influence of the material energy.

As Lord Krishna continues, once this is completed, one should move the life air upward, from the lowest Muladhara chakra to the heart, where the sacred syllable *Om* (*omkara*) is situated like the sound of a bell. One should thus continue raising the sacred sound upward, and then join the *omkara* with the fifteen vibrations produced with *anusvara*, the nasal passage. Being focused on the *omkara*, one should practice the *pranayama* system ten times at each sunrise, noon, and sunset. Thus, after one month one should gain control of the life air.

Keep the eyes half-closed and fix the gaze on the tip of the nose. Being alert, one should meditate on the lotus flower of the heart. This lotus has eight petals and is situated on a straight lotus stalk. Then one should meditate on the sun, moon, and fire, placing them one after the other within the whorl of that lotus flower. Placing My transcendental form within the fire, one should meditate upon it as the auspicious goal of all meditation. That form is perfectly proportioned, gentle, and cheerful. It possesses four beautiful long arms, a charming, beautiful neck, a handsome forehead, a pure smile, and glowing, shark-shaped earrings extending from the two ears. That spiritual form is the color of a dark rain cloud and is dressed in golden-yellow silk. The chest of that form is the abode of Shrivatsa and the goddess of fortune. That form is also decorated with a conchshell, disc, club, lotus flower, and a garland of forest flowers. The two brilliant lotus feet are decorated with ankle bells and bracelets, and that form exhibits the Kaustubha gem [on His chest] along with an effulgent crown. The upper hips are beautified by a golden belt, and the arms are decorated with valuable bracelets. All of the limbs of that beautiful form capture the heart, and the face is beautified by merciful glancing. Pulling the senses back from the sense objects, one should be grave and self-controlled and should use the intelligence to strongly fix the mind upon all of the limbs of My transcendental body. Thus, one should meditate upon that most delicate transcendental form of Mine.

Lord Kapila further describes that the Lord in the heart is superbly adorned with a pearl necklace, a crown, and pairs of armlets, bracelets, and anklets. He stands on the lotus of His devotee's heart. He is most charming to look at, and His serene aspect gladdens the eyes and souls of the devotees who behold Him. He is worshipable by all the inhabitants of every planet. He is ever youthful and always eager to bestow His blessings upon His devotees. One should meditate on the eternal form of the Lord until the mind becomes fixed.

In fixing the mind on this eternal form of the Lord, the yogi should not take a collective view of all His limbs, but should fix the mind on each individual limb of the Lord. The yogi should first start with the Lord's lotus feet, which are adorned with the marks of a thunderbolt, a goad, banner, and lotus. The splendor of their beautiful ruby nails resembles the moon and dispels any thick gloom in one's heart. The Lord's feet act like thunderbolts hurled to shatter the mountain of sin stored in the mind of the meditating devotees. One should therefore meditate on the Lord's feet for a long time.

Next the yogi should fix his mind on the Lord's thighs, the storehouse of all energy. They are whitish blue, like the luster of the linseed flower, and appear most graceful. The yogi should then contemplate His rounded hips, which are encircled by a girdle that rests on the exquisite yellow silk cloth that extends down to the ankles. The yogi should then meditate on His moonlike navel in the center of His abdomen. From His navel, which is the foundation of the universe, sprang the lotus stem that contained all the different planetary systems [from His form which is expanded in every universe as Garbhodakashayi Vishnu]. That lotus is the residence of Brahma, the first created being. Then the yogi should concentrate His mind on the Lord's nipples, which resemble a pair of most exquisite emeralds, whitish in hue because of the rays of the milk-white pearl necklaces adorning His chest.

The yogi should then meditate on the chest of the Supreme Personality, the abode of goddess Maha-Lakshmi, the goddess of fortune. The Lord's chest is the source of all transcendental pleasure for the mind and full satisfaction for the eyes. The yogi should then focus his mind on the neck of the Supreme Personality, who is adored by the entire universe. The neck of the Lord serves to enhance the beauty of the Kaustubha gem, which hangs on His chest. The yogi should then go on to meditate on the Lord's four arms, which are the source of power for the demigods who assist in controlling various aspects of the universal affairs. Next are the ornaments of the Lord, and the Lord's disc, the Sudarshan chakra, which contains a thousand spokes and a dazzling luster, as well as His conch shell that He holds in His hand. Then there is the Lord's club, Kaumadaki, which smashes the demoniac. One should also then concentrate on the Lord's nice garland that adorns the Lord's neck, and is surrounded by honey-seeking bumblebees that create a buzzing sound. The pearl necklace on the Lord's neck represents the pure living beings who engage in His service.

The yogi should then meditate on the lotus-like countenance of the Lord, who appears in this world out of compassion for His anxious devotees. The yogi next meditates upon the beautiful face of the Lord, which is adorned with curly hair and decorated with lotus-like eyes and dancing eyebrows. There is also the glances cast by the Lord's eyes that soothe the most fearful agonies of His devotees, and His smiles full of grace. The Lord's benevolent smile dries away the tears of grief for all those who bow to Him. Next is the Lord's arched eyebrows that are so charming they captivate the sex-god, Cupid, for the good of the [celibate] sages. The yogi can also meditate on the Lord's captivating laughter, which reveals His small teeth that resemble jasmine buds rendered rosy by the splendor of His lips. Once devoting his mind to this, the yogi should desire to see nothing else. Through this course of meditation, the yogi develops pure love for the Supreme and he feels excessive joy, and his mind withdraws from all material activity.

As Lord Krishna continues explaining to Uddhava, one should then pull the consciousness back from all the limbs of that transcendental body. At that time, one should meditate only on the wonderfully smiling face of the Lord. Being established in meditation on the Lord's face, one should then withdraw the consciousness and fix it in the sky. Then giving up such meditation, one should become completely established in Me and give up the process of meditation altogether.

One who has fixed his mind on Me in this way should see Me within his own soul and see the individual soul within Me, the Supreme Personality. Thus, he sees the individual souls united with the Supreme Soul, just as one sees the sun's rays completely united with the sun. When the yogi thus controls his mind by this intensely concentrated meditation, his illusory identification with material objects, knowledge, and activities is very quickly extinguished.

Lord Kapila concludes by describing that thus situated in the highest transcendental stage, the mind of the yogi ceases from all material reaction and becomes transcendental to all material conceptions of happiness and distress. At that time the yogi realizes the truth of his relationship with the Supreme. He discovers that pleasure and pain as well as their interactions are actually due to the false ego, or identification with the temporary body, a view that is a product of ignorance. Because he has achieved his real identity and is completely aware and focused on it, the perfectly realized soul has no conception of how the material body is moving or acting. He becomes a *jivanmukta*, a liberated soul while still in the body. The body of such a liberated yogi is taken charge of by the Supreme Person, and it functions until its destined activities are finished. The liberated devotee, being awakened to his spiritual constitutional position and, thus, situated in *samadhi* which is the highest stage of yoga, no longer accepts the by-products of the material body as his own. Thus, he considers his bodily activities to be like those in a dream. In this way, the yogi can be in the self-realized position after conquering the insurmountable spell of *maya*, illusion.

In Lord Krishna's instructions to Uddhava, He summarizes the goal of yoga in another way. He tells the story of a brahmana, in which the brahmana teaches that after perfecting the yogic sitting postures and the breathing processes, one should then make the mind steady by regulated practice of yoga and detachment from worldly concerns. Then fix the mind on the single goal of yoga. The mind can easily be controlled by focusing it on the Supreme Person. Once the mind is stable, it becomes free from polluted desires for material activities. That is when the mode of goodness increases, which empowers one to completely give up the modes of passion and ignorance. One can gradually even transcend the mode of material goodness [and enter pure goodness, the spiritual strata]. The fire of material existence is extinguished when the mind is free from the influence of the modes of nature. Then one can achieve the spiritual platform of directly relating with the object of meditation, the Supreme Lord. When one's consciousness is so fixed on the Absolute Truth, the Supreme Lord, one no longer perceives any duality or difference between external and internal reality. (*Bhag*.11.9.11-13)

LEAVING THE BODY THROUGH YOGA: THE ULTIMATE PERFECTION

By qualifying oneself for the spiritual dimension through the previously described method of meditation, the next step is to carry it through to its ultimate goal, which is to leave the body and all material tendencies and limitations behind, and become completely settled in the spiritual world.

In the *Bhagavata Purana* (2.2.15-38) Sukadeva Gosvami instructs King Pariksit on the means by which one attains the final and ultimate goal of yoga, and how to leave the body to reach the spiritual domain. He says that when a yogi desires to leave this planet, inhabited by human beings, he should not be concerned about the proper time and place, but should sit somewhere comfortably and begin regulating the life air and control the senses by the mind. The yogi should then merge his mind within himself by his intelligence, and then merge his spiritual identity into the Supersoul. Once this is done, one should feel fully satisfied so that he ceases from all other activities and awareness.

In that transcendental state there is no influence of time, which affects even the demigods in the celestial realms. Nor is there any influence from the modes of material nature, namely goodness, passion, and ignorance. One should then prepare to give up the body by first blocking the anus with the heel of one's foot. Then one needs to begin raising the life air from the base of the spine up through the different chakras, up from the navel to the chest, the heart, and on up to the root of the palate, and up between his eyebrows. [This is possible only after years of training in the yoga systems previously described in this book.] Then, blocking the seven openings in the head, from which the life air could leave, he should maintain his focus on going back to the spiritual realm. If he is completely free from all material desires, he should then lift the life air up to the cerebral hole at the top of the head, the crown chakra, and give up all material and bodily connections, focused on going back to the Supreme. However, if a yogi still has desires for material enjoyment, even to reach the higher and more refined planets like Brahmaloka, or to attain other perfections, then he takes with him the materially conditioned mind and senses. [This means that another birth in a material body somewhere in the universe will follow. Such material desires can only be accommodated with another material body.]

A true transcendentalist is concerned only with a spiritual body. Thus, as a result of their devotional service, austerities, and spiritual practices, they are unrestricted to move beyond the material worlds, but never can the fruitive workers or gross materialists attain such success.

On the way out of this material creation, the mystic passes over the star system known as the Milky Way by illuminating the Sushumna. The Milky Way leads toward the highest planet, Brahmaloka. Then the yogi reaches the planet of the fire deity, Vaishvanara. There he becomes cleansed of all material contaminations and can thus go still higher to the circle of Shishumara. This Sishumara is the universal pivot and is called the navel of Garbhodakashayi Vishnu. The yogi then goes to the planet of Maharloka, which is inhabited by pure saints, like Bhrigu, who enjoy a duration of life extending to 4,300,000,000 solar years. This planet is worshipable even by other purified saints.

On Maharloka, the yogi can see all the planets of the universe burning to ashes at the end of Brahma's life once they have been touched by the flame that emanates from the mouth of Anantadeva. Thereafter, the yogi leaves for and reaches Satyaloka (Brahmaloka), the topmost planet in the universe, by airplanes or vehicles that are used by the great purified souls. On Satyaloka, life is considered to be some 15,480,000,000,000 solar years. On this planet there is neither old age or death, nor pain or sadness. However, there may be a feeling of compassion when witnessing the many conditioned souls who have no knowledge of the spiritual process of devotional service to God, and who, therefore, undergo numerous miseries while in contact with the material energy.

On Satyaloka, the yogi is able to be released from the layers of material sheaths [*koshas*] that encompass his Self, and, thus, his form goes from earthly to watery, fiery, airy, and to the ethereal stage. In this way, he is relieved of the material subtle sense objects such as smelling, tasting, seeing, touching, hearing, and other organs for material activities. The yogi, thus relieved of both gross and subtle forms of covering, enters the final stage of false ego. Therein he neutralizes the material modes of goodness and passion and reaches ego in goodness. Thereafter, all egoism, or bodily identification of any kind, merges into the *mahat-tattva*, the unmanifest form of all the material ingredients, and the yogi reaches pure Self-realization. Then he attains freedom from all material influences and may leave the cosmic creation altogether. Only in that state can such a person attain the perfection of association with the Supreme Personality in complete bliss and satisfaction in his natural and spiritual state of being, free from all material limitations and identifications. Whoever is able to reach this stage of existence and devotional sentiment is never again attracted to the material manifestation and never returns to it. Thus, the yogi goes to the Vaikuntha spiritual world in which there are innumerable spiritual planets, each one hundreds of times larger than any material universe.

Sukadeva Gosvami concluded by stating the following: This knowledge was originally described by Lord Krishna to Lord Brahma. That great personality Brahma studied the *Vedas* three times with great attention and concentration. After such a scrutinizing examination he concluded that attraction for the Supreme Lord Sri Krishna is the highest perfection of religion. It is therefore essential that every human being hear about, glorify, and remember that Supreme Lord always and everywhere. Those who hear the nectarean message of Lord Krishna, the beloved of the devotees, thus become purified of the polluted aim of life of material desires and aims, and thus go back to the spiritual realm, back to the lotus feet of Lord Krishna.

THE STORY OF NARADA MUNI

In the previous conversation in the *Bhagavata Purana* on meditation, Uddhava had the same doubts as Arjuna had as described in the *Bhagavad-gita* about how effective this process of meditation could be. So, he questioned and said that he feared that the method of yoga that had been described by Lord Krishna is very difficult for one who cannot completely control his mind. Therefore, Uddhava requested Him to explain a simpler way of attaining spiritual perfection besides this very elevated form of meditation that Lord Krishna had described. Uddhava explained that many yogis who try to steady the mind in such a way experience frustration because of their inability to perfect the state of trance. Thus, they weary in their attempts to control the mind. Therefore, Uddhava expressed to Sri Krishna that swanlike men happily take shelter [through the process of bhakti yoga] of His lotus feet, the source of all transcendental ecstasy. But those who take pride in their accomplishments in yoga and karma fail to take shelter of You and are thus defeated by Your illusory energy. (*Bhagavatam*.11.29.1-3)

In this way, Uddhava suggested the process of bhakti yoga as the easiest means to effectively reach the goal of yoga. Therefore, in presenting the information regarding the process of spiritual realization and meditation that is recommended to work best for the mass of people in this age of Kali-yuga, we can listen to the most interesting story of Narada Muni, as related in the *Bhagavatam* (*Bhagavata*

Purana, Canto One, Chapters Five and Six) and hear how he achieved success, and what he also recommends for everyone in this age.

Narada Muni was someone who had become so perfect in meditation that He was completely God realized, and could directly see God. Nonetheless, even though the form of meditation that he used at first to achieve this enlightenment was the Lord in the heart as we have described, such as in raja yoga, it was not the process he used in the end. He chose a process of attaining God realization that is much more accommodating for the general mass of people in this age. So, let us hear his story and find out what he recommends.

While giving instructions to Sri Vyasadeva, the compiler of the Vedic literature, the great sage Narada Muni described his life and the process of his advancement to the level of spiritual and God realization. Narada Muni explained that in the last millennium he had been born as the simple son of a maidservant who was engaged in the service of brahmanas. They were devout followers of Vedanta, so they would settle as a group that would not travel in the rainy season. It was during this time that Narada was in the service of these Vedantists. Narada was a well-behaved boy and after some time the brahmanas gave him their mercy by once allowing him to take the remnants of their food. Taking the remnants of food from those who are spiritually advanced is sacred since their consciousness enters into the food and can help purify those who eat it. Once Narada had taken their food, he became purified in heart and he became attracted to the path of the transcendentalists.

At that time he could also hear them talking amongst themselves about the nature of the Absolute, the Supreme Being. Narada became attracted to their conversations. Narada could then realize that it was only in his ignorance that caused him to accept gross and subtle coverings as his real identity. The sages also instructed Narada in the most confidential of spiritual topics.

After the sages left for other territories, Narada stayed with his mother. Since he was her only son, he looked after her. She wanted to take care of him, but she was a simple woman and could not do much. Then once when she was going out one night to milk a cow, she was bitten on the leg by a serpent. After she died, Narada traveled north. He went through many towns, villages, valleys, dark forests, gardens, and more. He finally became exhausted and then took a bath in a river. After drinking some water, he felt relieved and found a banyan tree in an uninhabited forest.

Then in the shade he began to perform deep meditation. He focused on the Supersoul within him, as he had learned from the sages that he had served. His mind became filled with spiritual love, tears rolled down from his eyes, and not long afterwards the Supreme Lord Sri Krishna appeared in the lotus of his heart. He became overwhelmed by feelings of happiness. Being absorbed in an ocean of ecstasy, he could see both himself and the Lord. But then he suddenly lost the vision of the Lord within him and got up, being perturbed. Despite his attempts to concentrate again and regain the perception he had, he could not recapture his meditation and the vision of the Lord. Thus, he was much aggrieved.

However, the Lord then spoke to Narada from within. He said that He regretted that during this lifetime Narada would not be able to see Him anymore. But those who are incomplete in service and not completely free from all material taints can hardly ever see Him. Yet, the short vision Narada had of the Supreme was enough to increase Narada's hankering for Him. The more Narada desired to attain the vision of the Lord again, the more he would remain free from material desires. This would help in his progress. Such remembrance of the Supreme is itself a form of meditation. Through this sort of meditation, one's intelligence becomes fixed and it becomes a means that helps take one to the transcendental realm, out of the world of illusion. Then the Supreme Being, personified by sound but unseen by eyes, stopped speaking.

Narada then offered his obeisances to the Lord, bowing his head. Then, having experienced the unfruitful nature of his previous attempt to meditate, he started chanting the holy names of the Lord by repeated recitation. Thus, he was able to experience the beneficial and auspicious nature of the chanting and remembering of the spiritual pastimes of the Supreme. By so doing, Narada traveled all over the earth, satisfied, humble, and unenvious. In this way, he remained fully absorbed in thinking of the Supreme Being. Then, with no material attachments, Narada finally met with death, as lightning and illumination occur simultaneously. He thus quit the body made of the five elements, and then attained a spiritual body, fit for his transcendental consciousness, and befitting an associate of the Supreme.

Finally, at the end of the creation, all of the elements of the material manifestation were drawn into the form of the Lord as Garbhodakashayi Vishnu, the expansion of Lord Vishnu in each universe. This is described as the night of Brahma. Then when Lord Brahma again awoke from his night, he started the process of universal creation again. When the great sages reappeared in the world, so did Narada Muni. Since that time, Narada is the singing sage who travels everywhere without restriction, fixed in the devotional service of the Supreme Being, using his vina to accompany his songs. In conclusion to his story, Narada explains directly the benefit of the process of meditation that he now was using:

"The Supreme Lord Sri Krishna, whose glories and activities are pleasing to hear, at once appears on the seat of my heart, as if called for, as soon as I begin to chant His holy names and activities. It is personally experienced by me that those who are always full of cares and anxieties due to desiring contact of the senses with their objects of attraction can cross the ocean of nescience [illusory darkness] on a most suitable boat – the constant chanting of the transcendental names and activities of the Personality of Godhead. It is true that by practicing restraint of the senses by the yoga system one can get relief from the disturbances of desire and lust, but this is not sufficient to give satisfaction to the soul, for this [satisfaction] is derived from devotional service [bhakti yoga] to the Supreme Personality." (*Bhag*.1.6.33-35)

Herein Narada Muni described the benefit of the hearing and chanting of the activities and names of the Supreme Being as the ultimate form of meditation for giving the higher taste for which the soul is always hankering. Such names and pastimes of the Supreme are often put into the form of verses and mantras. Thus, mantras can also give one the easiest means and benefits that are often too difficult to attain by the attempt at controlling the mind to enter a deep state of meditation in *samadhi*. So, in a later chapter we will look more closely into the ways and benefits of using mantras for our meditation.

□

11

Bhakti Yoga

Bhakti yoga is one of the other main branches of yoga. Bhakti or devotion can also mean dedication, which is essential for any spiritual path. So, you find bhakti in many forms of spiritual practice and yoga systems. And since it has been mentioned at various points in the instructions about yoga earlier in this book, we should provide the information about what the process consists of and what are its advantages.

However, bhakti yoga, the process of simply developing loving devotional service to the Lord, is highly recommended in the *Bhagavata Purana* (*Srimad-Bhagavatam*) and other Vedic texts as the ultimate end of understanding Vedanta, and the most recommended process in this age of Kali-yuga. It is the prime avenue for developing one's loving relationship or unity with the Lord. This is what especially paves the way for freeing oneself from the attractions and attachments to the temporary material world, and, thus, provides the means for genuine liberation from the repeated cycle of birth and death in this cosmic manifestation. Bhakti yoga is a system that is generally practiced by the followers of Vedanta called Vaishnavas, or worshipers of Vishnu or Krishna. It is by far the easiest of all the yoga processes and has fewer requirements for the practitioners than any other process. Bhakti is the yoga that begins, continues, and ends with love and devotion to the Supreme. There is no stronger binding mechanism than love, and spiritual love is the natural sentiment that emanates from God and connects all living beings. Thus, it is said that attaining this sentiment of devotion to God holds the sum and substance of all other yoga processes and religions. This path is so powerful that even married people may practice it successfully, while in other systems of yoga it is expected that one should be celibate. There are no extreme austerities to undergo; yet, the results are sublime. It is a scientific method of expanding one's consciousness to perceptions of unlimited joy and inner peace. Bhakti yoga brings complete fulfillment to those who seriously practice it, and gives realizations and a perception of one's real identity as a spiritual being, and what one's relationship is with the Absolute. It can be practiced anywhere at anytime. However, as with any other form of yoga, one must still take it seriously.

In bhakti yoga, there is not much concern about the chakras and the practice for raising the life energy or *prana* up the Sushumna *nadi* or freeing oneself of the subtle body, as we find in other yoga systems. The reason for this is explained in *Srimad-Bhagavatam* (3.25.33), which states that bhakti, devotional service, dissolves the subtle body of the living entity without separate effort, just as fire in the stomach digests all that we eat. In other words, being focused on the Supreme through devotional service, which itself is a direct way of engaging in eternal spiritual activities, the yogi burns up the five coverings of the gross and subtle body, which includes the mind, through the fire of spiritual consciousness as he becomes more and more spiritualized. Thus, there is no need to struggle in the separate endeavor of trying to open the various chakras within the subtle body or becoming free of it when the subtle body is automatically dissolved. The bhakti-yogi naturally becomes free from ignorance, attachment to the body, false egotism, and material consciousness, and can rapidly reach the spiritual platform. In this way, in the deeper levels of bhakti yoga, when the subtle body begins to dissolve, there is a decreasing amount of interference from the mind up to the point when there is complete unity between the spiritual dimension, in which the soul exists, and the loving devotional service to God that is performed by the body and consciousness. Thus, the body becomes spiritually surcharged as a vessel in which the soul serves God. Therein, whatever *anarthas* or faults and unnecessary attractions and distractions we have of this material world, or *samskaras* such as mental impressions or memories of both pleasant times and heartache that we may have experienced from previous relationships, all become dissolved by the overbearing ecstasy of our reawakened loving relationship with Krishna. It is like a slate wiped clean from all previous markings. In this way, a person becomes absorbed in pure consciousness by reaching their natural spiritual identity, and, thus, is said to become a pure devotee. This is confirmed in *Bhagavad-gita* (14.26) where it states that one who engages in full devotional service and does not fall down transcends the material modes and reaches Brahman, the spiritual strata.

So, the process of bhakti yoga merely uncovers and releases to the highest degree the true loving potential of the soul. This inherent potential for full and unconditional love lies deep within all of us and is our ultimate motivation for all that we do, as most anyone can see in our propensity to serve those we love. Motivated by our need to love and be loved, when that need is interpreted through the body it becomes perverted and mistaken for the need for bodily affection or sensual desire, lust. When freed from this bodily and mental influence, the true needs of the soul stand revealed. This is an impetus for spiritual love, beyond all bodily desires, a pure love for God and all that is His.

The way this works is that within our material body and senses are our spiritual senses of the soul, which are lying dormant. They have no spiritual engagement while covered by matter. Devotional service, and the ultimate goal of any other yoga or religious system, involves freeing our real senses from the confines of matter and material consciousness, and engaging them in direct spiritual activities to the Supreme. When the contamination of materialistic consciousness has been removed and the senses act in purified God consciousness, we then have reached our eternal sensory activities which are spiritual and in relation with our real identity as an eternal spiritual servant of the Supreme Spirit. Eternal spiritual activities means to engage in serving the Supreme, which is our natural occupation, while temporary material activities means to engage in the attempt to satisfy our dull mind and senses, which keeps us a prisoner within matter.

While the yogis of other processes are struggling hard to artificially control their mind and senses, the senses of the bhakti yogi are automatically controlled and purified by engagement in loving devotional service. When the mind and consciousness are attracted to the Supreme Being through this loving service, it becomes easy to remain in such concentration without any other regulations, austerities, or mechanical processes.

One example of this from the Vedic literature is of Visvamitra. He was a great yogi, seriously practicing and performing many austerities. However, even though in meditation, simply by hearing the tinkling ankle bells of a beautiful woman walking nearby, named Menaka, he fell from his yogic trance and had sex with her. After many years of living with Menaka he realized the futility of his position. He angrily gave up married life and again took to his yogic practices. However, when Haridasa Thakura was tempted by a prostitute while he was engaged in bhakti yoga and chanting the Hare Krishna *maha-mantra*, he did not fall down. In fact, while the woman waited for hours in hopes of having sex with Haridasa, she became purified by hearing his chanting. She then gave up her interest in sex and also took up bhakti yoga. Therefore, by experiencing a higher taste, Haridasa Thakura was successful. This is the advantage of engaging in bhakti yoga. This is confirmed in *Srimad-Bhagavatam* (3.25.43-44), which states that those yogis who have spiritual knowledge and have renounced material interests engage in devotional service to the lotus feet of the Supreme Being for their eternal happiness. With their minds fixed in such devotional love and service, they are easily able to enter the spiritual kingdom. This is the only means for one to attain the final perfection of life.

Therefore, those yogis or mystics who engage in devotional yoga are considered first-class because, while living in this material universe, they engage in the same devotional activities that are going on within the Vaikuntha planets in the spiritual sky. In other words, deep within the great and unlimited Brahman are spiritual planets, called Vaikuntha planets. Within those planets are those souls, liberated through yoga, that are engaged in various spiritual activities that comprise loving relations centered around the Supreme. Thus, through bhakti yoga and though living in the material world, they have already attained their natural transcendental position. There is no higher perfection than this.

Presently, in bhakti yoga the Vaishnava sect is one of the three major divisions of Hinduism, the others being Shaivism (worship of Shiva) and Shakta (worship of the goddess). Vaishnavas have four major sects: the Ramanujas founded by Ramanujacharya; the Madhvas founded by Madhvacharya; the Vallabhas founded by Vallabhacharya; and the Gaudiya *sampradaya* or lineage, founded by Sri Chaitanya Mahaprabhu who is regarded as an *avatara* of Krishna Himself. This path of Vaishnavism or bhakti yoga is most clearly enunciated by Srila Vyasadeva within the teachings of his *Srimad-Bhagavatam* as the process for the most complete level of God-realization and liberation. This is also indicated in all the essential Vedic texts.

THE GRACE OF GOD

Many of the forms of yoga and spiritual enlightenment that have been described, such as raja yoga, were especially meant for previous ages, such as Satya-yuga, Treta-yuga, or even Dvapara-yuga. However, the fact is that due to the limitations and lack of ability we have in this age of Kali-yuga to accurately facilitate most of the above mentioned processes, they are basically impossible to allow most people to reach the ultimate level of spiritual success in this age. They may provide preliminary improvements and benefits in a person's awareness, realizations, health, and so on. But this is not meant to be the main focus or conclusion of such paths. Thus, because it can grant the practitioner the full range of spiritual development, the path of bhakti yoga is recommended for reaching spiritual success in this age of Kali-yuga. In this way, one should practice the path of bhakti yoga, or at least add it to whatever other path one prefers.

The biggest problem with the previously mentioned yoga processes is that a person, basically, is on his or her own when practicing them. By that I mean they are like mechanical processes that are either performed perfectly by one's own strength and determination, or they simply do not take you to the ultimate goal of that method. Of course, a person may have a guru and someone to guide him or her along that particular path. But it is explained in many places that you must have the help or the grace of God if you want to attain the kingdom of God or properly understand the Supreme. For that, God has to reveal Himself to you in the way you can understand. Otherwise, you cannot do it forcefully or without God's grace. So, it could be asked, how can you attain help from a formless energy, a mystical force, or the Brahman which has no qualities, personality, or the means of reciprocation? How can you attain personal assistance from God if you are convinced that God is formless and has no attributes to extend His help?

We have to understand that the divine virtues like God's love, protection, concern, and His grace, all come from His personality. That is why it is advised in numerous Vedic and religious texts, a few of which we are presenting here, that any spiritual practitioner, whether a *jnani,* a yogi, karma-yogi, kriya-yogi, raja-yogi, etc., should accept protection from God. At least at the final stage of a person's development in yoga, one should seek the grace and protection of God for the ultimate liberation. And no path other than devotion to God, bhakti yoga, can attract the reciprocation or grace of God so easily. Love naturally attracts the love of another. This is why no form of yoga or any spiritual path is complete without the practice of bhakti yoga.

The path of yoga alone is not necessarily protected by the mercy of God. In many places Lord Krishna explains that He is easily attained through bhakti or devotional love, and His devotees are protected because of that, even if they may accidentally fall from the proper standard. So, you could say that all other forms of yoga are the means of preparation and purification for freeing oneself from materialistic influences, and for reaching the stage of *shuddha-sattva,* or pure goodness. On that stage a person can perceive his or her spiritual identity, beyond the container of the body. Yet, this alone does not deliver one to the spiritual domain of *sat-chit-ananda-vigraha,* meaning the platform of eternal spiritual knowledge and bliss in activities that are in relation to our spiritual form. So, the above-mentioned paths are all steps of refinement after which one must include the path of bhakti yoga or devotion to the Lord to complete the path.

The point is that you cannot enter the kingdom of God by some mechanical or systematic process alone. You may as well try to build a stairway to heaven. You may get so far and be thrilled at the preliminary results, but in the end you must come back down. You can only enter the kingdom of God by God's grace, which is attained by pleasing God.

Then He will open the doors, so to speak, to bring you in. Similarly, you cannot see an important person like the president of the United States unless he agrees to see you. Once he agrees, there is little if anything that can stop you. As Lord Krishna says, for His devotees He preserves what they have and provides what they lack. In this way, they are protected. No other process provides that.

The advantage of bhakti yoga is explained as follows by Lord Krishna: "One who is thus transcendentally situated at once realizes the Supreme Brahman. He never laments nor desires to have anything; he is equally disposed to every living entity. In that state he attains pure devotional service unto Me. One can understand the Supreme Personality as He is only by devotional service. And when one is in full consciousness of the Supreme Lord by such devotion, he can enter the kingdom of God." (*Bg.*18.54-55)

In this instruction we can understand that through ordinary yoga one can attain the realization of one's spiritual identity as a pure soul, *aham brahmasmi*, and one's connection with God. One may even perceive the Brahman. On that level one is eligible to begin the path of bhakti yoga. Or one may simply start with bhakti alone and achieve these things as well. But it is especially through bhakti yoga which reveals God completely, or through which God reveals Himself to the pure devotee. This is how He can be understood.

So, through perfecting yoga and meditation, one begins to perceive the reflection of the soul, and one's real spiritual identity. Then through the perfection of bhakti yoga, the affinity for God Himself is developed and can give one the higher taste of Divine Love, and, thus, break the shackles of whatever remains of one's material attachments. Then the person clearly perceives the soul's eternal connection with the Supreme.

So, why is it that bhakti yoga delivers one to God? It is because of the devotional love that is developed, the Divine

Love that is exchanged between two living beings, namely the individual soul and the Supreme Soul. This connection is the ultimate goal of yoga. It is the reawakening of the real relationship between the soul and the Supersoul. This also naturally reveals the true characteristics and identity of the soul without the separate endeavors found in the other yoga processes, like *pranayama, asanas*, or raja yoga, astanga yoga, kriya yoga, etc.

When done sincerely, all of the practices in bhakti yoga are not only *sattvic* in nature, meaning in the mode of goodness, but more importantly they are purely transcendental to all material conditions, whether it be the chanting of the Lord's names, doing Deity worship, studying the *Bhagavad-gita*, or meditating on the Lord's form, etc. Such activities automatically engage the soul in its natural, spiritual loving service to the Lord, which earns one the grace and protection of the Lord that other spiritual processes may lack. As it is said: Do not try to see God but act in such a way that God will see you. Then He will reveal Himself to you. This is how the Infinite becomes submissive to the love of the finite *jiva* soul and reveals Himself. Then there is loving unity and reciprocation between you and God. Thus, the process of bhakti yoga is also the result.

Such loving activities in service to the Lord are also the type of activities that one finds in the spiritual Vaikuntha planets. So, the process of bhakti yoga is like a training to purify oneself and learn the nature of the spiritual world and the loving devotional activities that go on there. Thus, through such practice and spiritual perception, one can easily enter into the spiritual Vaikuntha worlds upon attaining liberation, or freedom from material and bodily existence.

However, another question that can be asked is, how can you tell Krishna is God? It is because of this loving reciprocation, this ecstatic exchange in the deeper aspects of bhakti yoga which far exceeds the typical feeling of awe, respect, reverence, or veneration that one generally develops toward the Lord in other spiritual processes or religions. This loving exchange provides a bliss that far surpasses the feeling one gets merely from the perception of one's spiritual identity as the eternal soul, or even from merging into the Brahman, which may also be achieved by perfecting other yoga processes. Such bhakti or love becomes unconditional. In other words, you become happy not for yourself but for Krishna's happiness. Your endeavors are to make Him happy, to make both Radha and Krishna happy. That is bhakti. However, the more you are dedicated to the service of God in this way, the more ecstatic you become from the attention and loving exchange with the Supreme. This is the reciprocation. Once you have this higher taste for the ever-increasing, ever-new sweetness and love of serving Krishna, Radha and Govinda, then you will not want to do anything that cannot be connected with Krishna in this way. Thus, within the path of bhakti yoga, all of one's actions can be performed with devotion to God. Through this process, and in His causeless mercy and limitless love, care, and protection, He remains with you to help you in your thoughts of Him. Then one's whole life is a means for one's spiritual upliftment. It is like a functional *samadhi*. In other words, you can remain in a state of such thought and meditation throughout the day though engaged in many activities.

So, through this system of yoga, such acts of devotion are a way of absorbing one's attention and consciousness on the forms of Krishna and His pastimes. It is a meditation based on loving service. Devotion is a way of extending concentration and meditation from a short period of time in the day to a long duration, even 24 hours a day, through love for God. This love is a natural flow of attraction for the most lovable object. Thus, the yogi never has to miss a moment in which he or she cannot be thinking of God through natural love and attraction.

As this loving service increases, what may have begun as a duty to spiritual life becomes an attraction, a higher taste, which increases through purification to go on to become love and reciprocation. There is no motivation or emotion that is more effective than love to draw one's attention and focus towards someone or something, just as a boy is naturally attracted to a girl. Similarly, on the spiritual level there is nothing more natural than the soul's attraction to the Supreme Soul. This love and attraction, which lies dormant in any conditioned soul, only needs to be reawakened, which is the purpose of bhakti yoga.

Krishna further clarifies in the *Bhagavata Purana* that whatever mystic perfections can be achieved by good birth, herbs, austerities, and mantras can all be achieved by devotional service to Him; indeed one cannot achieve the actual perfection of yoga by any other means. (*Bhag*.11.15.34) Everything that can be attained through fruitive or karmic activities, penance, knowledge, detachment, mystic yoga, charity, religious duties, or any other means of perfecting life can be easily achieved by His devotee simply through loving service to Him. If for some reason His devotee desires to be promoted to heaven or attain liberation, or a residence in His abode, such benedictions are easily achieved. (*Bhag*.11.20.32-33)

A similar point is reiterated by the Lord in His form as Kapiladeva when He explains that because His devotee is completely absorbed in thought of Him, the devotee does not desire such benedictions as going to the higher planetary systems, like Satyaloka, nor any of the eight mystic powers obtained from yoga, nor does he desire to be liberated into the kingdom of God. However, the devotee nonetheless enjoys all offered benedictions even in this life, even without asking for them. (*Bhag*.3.25.37)

In conclusion, everything that can be accomplished by separate endeavors in other processes are not left out of the path of devotion to the Lord. "A person who accepts the path of devotional service is not bereft of the results derived from studying the *Vedas*, performing austere sacrifices, giving charity, or pursuing philosophical and fruitive activities. At the end he reaches the supreme abode." (*Bhagavad-gita* 8.28)

This is the secret of the potency of bhakti yoga. (My book, "The Heart of Hinduism," gives advice and deeper directions into the practice of bhakti yoga.)

□

12
Using Mantras

For many people, the process of raja or astanga yoga may be a little too difficult for reaching complete spiritual perfection, or it may also take too long, even if you had nothing else to do. So, if this basic form of meditation that has been described does not seem like it would work so well for you, then it may be time to try or add something else. The most important alternative to this kind of inner meditation is the use of mantras. In fact, many of the Vedic texts proclaim that in this age of Kali-yuga, the age of quarrel, confusion, and distractions of all kinds, mantra meditation is the most dependable process of meditation and deliverance, not only to reach a higher consciousness, but also to make contact with the spiritual strata.

Mantra yoga is actually a mystical tradition found in almost every spiritual path in the world. It may involve the softly spoken repetition of a prayer or mantra for one's own meditation, or it may be the congregational singing of spiritually uplifting songs, prayers, or the sacred names of God. It all involves the same process, but in the Eastern tradition it is called mantra yoga because it is the easy process of focusing our minds on the higher levels of reality, or on Supreme through His names, which helps spiritualize our consciousness. *Man* means the mind, *tra* means deliverance. Therefore, a spiritual mantra is the pure sound vibration for delivering the mind from material to spiritual consciousness. This is the goal of any spiritual path. Although all spiritual traditions have their own prayers or mantras, the Vedic mantras are especially powerful and effective in uniting us with the spiritual realm. However, a complete yoga process is generally a blend of a few yoga systems, such as bhakti yoga with mantra-yoga, or raja yoga with bhakti yoga. Therefore, bhakti yoga also includes mantra yoga, or the process of concentrating on the sound vibration within a mantra. This is especially important in this age of Kali-yuga.

Many years ago the brahmana priests could accomplish many kinds of wondrous deeds simply by correctly chanting particular mantras. Many of these mantras still exist, but it is very difficult to find those who can chant them accurately. This is actually a safety measure because if the wish-fulfilling mantras were easily chanted, there would no doubt be many people who would misuse them. But other mantras that are available can easily help purify one's consciousness, give spiritual enlightenment, and put one in touch with the Supreme.

Mantras often consist of eternal sound energies, the *shabda-brahma,* that have always existed, both within the universe as well as beyond it, and before its manifestation and after its annihilation.

When it comes to mantras, the *Vedas* mention three types: *vedic*, *tantric*, and *puranic*. These can be further divided into *sattvic, rajasic,* and *tamasic*. The mantras that are *sattvic* or in the mode of goodness, are chanted for light, wisdom, compassion, divine love, or God realization. They help bring peace both individually and socially, destroy karma, and bring one to spiritual perfection. The mantras that are *rajasic,* or in the mode of passion, are chanted for material benedictions, like blessings for a healthy child, prosperity, certain talents, and so on. However, such mantras do not help one rise above karma, but force a person to take rebirth in order to acquire the results of his karma. The mantras that are *tamasic*, or in the mode of ignorance or darkness, are also called "black magic." These are used for the deliberate manipulation of the material energy for one's own purpose. Thus, they are sinful, and are often used to call spirits, or perform deeds that bring harm to others.

Saguna mantras (those that describe personal traits) often are like prayers that invoke certain deities or characteristics of the Absolute or the divinities they describe. *Nirguna* mantras (those that refer to the nature of the Absolute without qualities) often describe the person's identification with the Absolute or the Brahman. The *bija* or seed mantras are derived from the 50 prime sounds and are related to *Om*.

Some mantras hold certain powers in their vibratory formulas that are directly related to particular deities. In fact, they may represent the deity in full. When they do, they are considered non-different from the deity and the sound vibrations are spiritual in nature. By the repetition of the mantra, the person who chants it invokes the energy and mercy of the deity. Thus, the deity reveals Himself or Herself to the *sadhaka*, who then overcomes illusion and realizes the spiritual position of the deity and his or her relationship with the deity. The six kinds of mantras used in this connection are:

1. Dhyana Mantras – mantras for meditation to mentally invoke the deity's form, abode, or pastimes.
2. Bija Mantras – the seed mantras for meditation and purification, such as purifying the articles used in worship.
3. Mula Mantras – root mantras that are the essence of the deity, used when offering certain articles during the worship to address the Lord or the deity.
4. Stutis and Stotras – mantras or prayers chanted before, during, and after the worship to glorify the Lord's name, form, qualities, and pastimes.

5. Pranama Mantras – prayers offering obeisances to the Lord or the deity at the end of worship.
6. Gayatri Mantras – Vedic or Pancharatrika mantras used to worship the Lord and other Vedic divinities, and for invoking different moods and blessings.

The Vedic mantras, such as those coming from the four *samhitas* of the *Rig, Sama, Yajur,* and *Atharva Vedas,* are eternal or spiritual sound vibrations. They are not composed by any man at some particular point in history. They were passed down through an oral tradition and then compiled into the *samhitas* by Srila Vyasadeva. They are part of the *shabda-brahma,* the eternal, spiritual sound vibration, the eternal language of which Sanskrit represents. These mantras are like seeds of vast amounts of power and knowledge that are held within them. Thus, many scriptures explain that such powers cannot be fully revealed unless they have been received through the process of *diksha* or initiation from a spiritual master.

Besides this, the results of chanting a mantra depend on the chanter's conception or intent in the mind while chanting it. Thus, one should know the meaning or purpose of the mantra while reciting it. If one thinks the mantra is for attaining material goals, the person may get that. But if the inner purpose of the mantra is known to deliver one to the spiritual world, and a person chants it for that purpose, then that will be the reward rather than something minor or material if it is chanted correctly and sincerely.

Most Sanskrit mantras have several principles that you find in them. First they are often handed down or revealed by sages or authorities who have attained self-realization by its use. They also generally use a particular meter or rhythm. The mantra often represents a certain deity. It also has a *bija* or seed word that gives it additional power, and the sound formula it contains has a special *shakti* or energy. And finally, constant repetition of the mantra will open or activate the key of it which then can reveal pure consciousness in the one who has been initiated into its use. The practice of repeating or chanting it for one's personal use is called *japa*.

The mantra is thus a point of meditation for the mind, but also a formula or transcendental sound vibration like the holy name of God that releases its energy into one's consciousness. Thus, it prepares one for perceiving higher states of reality. With constant practice of the appropriate mantra, and with the proper pronunciation and sincere devotional mood, the mantra can reveal the Absolute Truth to the practitioner as well as one's own spiritual form as a spirit soul. Beyond that it can reveal the relationship that you have with the Supreme Being.

This is why it is best that one should receive and be initiated into the chanting of the mantra by a qualified guru. Then the mantra will be especially effective and powerful, and carry special means of invoking realizations into the devotee who uses it.

Mantras can be used in different ways. They can be chanted in whispers, or out loud, or silently within the mind. Generally, each mantra has a recommendation as to which way works best. Some mantras, like the Hare Krishna mantra, can be used in any of these ways, as well as sung as a song with a group or congregation. Most often this is done with a lead singer who sings the mantra in a particular melody, and then everyone else responds.

Some mantras are meant to be chanted only within the mind because their vibration or wavelength is beyond ordinary sound. So, the silent method helps invoke the energy within our consciousness. However, to first whisper it or softly speak the mantra correctly may help one be able to chant it silently.

When doing *japa* meditation for any length of time, or for a certain number of repetitions, it is best to use a set of chanting or *japa* beads. These are usually strings of 108 beads, called *japa mala*, plus one central or head bead. These are made from different substances, such as rudraksha seeds for Shiva mantras, lotus seeds for Devi mantras, tulasi wood for Vaishnava mantras, or other seeds and even crystal or glass. If you cannot find any beads made from these materials, you can also simply get any wooden beads from a craft shop and string them together with a knot in between each bead, and then pull the ends of the cord through the head bead and tie a knot to secure the ends on the other side of the head bead, cut the excess cord off leaving a tassle, and there you go.

Often times when a person is initiated into the chanting of a mantra, the guru may give him or her a *japa mala* after the guru has chanted on the beads. This purifies the beads and also, after hearing the mantra from the guru, helps activate the mantra to help transform one's consciousness.

There are many mantras to choose from for various purposes, but we will take some time here to explain the techniques for the most important ones that are used for spiritual advancement.

THE OM MANTRA MEDITATION

The *Om* mantra is a most sacred syllable in Vedic culture. The *Vedas* glorify *Om* as the origin of the *Vedas*, or the seed from which all of the *Vedas* grew. This is why *Om* precedes important Vedic mantras. *Om* expands into the *vyahritis* (*bhuh*, *bhuvah* and *svaha*) which indicates the three planetary levels of the universe, or the whole creation. The *vyahritis* expand into the Brahma gayatri mantra, and this expands into all the Vedic literature, including the *Bhagavata Purana*.

The importance of the *Om* mantra is shown in this Sanskrit verse:

Omkaram bindu samyuktam
Nityam dhyayanti yoginah
Kama-dam moksha-dam chaiva
Omkaraya namo namah

"The yogis meditate constantly on the syllable *Om* composed of the sounds O and M. This *Om* fulfills all our desires and leads to liberation. Salutations again and again to this syllable *Om*."

"*Om* is the Akshara, the imperishable syllable. *Om* is the universe, the past, present, and future. *Om* is all that was, is, and all that will be. *Om* is also all that exists beyond the boundaries of time." (*Mandukya Upanishad*)

Om is the sound substance of the Absolute, the seed of the universal manifestation, and connected to the infinite Brahman. It is also a name of God. It is also composed of the letters A, U, and M. Several meanings for these have been written in the Sanskrit texts. "A" represents that which is observed in the state of wakefulness, or the experience of the body and senses. "U" represents that which is observed in the dream state, or the inner astral realm. "M" represents that which is in the state of deep sleep as well as that which is beyond the perception of the senses in the wakeful state. The silence, which is like the fourth letter of AUM, is the basis and underlying reality found in all states of consciousness, whether waking, dreaming, or deep sleep. This is the Brahman, which is all that is manifested and all that is unmanifest.

However, *Om* also reveals itself according to the depth of consciousness and realizations of the practitioner or *sadhaka*. In other words, *Om* or AUM is like the signal, but its affects also depend on the quality of the receiver, the one who chants it. For example, another interpretation by the Gosvamis of Vrindavana is that the letter A (*a-kara*) refers to the Supreme Being, Krishna, the master of all living beings and all material and spiritual worlds. He is the Supreme Leader. The letter U (*u-kara*) represents Radharani, or the pleasure potency or spiritual energy of the Supreme, otherwise known as the feminine aspect of God. The M (*ma-kara*) represents the living beings, the marginal energy of the Supreme. Thus, *Om* is the complete combination of the

Absolute Truth. In other words, *omkara* or *Om* represents the Supreme Being, His name (Krishna), fame, pastimes, entourage, expansions, energies, and everything else. Thus, *Om* is also the resting place of everything and the full understanding of the *Vedas*.

Further information relates that *omkara,* as the representation of the Supreme Lord, delivers one back to the spiritual dimension if one remembers or chants it at the time of death. Srila Jiva Gosvami, in his *Bhagavat-sandarbha,* says that *omkara* is considered the sound vibration of the holy name of the Supreme Lord. The *Srimad-Bhagavatam* also begins with *omkara*. Thus, it is considered the seed of deliverance from the material world. Since the Supreme is absolute, then both He and His name are the same. In this way, contact with the name is also contact with the Lord Himself.

The image of *Om* looks something like the number 3 with an extra curve. The largest lower curve represents the waking state. The upper curve signifies deep dreamless sleep. The additional lower curve that goes to the right is the dream state. [Some say the large lower curve is the dream state, the upper curve is the waking state, and the side lower curve is the deep dreamless sleep.] The dot represents the Absolute Reality which is separated from the other curves (or states of consciousness) by a half-circle. This half-circle signifies the curtain of *maya,* the illusion or material energy. It is *maya* which keeps us focused on various states of consciousness within the realm of the material manifestation which then veils the Absolute from our experience or awareness. The half-circle, open on top, indicates the infinite and unbounded nature of the Absolute, which is always separate from *maya.*

Om, therefore, is the indescribable reality. It is the encapsulated form of all that is. When it is pronounced properly, the "A" begins from the base of the spine, the Muladhara chakra. As the sound moves up, the "A" or *A-kara* activates the area of the naval and the digestive system.

The "U" sound comes from the heart area, so our blood circulation becomes activated. The heart gets the extra supply of oxygen, which then spreads through other parts of the body. The sound of "U" is pronounced in the throat region, ending at the tongue's tip. The "M" is focused at the lips, or the end of the vocal mechanism. It goes in our head and comes out through our nose, which stimulates the vibrations in the brain. This also helps activate the pituitary gland and helps the over-all improvement of the body. Plus, the psychic abilities are awakened. Thus, when *Om* is chanted or pronounced correctly, it includes all the sounds or vowels of the alphabet.

In the last part of the mantra is the silence into which the *Om* culminates. It is the *Om* without the distinction of parts. It has no name and, thus, does not come under the purview of empirical usage. It is the self or pure consciousness, the *turiya,* which transcends all distinctions.

Om is also said to be the vibration or sound of the universe, or the movement of the energy which flows through it. Thus, to meditate on *Om* in deep attention leads one's mind into profound states of higher consciousness.

OM MEDITATION TECHNIQUE

The correct procedure for chanting *Om* is as follows:

1. Sit in your meditation posture with eyes closed and your mind at peace. The head, neck and spine must be straight. Prepare yourself appropriately with relaxation, deep breathing, and *pranayama*.
2. When ready, take in a deep breath slowly until it reaches the naval, hold it comfortably.
3. Then begin to utter *Om* with a long exhale, going ooooooommmmm or aaaaauuuuummmmm. You first chant the "A" or "aaahhh" sound during the main portion of the exhale, and then go to pronouncing the "U" or "uh" sound, and conclude with the "M" sound. The "A" is chanted through parted lips, slowly ascending in volume. The "U" is chanted through lips that are closer together. The time taken for chanting the "U" should be double the time taken for chanting "A". The last sound "M" is uttered through the nose with lips closed. The time for chanting "M" should be double that for "U". As you chant the "M" the volume of the sound should descend as slowly as it rose during the "A", taking as much time as it took to ascend.
4. Chant it like this several times for a total of at least nine times. You chant it three times when starting your yoga session, but nine times when using it for meditation.
5. As you chant, do it more quietly until it is a whisper, bringing your awareness deeper within yourself each time.

6. Then chant even more deeply, but only mentally, not out loud. Let the sound pervade and resonate in your mind. It should be the only thing that you hear.
7. The last step is when this form of meditation gets more difficult. Now cease the mental chanting while still listening to the sound within your awareness. Let yourself flow into that sound, losing all other identity, and all other awareness. You should be aware of nothing else. Only you and *Om*, the vibration of God. Within that vibration is all there is. If you can reach this level of awareness, then for several minutes or as long as you can, if you are aware of time at all, sit in that awareness of God, the Absolute, the Pure, the Omniscient and Supreme Being. This meditation can certainly give one spiritual inspiration and clarity. Continue to practice this routine once, twice, or three times a day. Or add it to the conclusion of your hatha yoga session. It will become increasingly significant with practice.

However, to chant *Om* properly in order to actually reach the full perfection of *moksha* or liberation into the spiritual dimension is not easy. The mantra has full capacity to do that, but whether we have the ability to use it to that degree depends on us. This is why some sages feel, and some references in the Vedic *shastra* state, that this can be a nice preliminary form of practice, but should not be expected to take average people to the deepest level of realization, simply because most people in the age of Kali-yuga will find it too difficult. There are simply too many distractions to reach the desired success with it, and the mental strength and concentration needed are rarely to be found these days. Thus, other mantras have been recommended for this age. So, we will give one more mantra technique in the next chapter, one that is far easier and far more advantageous and recommended for this age.

□

13
The Hare Krishna Mantra

In *Bhagavad-gita* (10.25) Sri Krishna explains that He is the transcendental *Om* mantra and that the chanting of *japa* (chanting a mantra quietly for one's own meditation) is the purest of His representations and sacrifices. It is understood that by chanting *japa* and hearing the holy sounds of the mantra, one can come to the platform of spiritual realization. This is the process of mantra yoga, as previously explained. Even though the mantra is powerful in itself, when the mantra is chanted by a great devotee, it becomes more powerful. This is the effect when a disciple is fortunate enough to take initiation from a spiritually powerful master who gives him a mantra for spiritual purposes. Then the disciple can make rapid progress by utilizing the mantra.

It is explained in the Vedic texts that in this age of Kali-yuga the process of chanting *japa* or mantra meditation is much more effective than practicing other spiritual paths that include meditating on the void or Brahman effulgence, or trying to control the life air within the body as in raja yoga. And only a very few can become perfect at raising the kundalini force up through the various chakras, or moving the life air up to the top of the head for full enlightenment and then have it leave the body at the right time to achieve liberation. Plus, meditating on the void becomes useless as soon as there is the slightest distraction that pulls you out of it, which in this age of Kali is a continuous thing.

There is certainly no harm in trying these yoga systems, and many benefits are to be found in them. But, in reaching the perfection of attaining *moksha,* or entering the spiritual dimension after death, is most challenging in these systems. Therefore, it is said that the most effective means of focusing the consciousness on the spiritual strata is to concentrate on the sound vibration of a mantra.

There are two mantras that are especially recommended in the Vedic literature. One is *omkara* or the *Om* mantra, as we have previously explained, and the other is Hare Krishna, Hare Krishna, Krishna Krishna, Hare Hare/Hare Rama, Hare Rama, Rama Rama, Hare Hare. This is known as the *maha* or great mantra. It is explained that these two mantras can deliver one to the realm beyond material existence.

The mantra that is especially meant to be chanted in this age is easy and is actually more directly connected with the Supreme than the sound vibration of *omkara* because it contains the direct holy names of the Lord. So, the mantra especially for Kali-yuga is the *maha-mantra,* or great mantra for deliverance, which is Hare Krishna, Hare Krishna, Krishna Krishna, Hare Hare/Hare Rama, Hare Rama, Rama Rama, Hare Hare.

THE IMPORTANCE OF CHANTING THE MAHA-MANTRA

There are many Vedic references which specifically recommend the chanting of the Hare Krishna *maha-mantra* as the most effective and advantageous means of reaching spiritual realization and counteracting all the problems of this age. Some of these verses are the following:

"These sixteen words – Hare Krishna, Hare Krishna, Krishna Krishna, Hare Hare/Hare Rama, Hare Rama, Rama Rama, Hare Hare – are especially meant for counteracting the ill effects of the present age of quarrel and anxiety." (*Kali-santarana Upanishad*)

"All mantras and all processes for self-realization are compressed into the Hare Krishna *maha-mantra*." (*Narada-pancaratra*)

"Chant the holy names, chant the holy names, chant the holy names. In this age of Kali [the age of quarrel and confusion] without a doubt there is no other way, there is no other way, there is no other way." (*Brihan-naradiya Purana* 38.126)

"In this age there is no use in meditation, sacrifice and temple worship. Simply by chanting the holy name of Krishna – Hare Krishna, Hare Krishna, Krishna Krishna, Hare Hare/Hare Rama, Hare Rama, Rama Rama, Hare Hare – one can achieve perfect self-realization." (*Vishnu Purana* 6.2.17)

"The self-realization which was achieved in the Satya millennium by meditation, in the Treta millennium by the performance of different sacrifices, and in the Dvapara millennium by opulent worship of Lord Krishna [as the deity in the temple], can be achieved in the age of Kali simply by chanting the holy names, Hare Krishna." (*Bhag.*12.3.52) (Verses similar to this are also found in the *Padma Purana, Uttara-khanda* 72.25, and the *Brihan-naradiya Purana* 38.97)

"Living beings who are entangled in the complicated meshes of birth and death can be freed immediately by even unconsciously chanting the holy name of Krishna, which is feared by fear personified." (*Bhag.*1.1.14)

When instructing King Pariksit, the great sage Sri Shukadeva Gosvami said, "O King, constant chanting of the holy name of the Lord after the ways of the great authorities is the doubtless and fearless way of success for all, including those who are free from all material desires, those who are desirous of all material enjoyment, and also those who are self-satisfied by dint of transcendental knowledge. What is the value of a prolonged life which is wasted, inexperienced by years in this world? Better a moment of full consciousness, because that gives one a start in searching after his supreme interest." (*Bhag*.2.1.11-13)

The reason that chanting the Lord's names is such an effective process is because the Lord and His names are identical: they are the same spiritual energy. By chanting Hare Krishna we are in immediate contact with God. The more purely we chant the names, the more direct is the contact. If we chant someone else's name, we cannot enjoy their association because the name and the person are different, as is typical with material energy. For example, by chanting "water, water, water," we do not quench our thirst because water and the name are two different things. But in the spiritual world everything is absolute. Krishna is non-different from His names and, therefore, we can feel His presence simply by chanting His names. This is further elaborated in the *Caitanya-caritamrta* (*Madhya-lila*, 17.131-133), which explains that there is no difference between the Lords name, form, or personality, and they are all transcendentally sweet. Krishna's name is the same as Krishna Himself, and is not material in any way. It gives spiritual benedictions and is full of pleasure. But in the material world everything is different. Furthermore, in *Caitanya-caritamrta* (*Adi-lila*, 17.22, and the *Padma Purana*), the Hare Krishna *maha-mantra* is said to be the sound incarnation of Krishna, and anyone who chants this mantra is in direct association with Krishna and is delivered from the clutches of the material energy.

It is also explained that because chanting the names of God brings us in direct contact with God in proportion to the chanter's purity, this process of self-realization is the way of success for anyone and everyone. The *Bhagavatam* (2.1.11) discloses that the chanting of God's names in the manner of the great authorities is the doubtless way to spiritual success for everyone, no matter whether they are full of material desires or free of all desires or self-satisfied because of their spiritual knowledge.

Simply by relying on the chanting of the holy names of God, one need not depend upon other processes, rituals, paraphernalia, or persons. One does not even have to be initiated by a spiritual master to chant the *maha-mantra.* As the *Caitanya-caritamrta* (*Madhya-lila,* 15.108) says, one does not have to take initiation, but only has to chant the holy names. Thus, deliverance is available to even the lowest of people. Furthermore, Rupa Gosvami writes about the potency of the holy name in his *Padyavali*:

"The holy name of Lord Krishna is an attractive feature for many saintly, liberal people. It is the annihilator of all sinful reactions and is so powerful that save for the dumb who cannot chant it, it is readily available to everyone, including the lowest type of man, the *chandala.* The holy name of Krishna is the controller of the opulence of liberation, and it is identical with Krishna. Simply by touching the holy name with one's tongue, immediate effects are produced. Chanting the holy name does not depend on initiation, pious activities, or the *purascarya* regulative principles generally observed before initiation. The holy name does not wait for all these activities. It is self-sufficient." (*Padyavali* 29)

Herein is scriptural evidence that the Hare Krishna *maha-mantra* is so powerful that one who sincerely takes shelter of it will attain all the desired results of connection with the Supreme. The *Skanda Purana* gives further evidence of how powerful is the *maha-mantra*:

"The name of the Lord need not be chanted with regard to place, time, circumstantial conditions, preliminary self-purification, or any other factors. Rather, it is completely independent of all other processes and rewards all the desires of those who eagerly chant it." (*Skanda Purana*)

Therefore, without a doubt, the Hare Krishna mantra is the most potent mantra one can utilize for spiritual upliftment. The *Caitanya-caritamrta* (*Madhya-lila,* 15.107) also points out that one is freed of all sinful reactions simply by chanting Krishna's names. And all the nine types of devotional service are completed by this process. Thus, in Kali-yuga only the chanting of the holy names is necessary for worshiping the Lord. However, if one is not able to chant purely or follow the regulations for chanting, it is recommended that one get further guidance from a bona fide spiritual master.

In Kali-yuga, the chanting of the holy names is certainly the most practical and effective process for the conditioned souls. It is also the easiest process whether one finds himself in Kali-yuga, Satya-yuga, Treta-yuga, or Dvapara-yuga. Regardless of what age one may be living in, the process of chanting the holy names is always recommended for everyone. "The names of the Supreme Lord who has the disc as His weapon should be glorified always and everywhere." (*Vaisakha-mahatmya* section of the *Padma Purana*) But since the age of Kali is the most difficult, where men have short durations of life, it is also the most fortunate age. This is explained in *Srimad-Bhagavatam* (11.5.36-37 and 12.3.51) which states that those who are wise know the value of this age of Kali because, in spite of the fallen nature of this age, the spiritual perfection of life can be attained by the easy process of *sankirtana*, the congregational chanting of Krishna's holy names. No better position can be found to attain freedom from material existence and entrance into the spiritual kingdom than joining the Lord's *sankirtana* movement (for the congregational chanting and singing of the Lord's holy names).

Even those living in other ages desire to take birth in Kali-yuga to take advantage of this special concession of a speedy delivery from the cycle of birth and death through the process of *sankirtana*. This is confirmed in *Srimad-Bhagavatam* (11.5.38) where we find it said that those who live during Satya-yuga and other ages wish to be born in Kali-yuga just to take advantage of associating with the devotees of Lord Narayana [Vishnu], who are especially found in South India.

The *Srimad-Bhagavatam* (11.5.32) also explains that intelligent persons perform congregational singing of Krishna's names to worship the *avatara* of Krishna who sings His own names, and who is accompanied by His associates and confidential companions [which indicates Lord Sri Caitanya Mahaprabhu]. Therefore, as the *Caitanya-caritamrta* (*Adi-lila*, 7.74) specifically says, the essence of all scriptural teachings is that the only religious principle in the age of Kali is to chant the Lord's holy names, which are the basis of all Vedic hymns. "In this way the most perfect penance to be executed in this world is the chanting of the name of Lord Sri Hari. Especially in the age of Kali, one can satisfy the Supreme Lord Vishnu by performing *sankirtana* [The congregational chanting of the Lord's holy names]." (*Caturmasya-mahatmya* section of the *Skanda Purana*)

The fact of the matter, as explained in *Srimad-Bhagavatam* (3.33.6-7), is that regardless of what one's present situation is, if a person once speaks about the activities and chants the holy names of the Supreme, or hears about and remembers Him, he becomes eligible to engage in the Vedic rituals. And how much more glorious are those who regularly chant the holy names. Such people are indeed worshipable, for they must have performed all kinds of austerities, achieved the characteristics of the Aryans, studied the *Vedas*, bathed at all the holy places of pilgrimage, and done whatever else is required.

When the great sage Narada Muni was explaining to Srila Vyasadeva the means by which he became enlightened, he said, "It is personally experienced by me that those who are always full of cares and anxieties due to desiring contact of the senses with their objects can cross the ocean of nescience [illusory darkness] on a most suitable boat – the constant chanting of the transcendental activities of the Personality of Godhead. It is true that by practicing restraint of the senses by the yoga system one can get relief from the disturbances of desire and lust, but this is not sufficient to give satisfaction to the soul, for this [satisfaction] is derived from devotional service to the Supreme Personality." (*Bhag*.1.6.34-35)

Lord Krishna goes on to explain to Uddhava that in the association of saintly devotees, there is always the discussion about Him, and those who partake in such hearing and chanting about the Lord's glories are certainly purified of all sins. In this way, whoever hears, chants, and respectfully opens his heart to these topics about the Lord becomes faithfully dedicated to Him. Thus, he achieves devotional service to Lord Krishna. Then, as Lord Krishna Himself asks, "What more remains to be accomplished for the perfect devotee after achieving devotional service unto Me, the Supreme Absolute Truth, whose qualities are innumerable and who am the embodiment of all ecstatic experience?" (*Bhag*.11.26.28-30)

As further related by Sukadeva Gosvami, "A person who with faith engages in chanting the glories of these various pastimes and incarnations of Vishnu, the Lord of lords, will gain liberation from all sins. The all-auspicious exploits of the all attractive incarnations of Lord Shri Krishna, the Supreme Personality of Godhead, and also the pastimes He performed as a child, are described in this *Srimad-Bhagavatam* and in other scriptures. Anyone who clearly chants these descriptions of His pastimes will attain transcendental loving service unto Lord Krishna, who is the goal of all perfected sages." (*Bhag*.11.31.27-28)

Sri Suta Gosvami also relates a conversation between Narada Muni and Sanatkumara, wherein Sanatkumara explained the way to attain freedom from this world, even for the most wayward sinners. He says that even all those mean men who are destitute of all good ways of behavior, who are of a wicked mind, who are outcaste, who deceive the world, who are intent upon religious hypocrisy, pride, drinking liquor, and wickedness, who are sinful and cruel, who are interested in another man's wealth, wife and sons, become pure if they resort to the lotus-like feet of Vishnu. The name of Vishnu, sure to succeed here, protects those sinful men who transgress even Him who causes divinity, who gives salvation to the immobile beings and the mobile beings. A man who has done all kinds of sins is freed if he resorts to Vishnu. If a contemptible, wicked biped would commit sin against Vishnu and by chance resorts to chanting His name, he is emancipated due to the (power of the) name (of Vishnu). However, a man falls down due to his sin against (Vishnu's) name, which is the friend of all. (*Padma Purana* 4.25.8-13)

The sage Kavi instructed King Nimi that the holy names of the Supreme Lord are all-auspicious because they describe His transcendental birth and pastimes, which He performs for the upliftment and salvation of all conditioned souls. For this reason the Lord's holy names are sung throughout the world. By chanting these holy names of the Supreme, one reaches the level of love of God, in which one becomes fixed as an eternal servant of the Lord. Then such a devotee becomes very attached to a particular name and form of the Lord in his service. As his heart melts in ecstatic love, he may laugh loudly or cry or shout. Sometimes he may even sing or dance like a madman in such ecstasy because he becomes indifferent to the opinion of others. (*Bhag*.11.2.39-40)

In this way, we can begin to understand how elevated the writer of the Vedic scripture considers those who have adopted the process of chanting Krishna's holy names. However, for those who do not like the chanting of the holy names and blaspheme the process and criticize or try to restrain those who do chant, we can understand that their sentiment is due to their sinful and offensive activities. Such people are said to have no intelligence and work for no useful purpose and simply contribute to the chaos and confusion within society. The *Bhagavatam* (3.9.7) confirms that "those who do not engage in the blessed chanting and hearing about the activities of the Supreme are bereft of intelligence and good fortune. They perform sinful activities to enjoy sensual pleasure which lasts only for a short time."

Therefore, let us re-emphasize that it is impossible to realize the Supreme without having spiritual experience. What level and type of experience you have will depend on the process you take. Regardless of what method you accept, in order to obtain such an experience, the best method is through intense concentration or a flowing meditation in which we can forget the outer world of sensual stimuli. As we can see, many portions of the Vedic literature recommend that in this age one can most easily reach this ultimate goal through japa, or chanting the simple mantra consisting of the Lord's holy names. When this is chanted with faith, sincerity, and determination, and especially with love toward the object of your meditation, then progress can develop very quickly.

In the beginning, the sounds of the japa practice of chanting the mantra may seem like ordinary sounds. However, the power of the names will soon begin to reveal their personality and the fact that the Supreme also resides within them. Thus, the sound becomes transformed as does the person who chants the names. It is this practice of *japa* yoga, or *japa* meditation, which can bring the person to the highest goal of realization and experience. Thus, whatever could be achieved in previous ages through the arduous discipline of raja yoga and similar techniques can easily be attained through diving into the joyous path of chanting the holy names of the Supreme.

HOW TO CHANT THE MAHA-MANTRA

To begin progressing on the path of chanting the *maha-mantra,* it is prescribed that the practitioner chant on beads called *japa-mala,* similar to a rosary, that consists of 108 beads with one extra head bead, which is larger than the others. This represents the 108 *Upanishads,* or, as described elsewhere, Krishna in the form of the head bead surrounded by 108 of His most advanced devotees.

You may be able to purchase a set of *japa* beads at certain import shops or temples. If you cannot find them anywhere, you can also make them. Simply go to a crafts shop and purchase 108 beads, all of the same size in the style you want, and one larger bead of your choice for the Krishna bead. Also, get a length of durable nylon cord. String the 108 beads with a knot in between each one and bring the two ends of the cord through one hole of the Krishna bead and out the other side where you tie the two ends of the cord together in a firm knot. Then cut the remaining lengths of the cord so you have a small tassel. Now you have got your own set of beads for *japa* meditation.

One chants the Hare Krishna mantra once on each bead from the head bead all the way around the 108 beads. With your beads in hand, you hold the *japa mala* between your thumb and third finger. You start chanting the mantra on the first bead next to the head bead, and chant the mantra on each bead all the way through the 108 beads to make one "round." Then when you reach the head bead you do not chant the mantra on it, but you turn the beads around and chant on the beads in the opposite direction until you reach the head bead again for another 108 repetitions. This would be your second "round." It is usually prescribed that the mantra be chanted a certain number of times, or so many "rounds" in a day. One such "round" of chanting a typical mantra will take an average of seven to ten minutes.

One should chant each day, preferably in the morning, and peacefully sit down or walk and chant the particular number of rounds you have set for yourself. As with any form of meditation, it is best to do your chanting in the early morning when it is quiet and peaceful, and before your mind starts with the activities of the day. However, you can do it anytime or even at a few different times throughout the day. A person may even walk while he or she chants.

There are no hard rules and as long as one listens to the mantra, and the mind and consciousness are focused in such *japa* meditation. A person may chant two rounds, four rounds, or whatever one can do.

For those who are serious, it is prescribed that they chant a total of at least sixteen rounds everyday. With a little practice, this normally takes about two hours. Two rounds will take about fifteen minutes. But one should set a fixed number of rounds to chant everyday. Then one can also spend some time, such as a half-hour or more, reading *Bhagavad-gita* or *Srimad-Bhagavatam* to enhance his or her spiritual development. A daily program of chanting and reading will produce definite results very quickly. The key is to never give up. It is the sincerity that is the essence of purity.

When you are ready to use the mantra, it does not hurt to calm the mind through the basic yoga steps of preparation that have already been described, such as some hatha yoga exercises, a few *pranayama* breathing techniques, and so on. These are, after all, steps for preparing the body and mind to attain deeper levels of awareness and consciousness. Then take your *japa* beads and begin intently chanting the Hare Krishna mantra. When the mind is calm and focused, it will especially be able to concentrate on the vibrations of the mantra. As you chant it with your voice, it is received through the ear and considered by the intelligence. From there it goes deeper into the consciousness. Let no other thoughts enter the mind so that the mantra is all there is. You should be aware of nothing else. Dive deep into the sound of your chanting and feel the vibration of the holy names and the energy they emit.

As you become regulated at this, doing it everyday, changes will begin to manifest in your consciousness that may be imperceptible at first, while other changes begin that will be noticeable from the start. You will often notice an internal energy or even strength within you that was not there before. Amongst other things, you may also feel more sure of your own position and purpose in life, and a closer affinity with God and all beings. Of course, this is just the beginning, so if you do this regularly, deeper insights and realizations will occur as your consciousness acquires more clarity and purification, and as the holy names begin to reveal themselves and their real character to you.

In my own experience when I first started chanting the *maha-mantra* everyday many years ago, I noticed a certain power that came over me that I did not have before. I was a musician at the time, so I occasionally smoked cigarettes when around friends. So, when I started taking my spiritual life more seriously, and I felt this new inner strength that I got from chanting, I decided to direct it toward quitting this nasty habit of smoking cigarettes. I do not know if this would work for everyone, but it could certainly help. So, I directed this new power and strength at giving up cigarettes and I quit completely and never went back. That was just the first of many other extraordinary and positive experiences that unfolded in my life from chanting this mantra.

Of course, this short description on the chanting of the *maha-mantra* does not include more developed information. For example, you can easily get a real and higher taste for the nectar within the Lord's holy names themselves as you can begin to perceive a reciprocation between yourself and the Lord in His names every time you begin to chant. That is only a small part of the new strength you can get, as described above. When this happens, this takes on a whole different perspective of spiritual growth which more closely links one to God, which, after all, is the whole purpose of any sort of yoga or religion.

* * *

This chapter contains only brief descriptions of the glories and effectiveness of chanting the *maha-mantra*. Those who are sincere will certainly add this spiritual practice to their lives. By taking it seriously, they will soon notice a change in their disposition. They are most likely to feel more peaceful, content, happy, etc. One trait that is always noticeable in a person who seriously takes to bhakti yoga and the chanting of the *maha-mantra* is a decrease in such feelings as anxiety and distress, up to the point of attaining complete fearlessness. Once someone is no longer afraid of death, then what is there to be afraid of in this material world? One loses such fear when he or she is spiritually self-realized and knows he or she is not this body and, therefore, not actually subject to death, but merely undergoes a transformation of giving up the body, and with spiritual advancement attains the means of entering the spiritual dimension. Thus, by taking shelter of the protection of the holy names of Krishna, one will remain spiritually safe in any condition of life.

□

14

What is Spiritual Enlightenment

There are many explanations of what is enlightenment, and many are rather unclear or even misleading, often appearing to come from someone who is not truly or deeply experienced. So, I wanted to try and offer something that is more apparent and direct. After all, enlightenment is a goal of yoga and meditation, and we should know something of what we are trying to attain.

First of all, the thing we need to understand is there are different levels of enlightenment. There is the enlightenment concerning our spiritual position or identity known as the *jiva* or spirit soul. That is enlightenment of our higher self. Then there is the more developed enlightenment of God, of which there are three aspects. There is enlightenment of the all-pervading spiritual force, or the effulgence known as the Brahman. This is also the spiritual atmosphere or dimension that is beyond all material influence.

Then there is the realization or enlightenment of the Paramatma or Supersoul within all beings. Most forms of yoga focus on the eventual or ultimate realization of the soul and Supersoul and their connection. Then the third aspect is enlightenment of Bhagavan, the ultimate Supreme Personality who displays His real characteristics, qualities, and pastimes to His most confidential devotees.

Great sages have explained that for one to be completely enlightened, he or she must be realized in all three of these aspects of God; namely the Brahman, Paramatma, and Bhagavan if their enlightenment is to be complete. However, before reaching this stage, a spiritual *sadhaka* or practitioner is likely to go through other preliminary stages of understanding and realization that, without proper experience or training, may lead one to think they are fully realized or enlightened.

This leads us to understand that there are different levels of enlightenment, such as realization on the mental level. For example, the mental level of enlightenment is when something makes sense or resonates with you, and makes you want to know more. You can relate with it or feel a connection. It may even be something that you somehow recall from a previous existence. It is like peaking through the door and seeing something attractive, and then realizing that this may be something you have been looking and waiting for over the course of many years, or even lifetimes. But this realization is of the importance of something and your connection with it, it is not spiritual enlightenment.

Then there is enlightenment on the intellectual level with the use of cultivated knowledge, known as *jnana*. The intellectual level of realization is based on collected information when you study and gather facts and details so you understand the subject better, or comprehend it and even explain it to others. You may develop full faith and accept the reality of its existence, but have not quite seen it directly yet.

Then there is realization of that collected knowledge when *jnana* is called *vijnana*. In other words, it is like seeing through the spectacles of knowledge, you can actually see what the *shastra* or spiritual texts have been talking about. Actual realization is beyond theory or cultivated information alone, but is when you actually perceive the knowledge in action. It is when you can begin to see how the concepts of spiritual knowledge work around you. You recognize the effects of karma, or how the modes of nature are pushing people to do various things. You begin to see what others cannot when they have no spiritual insights or training. However, even such realizations can be on various levels. For example, you may have the realization of how temporary everything is in this material world by recognizing direct evidence of this fact. You may realize the need to learn the process for attaining freedom from this world. You may realize the need to regain your spiritual position and identity. Then, on a higher level you may realize how you are not this temporary body and how you are a spirit soul, and how everyone is essentially spiritual in nature. Then you may go on to realize or recognize the Supersoul or Paramatma within all beings. These are certainly steps toward full spiritual enlightenment.

Higher than this kind of realization is the direct perception or experience. This is when life is no longer a mystery to solve but it becomes a reality to experience. This experience, however, must be as clear as when you see the sun rise in the east. Someone may tell you the sun rises in the east, but until you see it clearly yourself, it is still only theory, or knowledge from someone else's experience. But direct perception takes place after what can be years of spiritual practice. Then you may begin to see the different aspects of the spiritual dimension. It is by constant and serious practice that your consciousness becomes purified or spiritualized so that the spiritual strata begins to reveal itself to you, or you begin to attain direct access to the spiritual dimension.

Perception or experience is like eating a nice meal after being hungry and experiencing the relief from hunger. You can analyze how to cure your hunger in so many ways, but the experience is in eating a nice meal. And that experience is universal. You may use different types of food, such as Italian, Mexican, Chinese, Indian, or whatever, but the experience of feeling the relief from hunger, or the satisfaction of a full stomach, is the same for everyone, after which there are no more arguments about what it takes to relieve one's hunger. This is similar to spiritual enlightenment.

One has to proceed through all of the steps or one's progress may become encumbered by misjudgment and a lack of understanding and proper training. Otherwise, a person may think they are fully enlightened when they actually have a long way to go.

Enlightenment is also the freedom from our karma, or the reactions of one's past deeds. Being forced to deal with our karma and undergo the consequences from past actions can be an obstacle and hinders our ability to reach self-realization. It can keep one motivated toward areas of past familiarity and desires. Yet, the more spiritual you become, the more you become free from the base tendencies or sensual addictions that often linger because of one's karma. How this happens is explained in the *Bhagavad-gita*. With freedom from one's past karma, one can reach enlightenment. But it also works both ways. In other words, the purification one acquires by spiritual practice which gradually paves the way to enlightenment also slowly nullifies a person's past karma. The practice of the yoga system, particularly bhakti yoga, purifies one's consciousness, which also evaporates one's subtle body of mind, intelligence, and false ego. These are all considered material elements according to the Vedic philosophy, and where one's material desires reside. Freedom from such material desires is also a part of becoming free from one's past karma, which tends to lock us into those desires. And such freedom paves the way to complete spiritual enlightenment.

Therefore, if one is truly becoming enlightened, that person will also become free from the sensual desires that are widespread amongst materialists or common men. However, if someone who poses as a spiritual authority, teacher, or guru continues to exhibit the same desires for sensual pleasures that should have been surpassed, then it is obvious that he has not attained enlightenment or mastered the art of spiritual practice.

We need to remember that the *yamas* and *niyamas*, or the dos and don'ts and the regulative principles of the yoga system are not rules to stifle our style or limit our activities from those things we would otherwise like to do. Nor are they meant to force us to adopt habits or restrictions that are artificial or abnormal to us. But they are actually a natural state of being for those who are spiritually realized. Why should one not follow *ahimsa* or nonviolence, or be content, peaceful, materially detached, etc., if he or she is truly enlightened? Once a person becomes enlightened, he or she will rise to the level of awareness in which these qualities, or the regulative principles, automatically manifest in the content of one's character. If these qualities are not evident, then it shows the degree to which that person has remained attached to sensual pleasure or absorbed in materialistic consciousness. Thus, such a person is not spiritually enlightened and cannot become so as long as this is the case.

Spiritual awakening means to awaken from the illusion of temporary material existence, and to see the spiritual essence and the Absolute or Supreme Creator within and behind every aspect of the creation. It is not that this material world is unreal, but it is like an ephemeral dream we have. The dream is real, and it may indeed affect us, but it has influence over us only as long as we do not wake up. Once we wake up from the dream, we realize what is genuinely real and then we remember our actual situation and what we are meant to do. Spiritual awakening is the same thing in which we awaken from our materialistic dream to our real spiritual identity and become free from the influence of temporary material existence, and then we remember who we really are.

In such a consciousness and full awareness of spiritual reality, there is no time when we forget God. That is the essence of Krishna or God consciousness. Thus, you see everything as a display of the energy of God. You recognize the Creator behind all created things. This is when you become one with the universal Self, and you see your self as one or the same as all others. In this unity, we find peace, calmness, acceptance, and the highest bliss.

In this way, spiritual enlightenment is perceiving and honoring the inner sacredness of ourselves and all other beings, in fact all of creation. It is knowing we are all divine emanations from the same source. It is through this perception that allows us to undergo the challenge of constant changes in this material existence, or to weather the storm so to speak, with balance, equilibrium, and grace, knowing that all problems or reversals in life are but temporary illusions.

At the spiritual level, the soul has no evil. The soul only wants what it ought to want, or desires what it ought to desire, and does not undergo extremes of unnecessary happiness, exuberance, or sadness, or depression. When we have regained our natural spiritual position and are free of the influence from the externals around us, along with the various changing emotions or dualities that are seen and engaged in on the mental state in our material existence, then we are eternally balanced in *sudha sattva*, ultimate pure goodness. This is our natural state of being that becomes clear and is perceived in the state of complete self-realization or actual enlightenment. And this flows from us on a continual basis to the degree in which we are spiritually awakened.

Self-realization or enlightenment is also surrendering our false identity, our material conceptions and attachments into the ocean of nectar that is our devotion and love for God. This *rasa* or taste in the relationship we have with the Supreme can outweigh all other desires or cravings, and is that for which we all are ultimately searching. That is our home, and the basis for all our other longings. Once you attain that awakening, you are complete and whole in your self because you have established your connection with the Complete, as explained in the *Sri Isopanishad*.

So, how do we get there? How do we attain this level of enlightenment and spiritual awakening? Through *sadhana*, regulated spiritual practice, which is part of and the purpose of the yoga system. To purify our consciousness starts with purifying or spiritualizing our activities. For example, if we have a cup and we want to fill it with nectar, but it is filled with dirt, we first have to start taking out the dirt. The more dirt we take out, the more nectar we can put into it. Similarly, the more nectar or bliss we want to put into our life, the more we have to start changing our activities to those which are based on or conducive to spiritual progress. This changes our consciousness. When our activities are purified, then our mind becomes purified or spiritualized. Thus, our desires are purified. When that happens, our consciousness becomes spiritualized. When that happens, material existence has nothing more to offer us. It is neither attractive nor repulsive to us—we are simply indifferent, or no longer interested.

In this way, spiritual realization, awakening, or enlightenment is the aim, goal, and success of human life. Only human existence offers the facility for the living entity to become spiritually enlightened. Therefore, we should not waste this life on mere animal or trivial base pursuits.

Actual enlightenment is the stage when one's realizations have matured into a way of life, not glimpses of the truth, but a constant reality that directs one's every action. This is when you know exactly what is to be done, the purpose of life, and can do nothing else but what takes you toward that goal. Others may or may not always understand such actions, but an enlightened person has complete singleness of purpose in all of his or her endeavors.

Spiritual enlightenment does not mean that you are always in a state of being blissed-out, and otherwise dysfunctional to being able to do anything else. But it means you now clearly see what is to be done in this life and can joyfully do it. When you have such clarity and you sincerely try to arrange your life to do what is essential, then the universe or even the Divine will give you the opportunity to act in such a way, or give you the means to perform such activities. In such a state, when there is unity between one's soul and the Supreme within, then the Divine may even work through such a person for the benefit of others.

With this kind of clarity you will know your true purpose and what you are meant to give to the world. Then you will also know there is no time to waste and will want to work diligently to accomplish what you are meant to do in this life.

Death is not the experience that automatically gives enlightenment or provides all the answers, as some people think. The experience of death will certainly provide additional insights and understanding. But, for the most part, the consciousness you develop in this life is carried over into the next, and from there you continue your development, and, ultimately, your search or quest for spiritual awakening. It is your state of mind and consciousness which attracts you to the situation in your next life that best accommodates you. That is why it is important to attain the highest level of enlightenment now, in this life, to attain the best possible situation in your next existence.

Once you have attained pure spiritual consciousness, either in this or some future existence, there will be no need for further births in the cycle of *samsara*, or life and death in this material world. You achieve the ultimate success by entering directly into the spiritual dimension and eternal life. This is real freedom and the attainment of real life, our natural spiritual state, which is above and beyond the emotional, mental, intellectual, or even subtle realms of this temporary material existence. Such a *jivanmukta* or liberated soul will have attained his or her status of enlightenment through the process of steady *sadhana* or spiritual practice, then realization, illumination, direct perception, and then full transcendental freedom. That is enlightenment.

□

Conclusion
The Greatest Adventure

This book has provided an essential description of the process of yoga and meditation, from the basic purpose up to the preparations and techniques for attaining enlightenment and spiritual perfection. This, along with which processes are most recommended, and which ones work the best for the particular age of Kali in which we presently find ourselves, gives the average person a quick understanding on how to begin and what to expect, and how to get the most out of it. Regardless of whatever your personal aims in life may be, yoga can help you become more efficient, peaceful, and aware. It can definitely transform your life into a more exciting adventure – a journey to inner enlightenment and spiritual unfoldment.

The greatest adventure is man's (or woman's) journey back to our Creator. Thus, it is not too much to ask that we do what we can to balance our mind, body, senses, intellect, will, and soul to reach the Supersoul, God. If we cannot do that, then no matter what else we may accomplish, we have not used this human existence to its ultimate advantage.

The yogi knows that the path of sensual pleasure is wide and long, and it never ends, just like a fire that will never stop burning as long as it has fuel to consume. Thus, the senses also will never stop wanting more as long as they have objects to enjoy. They will always distract us in this way. Therefore, the path of sensual pleasure leads to destruction because it occupies and consumes all the time we give it and never returns us to the real goal of life, unless somehow we can break away from the false aim of existence. But many are those who prefer the materialistic path that ultimately leads to nowhere except the constant highs and lows, and ups and downs of life.

Whereas the path of yoga is pointed, narrow, and considered to be like a razors edge. Few are those who can find it, and fewer are those who can actually follow it closely. But, as the *Bhagavad-gita* explains, that which may be full of pleasure at first becomes like poison in the end, whereas that which may be difficult and bitter at first becomes like nectar in the end. This is the difference between material life and spiritual practice. Material life, or satisfying our mind and senses, may be thrilling at first, but gradually it becomes boring and works against us. But spiritual life may not be what we are spontaneously drawn to at first, but the bliss increases.

Spiritual life will ultimately end all the problems of existence and open the doors to unlimited spiritual happiness, whereas with material life, what you have is all that you get, and the problems that come with it never completely go away, but rise up again and again with time. Through the process of yoga we can reach the heights of our real potential as spiritual beings, which is our real identity and constitutional position. It is just a matter of reawakening it and returning to that consciousness and awareness. That is the advantage of being a human being and going toward the real goal of human life.

The final result of our spiritual quest and self-realization is to understand that we are all spirit souls, a part of the spiritual realm, a part of the Supreme Spirit. Nothing can change that or take that away from us. That is our eternal position, though we may have temporarily forgotten it. Therefore, all we really need to do is simply reawaken our transcendental nature and attraction for the Supreme, and learn the art of such devotional service. Then we merely regain our real and eternal identity that has been waiting for us for unknown lifetimes. It is like returning to our long lost home.

More information and a complete course in understanding these points of spiritual realization is available and presented in "The Heart of Hinduism: The Eastern Path to Freedom, Empowerment and Illumination" and my other books. All the best on your spiritual path.

OM SHANTI SHANTI SHANTIHI
HARI OM HARI OM HARI OM
HARE KRISHNA

Glossary

Acarya – the spiritual master who sets the proper standard by his own example.

Advaita – nondual, meaning that the Absolute Truth is one, and that there is no individuality between the Supreme Being and the individual souls which merge into oneness, the Brahman, when released from material existence. The philosophy taught by Sankaracharya.

Agni – fire, or Agni the demigod of fire.

Agnihotra – the Vedic sacrifice in which offerings were made to the fire, such as ghee, milk, sesame seeds, grains, etc. The demigod Agni would deliver the offerings to the demigods that are referred to in the ritual.

Ahankara – false ego, identification with matter.

Ahimsa – nonviolence.

Amrit – psychic nectar.

Ananda – spiritual bliss.

Ananta – unlimited.

Arati – the ceremony of worship when incense and ghee lamps are offered to the Deities.

Arca-vigraha – the worshipable Deity form of the Lord made of stone, wood, etc.

Aryan – a noble person, one who is on the Vedic path of spiritual advancement.

Asana – postures for meditation, or exercises for developing the body into a fit instrument for spiritual advancement.

Asat – that which is temporary.

Ashrama – one of the four orders of spiritual life, such as *brahmacari* (celibate student), *grihastha* (married householder), *vanaprastha* (retired stage), and *sannyasa* (renunciate); or the abode of a spiritual teacher or *sadhu*.

Astanga-yoga – the eightfold path of mystic yoga.

Atma – the self or soul. Sometimes means the body, mind, and senses.

Atman – usually referred to as the Supreme Self.

Avatara – an incarnation of the Lord who descends from the spiritual world.

Avidya – ignorance or nescience.

Aum – *om* or *pranava*

Ayurveda – the original wholistic form of medicine as described in the Vedic literature.

Bandha – an energy block the redirects the flow of prana or kundalini.

Bhagavan – one who possesses all opulences, God.

Bhajan – song of worship.

Bhakta – a devotee of the Lord who is engaged in *bhakti-yoga*.

Bhakti – love and devotion for God.

Bhakti-yoga – the path of offering pure devotional service to the Supreme.

Bindu – the psychic center at the top back of the head.

Brahmacari – a celebate student, usually five to twenty-five years of age, who is trained by the spiritual master. One of the four divisions or *ashramas* of spiritual life.

Brahma granthi – a subtle knot in the shushumna nadi near the perineum in the muladhara chakra connected with material and sensual attachment.

Brahmajyoti – the great white light or effulgence which emanates from the body of the Lord.

Brahman – the spiritual energy; the all-pervading impersonal aspect of the Lord; or the Supreme Lord Himself.

Brahmana or brahmin – one of the four orders of society; the intellectual class of men who have been trained in the knowledge of the *Vedas* and initiated by a spiritual master.

Chakra – a wheel, disk, or psychic energy center situated along the spinal column in the subtle body of the physical shell.

Darshan – the devotional act of seeing and being seen by the Deity in the temple.

Deva – a demigod, or higher being.

Devaloka – the higher planets or planes of existence of the devas.

Devas – demigods or heavenly beings from higher levels of material existence, or a godly person.

Dham – a holy place.

Dharma – the essential nature or duty of the living being.

Diksha – spiritual initiation.

Dwaita – dualism, the principle that the Absolute Truth consists of the infinite Supreme Being along with the infinitesimal, individual souls.

Gayatri – the spiritual vibration or *mantra* from which the other *Vedas* were expanded and which is chanted by those who are initiated as *brahmanas* and given the spiritual understanding of Vedic philosophy.

Ghat – a bathing place along a river or lake with steps leading down to the water.

Goloka Vrindavana – the name of Lord Krishna's spiritual planet.

Gosvami – one who is master of the senses.

Granthis – the three psychic knots in the *sushumna nadi* which hinder the upward passage of the *kundalini*, namely *brahma granthi*, *vishnu granthi* and *rudra granthi*.

Grihastha – the householder order of life. One of the four *ashramas* in spiritual life.

Gunas – the modes of material nature of which there is *sattva* (goodness), *rajas* (passion), and *tamas* (ignorance).

Guru – a spiritual master.

Hare – the Lord's pleasure potency, Radharani, who is approached for accessibility to the Lord.

Hari – a name of Krishna as the one who takes away one's obstacles on the spiritual path.

Hatha-yoga – a part of the yoga system which stresses various sitting postures and exercises.

Hinayana – Lesser Vehicle, the Buddhist school that stresses achieving one's own enlightenment.

Impersonalism – the view that God has no personality or form, but is only an impersonal force (Brahman) which the individual souls merge back into when released from material existence.

Impersonalist – those who believe God has no personality or form.

Japa – the chanting one performs, usually softly, for one's own meditation.

Japa-mala – the string of beads one uses for chanting.

Jiva – the individual soul or living being.

Jivanmukta – a liberated soul, though still in the material body and universe.

Jnana – knowledge which may be material or spiritual.

Jnana-yoga – the process of linking with the Supreme through empirical knowledge and mental speculation.

Jnani – one engaged in *jnana-yoga,* or the process of cultivating knowledge to understand the Absolute.

Kali-yuga – the fourth and present age, the age of quarrel and confusion, which lasts 432,000 years and began 5,000 years ago.

Kalki – future incarnation of Lord Vishnu who appears at the end of Kali-yuga.

Karma – material actions performed in regard to developing one's position or for future results which produce *karmic* reactions. It is also the reactions one endures from such fruitive activities.

Karma-yoga – system of yoga for using one's activities for spiritual advancement.

Kirtana – chanting or singing the glories of the Lord.

Krishna – the name of the original Supreme Personality of Godhead which means the most attractive and greatest pleasure. He is the source of all other incarnations, such as Vishnu, Rama, Narasimha, Narayana, Buddha, Parashurama, Vamanadeva, Kalki at the end of Kali-yuga, etc.

Kshatriya – the second class of *varna* of society, or occupation of administrative or protective service, such as warrior or military personel.

Maha-Vishnu or Karanodakasayi Vishnu – the Vishnu expansion of Lord Krishna from whom all the material universes emanate.

Mahayana – Great Vehicle, the Buddhist school that stresses giving aid to all living beings toward enlightenment.

Mantra – a sound vibration which prepares the mind for spiritual realization and delivers the mind from material inclinations. In some cases a *mantra* is chanted for specific material benefits.

Maya – illusion, or anything that appears to not be connected with the eternal Absolute Truth.

Moksha – liberation from material existence.

Nirvana – the state of no material miseries, usually the goal of the Buddhists or voidists.

Om or *Omkara* – *pranava,* the transcendental *om mantra,* generally referring to the attributeless or impersonal aspects of the Absolute.

Paramatma – the Supersoul, or localized expansion of the Lord.

Parampara – the system of disciplic succession through which transcendental knowledge descends.

Patanjali – the authority on the *astanga-yoga* system.

Prana – the life air or cosmic energy.

Pranayama – control of the breathing process as in *astanga* or *raja-yoga.*

Pranava – same as *omkara.*

Prasada – food or other articles that have been offered to the Deity in the temple and then distributed amongst people as the blessings or mercy of the Deity.

Puja – the worship offered to the Deity.

Pujari – the priest who performs worship, *puja*, to the Deity.

Rudra granthi – the subtle or psychic knot within the ajna chakra connected with higher mental attributes and siddhis.

Raja-yoga – the eightfold yoga system.

Sadhana – a specific practice or discipline for attaining God realization.

Sadhu – Indian holy man or devotee.

Samadhi – trance, the perfection of being absorbed in the Absolute.

Sanatana-dharma – the eternal nature of the living being, to love and render service to the supreme lovable object, the Lord.

Sannyasa – the renounced order of life, the highest of the four *ashramas* on the spiritual path.

Sattva-guna – the material mode of goodness.

Satya-yuga – the first of the four ages which lasts 1,728,000 years.

Shakti – energy, potency or power, the active principle in creation. Also the active power or wife of a deity, such as Shiva/Shakti.

Shastra – the authentic revealed Vedic scripture.

Srimad-Bhagavatam – the most ripened fruit of the tree of Vedic knowledge compiled by Vyasadeva.

Sruti – scriptures that were received directly from God and transmitted orally by *brahmanas* or *rishis* down through succeeding generations. Traditionally, it is considered the four primary *Vedas*.

Tapasya – voluntary austerity for spiritual advancement.

Treta-yuga – the second of the four ages which lasts 1,296,000 years.

Vanaprastha – the third of the four *ashramas* of spiritual life in which one retires from family life in preparation for the renounced order.

Varna – sometimes referred to as caste, a division of society, such as *brahmana* (a priestly intellectual), a *kshatriya* (ruler or manager), *vaisya* (a merchant, banker, or farmer), and *sudra* (common laborer).

Varnashrama – the system of four divisions of society and four orders of spiritual life.

Vedas – generally means the four primary *samhitas; Rig, Yajur, Sama, Atharva.*

Vishnu granthi – is in the region of the anahata chakra, and connected with emotional attachments and attachments to people and inner psychic powers, and ambition.

Yoga – linking up with the Absolute.

Yoga-*siddhi* – mystic perfection.

References

Art of Sadhana: A Guide to Daily Devotion, by Swami B.P. Puri Maharaja, Mandala Publishing Group, San Francisco, CA

Bhagavad-gita As It Is, translated by A. C. Bhaktivedanta Swami, Bhaktivedanta Book Trust, New York/Los Angeles, 1972

Bhagavad-gita, translated by Swami Chidbhavananda, Sri Ramakrishna Tapovanam, Tiruchirappalli, India, 1991

Brahma-vaivarta Purana, translated by Shanti Lal Nagar, edited by Acharya Ramesh Chaturvedi, Parimal Publications, Delhi, 2005

Caitanya-caritamrta, translated by A. C. Bhaktivedanta Swami, Bhaktivedanta Book Trust, Los Angeles, 1974

Caitanya Upanisad, translated by Kusakratha dasa, Bala Books, New York, 1970

Chakras Energy Centers of Transformation, by Harish Johari, Destiny Books, Rochester, Vermont, 1987

Chandogya Upanishad,

Divine Yoga Sadhana, by Yogi Bharat J. Gajjar, Rupal International, Hockessin, Delaware, 2009

Gheranda Samhita, translated by Rai Bahadur Srisa Chandra Vasu, Munshiram Manoharlal, New Delhi, 1980

Hatha Yoga Pradipika, by Swami Muktibodhananda, Yoga Publications Trust, Munger, Bihar, India, 1993

How to Know God, The Yoga Aphorisms of Patanjali, translated by Swami Prabhavananda and C. Isherwood, New American Library, 1969

Kundalini Tantra, by Swami Satyananda Sarasvati, Yoga Publications Trust, Munger, Bihar, India, 1984

Kundalini The Arousal of the Inner Energy, by Ajit Mookerjee, Destiny Books, New York, 1982

Light on Yoga, B.K.S. Iyengar, Schocken Books, New York, 1966

Mahabharata, Sanskrit Text With English Translations, by M.N. Dutt, Parimal Publications, Delhi, 2001

Mantras, Yantras and Fabulous Gems, by Howard Beckman, Balaji Publishing, Pecos, New Mexico, 1997

Meditation for Higher Consciousness, by Professor Bharat J. Gajjar, Rupal International, Wilmington, Delaware, 2008

Pranayama: The Yoga of Breathing, Andre van Lysebeth, Unwin Paperbacks, London, 1979

Seven Systems of Indian Philosophy, by Rajmani Tigunait, Ph.D., Himalayan Publishers, Honesdale, Pennsylvasnia, 1953

Sri Isopanisad, translated by A. C. Bhaktivedanta Swami, Bhaktivedanta Book Trust, New York/Los Angeles, 1969

Srimad-Bhagavatam, translated by A. C. Bhaktivedanta Swami, Bhaktivedanta Book trust, New York/Los Angeles, 1972

The Practice of Meditation, Swami Ritajananda, Sri Rama Krishna Math, Mylapore, Madras, India

Vedic Tantrism, [*Rigvidhana of Saunaka*], by M.S. Bhat, Motilal Banarsidass, Delhi, 1987

□□□